Order this book online at www.trafford.com
or email orders@trafford.com

Most Trafford titles are also available at major online book retailers.

Printed in the United States of America.

ISBN: 978-1-4669-6962-9 (sc)
ISBN: 978-1-4669-6960-5 (hc)
ISBN: 978-1-4669-6961-2 (e)

Library of Congress Control Number: 2012921946

Trafford rev. 11/26/2012

 www.trafford.com

North America & international
toll-free: 1 888 232 4444 (USA & Canada)
phone: 250 383 6864 ♦ fax: 812 355 4082

Dedication

This novel would never have been finished except for the unflagging interest, major commitment, and sincere confidence in the potential of this novel by my wonderful friend and mentor, Jamie Pettigrew. To her, I credit three complete editings, numerous arguments and discussions over an extended period of time, and the incalculable benefit of her great knowledge and love of the English language. Her endless patience as I struggled, in my inexperience, to do this is appreciated to an extent I cannot express. My friend is now ninety-seven years old, and I don't know if she will be able to understand that this book is going to be published, which saddens me, but she never doubted that it would be, which was her invaluable gift to me. I also wish to thank my family and friends for their encouragement, and particularly to the Kookaburras, who insisted that I try *just one more time* to get this published.

Chapter 1

$\mathcal{M}$aggs picked up her third cup of coffee and carried it outside to the terrace. She thought she might be able to finish this one now that Stephen had gotten off to work. She munched a bagel as she went over her appointment book and sighed, wondering where she would find the energy to get everything done. And the only difference between today and tomorrow seemed to be the nature of the obligations. Today, she had to mail Greg's birthday present, go to the market, stop at the cleaners, and pick up Sassie's dress from the alteration shop. She had a writing class at ten and lunch with Leah at noon. She had promised to take her four-year-old granddaughter to a matinee. Then home to refresh her makeup, start dinner, and chill some martinis before Stephen got home.

If he made it home before she went to bed. These days she could never be sure. Success had brought many demands with it, most of them to do with time, and Maggs longed sometimes for the simplicity of their early years together. The children were small, she was a working mother, Stephen was struggling financially while stubbornly hanging on to his dream of building his own business importing the expensive foreign sports cars he so loved, a dream which eventually brought him the twin rewards of prosperity and personal satisfaction. Those problems had sometimes seemed monumental, but looking back after thirty years, it all seemed easier than the schedules they kept now.

Realizing she had no time for such reflections today, she took her dishes into the kitchen, started the dishwasher, and went upstairs to wake Sassie, who lay in a tangle of tanned arms and legs and flowered sheets. Maggs lifted Sassie's heavy dark hair from over her eyes and shook her gently.

"Up, lazybones, it's getting late and you have morning classes. What time did you come in last night, anyway?"

Sassie grumbled her disapproval at being disturbed but finally unwound herself from the tangled bedclothes, kissed her mother, and went into her bathroom to shower.

"I don't know, exactly, Mom. I don't think it was too late. A bunch of us decided to go out to the beach and cook steaks. It was really nice out there last night. You and Dad should open the cottage soon. We didn't leave a mess, I promise." From the shower she chattered on about the evening while Maggs half-listened as she straightened the room and gathered clothes for the laundry.

"Will you be home for dinner, Sass?" Maggs asked when Sassie paused long enough for her to get a word in. "I have tons of errands and won't be here much today, so I need to know."

"Jeff and I are going out to dinner and a movie, Mom. I shouldn't be late. Are you going to pick my dress up, or do you want me to?" asked Sassie as she unselfconsciously stepped from the shower and reached for a towel.

"I plan to, but it will help me out if you have time to do it, sweetie, could you?"

"Sure, no problem. Oh, and, Mom, I have an early lab tomorrow, so will you make sure I'm up by nine o'clock?"

Maggs nodded as she closed the door and went to her own bedroom, feeling somewhat as though she had just stepped out of a wind tunnel. Sassie has a way of leaving people a little breathless, Maggs reflected, as she considered her youngest child with satisfaction.

Alexandra Masters was the baby of the family and the only one who had chosen to stay at home while going to school. She had worked a year before enrolling at the University of South Alabama; she would soon complete her freshman year, and as was the case with everything she set her mind to, she had done very well. She had a summer job lined up; she and a girlfriend planned to rent an apartment, and if it worked out, they could extend the lease for next year. Maggs had mixed feelings about Sassie's moving out. The freedom it meant for her and Stephen would be nice, but Maggs wondered uncertainly about redefining her role once the last chick had left the nest.

In addition to her other qualities, Sassie was breathtakingly lovely. Sometimes Maggs watched her and wondered how she could be so unaware of the fact. But vanity was as foreign to Sassie's nature as the idea that her beauty made any difference in the flow of her life. She didn't judge others by their appearance and would have been surprised and disapproving to realize what an advantage her looks were. Unlike Maggs's tall, blonde slimness, Sassie was petite, voluptuous, and brunette with thick dark hair that had just the right amount of curl, flashing black eyes, a ready smile, and the prettiest skin Maggs had ever seen. She felt a little guilty about taking pride in something as superficial as her daughter's physical beauty when there were so many more important qualities Sassie possessed. But only sometimes.

It was occasionally a problem to Leah that Sassie and Maggs were so close. Leah felt excluded from their easy, affectionate acceptance of each other, perhaps because she was incapable of such a relationship. Sassie was aware of her sister's feelings and attempted to assuage them whenever possible, understanding that Leah's feelings sprang from envy that Sassie's future was open to all kinds of choices which were no longer open to her. But it wasn't a malicious envy, and Sassie realized that too.

Sassie played hard, worked hard, and rarely worried about anything. Life seemed destined to grant her every wish, but she was so undemanding and so loving that no one ever minded.

Maggs smiled at the thought as she took a deep breath and stepped into the shower, ready to get on with another day.

This Wednesday in the life of Mary Margaret Masters began, as had so many others before it, another in a long succession of days filled with endless minor details which required her attention, days which left her feeling that she had run all day and had little to show for it. *How did I get here,* she wondered often at the close of such days, and *where do I go from here?* She felt like a hamster running inside one of those brightly colored little wheels, not knowing where she was going or how to get off, but almost always exhausted at not getting anywhere.

A few hours later, Maggs sat in a small trendy restaurant, contemplating the menu. Leah was late, as usual. Maggs ordered for them, and as she waited, she spent the time thinking about Leah's life.

Maggs's love for Leah was both defensive and protective, born of a lamentable but realistic maternal conviction that Leah was either not willing or not able to protect herself. Probably a little of both, Maggs believed. Sometimes she fiercely resented Leah's dependence and questioned the wisdom of continuing to be her buffer. But so far she had, and for several reasons.

The oldest of Stephen and Maggs's four children, Leah was twenty-eight years old. She was employed by an accounting firm where she made a substantial salary but had little chance of advancement. Her two children were a continuing source of pleasure to Maggs: four-year-old blonde and blue-eyed Melody and fat and sassy two-year-old Jason, who had Maggs's heart firmly clutched in his chubby little hands. For their sake, Maggs had played a more involved role in Leah's life than she really felt was good for any of them.

Maggs privately suspected that Leah's marriage was in trouble. Leah had married while she was still in college; and, as with most of her choices, she had refused to listen to Maggs's and Stephen's advice to wait. They instinctively knew she had made a bad choice in Matt Sterling, but Leah would hear nothing they had to say. Matt wasn't a bad person, just spoiled and immature. Leah was more than a little spoiled and immature herself as Maggs fully understood, and the result was an inevitable clash of wills, which occurred frequently and often tempestuously. Leah remained resolutely committed to Matt but resented him much of the time because she got few paybacks for her loyalty.

She confided once to Maggs that she had thought children would foster a sense of responsibility in Matt, but soon after Melody's birth, Leah realized that would not be the case. By the time Jason came along, she realized she had merely increased her own responsibilities; the children's existence did not much affect Matt. Although he loved his children, his inclination to put himself first didn't change. Leah had little fun in her life and was likely to project her misery on to all those around her, particularly Maggs. As she juggled her devotion to Matt, her responsibility to the children, and a job situation she wasn't happy with, Leah made Maggs the repository for all her woes. Maggs accepted her role, sometimes willingly and sometimes not. In spite of her concern for Leah, she sometimes avoided her when it got to be too much.

Distracted from her contemplative mood by a ripple of laughter, Maggs looked up as Leah breezed in on a cloud of perfume and a wave of excuses for her tardiness. They always played this game, affectionately and comfortably: Leah was never on time anywhere, and Maggs accepted the fact as well as the excuses because to do otherwise required too much effort and changed nothing.

"I ordered for us, in the interest of time, is that okay?" Maggs asked. "I have a tight schedule this afternoon, but I'm glad we can have lunch. How are you?"

"Oh, Mom," Leah sighed as she settled into her seat. "Everything's okay, I guess. At least as okay as it ever gets anymore. I don't know where all the time goes. I can't seem to get everything done anymore, and I don't ever seem to find time to do anything just for me, you know?"

She unfolded her napkin and placed it in her lap as the waiter brought their lunch.

"Yes, dear, I know," Maggs replied automatically, barely managing to conceal her annoyance—were they really going to have this conversation again?

In an attempt to divert Leah before she began an all-out recital of her latest troubles, Maggs asked, "Do you have your dress for the dance this weekend? You haven't told me what you're wearing."

"I guess the dark blue satin I wore to the Christmas dance. I can't afford to buy anything new right now. Matt just bought a motorcycle, and we're kind of strapped. I'm not too keen on going this year anyway, Mom, and Matt really wants to beg off. Would you be terribly upset if we didn't come?"

"Oh, Leah, of course you don't have to come if you really don't want to, but your father has been counting on you and Sassie to be there. It's so seldom that we're all together anymore. And you've already accepted the invitation. Please try to work it out, for his sake."

"I know he'll be disappointed, but I really don't feel like battling Matt about this, Mom. It seems like all we do is argue lately. Fix it with Dad, won't you, please—for me?" she pleaded in her best little-girl voice. She looked at her watch and pushed back her plate. "Gosh, I've got to run, I can't be late again. I'm in hot water at the office already. See you later, Mom," she said bending over to kiss Maggs. "Talk to Dad, please? I'll see you when you bring Melody home. Thanks for lunch."

Leah departed in the same rush in which she had arrived, blowing a kiss over her shoulder as she made her way through the crowded room.

As Maggs gave the waiter her credit card, she heard someone say, "Maggs, is that you? I swear you never change. You look marvelous."

Maggs looked up and into the incredibly blue eyes of Delaine Packard. Delaine had been her best friend/best enemy since childhood. They had played jacks together, gone to each other's spend-the-night parties, graduated from high school together, and pledged the same sorority in college. They had even competed for Stephen's attention at one point, and although Maggs had won that particular contest, Delaine had always made it seem as if she had conceded the prize.

Maggs had come home to Mobile after college. Instead of getting her master's degree, she had married Stephen, and graduate school was put on the back burner. Maggs accepted a temporary position as Girl-Friday in the newly established law firm of Patrick

Delaney, a fraternity brother of Stephen's. That temporary position lasted twenty-three years. Maggs had retired four years ago.

Delaine, on the other hand, following her natural flair for the dramatic and her dedicated pursuit of being the center of attention, went to California and became an actress. A striking beauty, she had the good fortune to be in the right place at the right time and caught the eye of a television producer who auditioned her for a small part in a new dramatic series. The bit part showed her to great advantage, and soon she parlayed it into one of the leading roles in the series. The camera fell in love with her, and so did the public. From that modest beginning she had become a celebrity whose name brought to mind a considerable number of acting credits of worthy note as well as a better-known personal history. Delaine's life had been stormy on-screen and off and unfortunately played out almost entirely in the glare of publicity.

As they embraced and exchanged pleasantries, Maggs was conscious that Delaine's vivid beauty had not lessened over the years. She was sophisticated, confident, gorgeous. The attention of the entire room was focused on her; she knew it and played to it instinctively. She couldn't help it. She never could.

"Are you leaving?" Delaine said. "Please stay and have a drink with me. It's been years since we've had a good gossip. I'm home to celebrate Pop's birthday and then I have to fly back to LA first thing Sunday morning. I had to have a drink before facing all that, and you know how Mother is about alcohol in the house. Please?"

Maggs sat back down, knowing that she couldn't really spare the time. But she could never resist Delaine, and as they talked, Maggs couldn't help comparing her life to the dazzle and glitter of Delaine's. Well aware that Delaine had paid a dear price for the dazzle, Maggs knew she wouldn't trade lifestyles but still felt a twinge of something (envy, perhaps?) as Delaine chatted on, dropping famous names and telling hilarious tales of her encounters.

Engrossed with Delaine's make-believe world, Maggs looked at her watch and was shocked to discover the time. Hurriedly calling for the check, she explained that she had to pick Melody up and be at the theater in half an hour. She was both relieved and reluctant to leave Delaine, promising to keep in touch but knowing it wouldn't happen. Their worlds were separated by much more than miles.

The theater was predictably packed, and the movie was just starting as she and Melody slipped into their seats. Maggs had adored Melody from the first moment she had held her in her arms, in large part because, even as an infant, Melody had an inner contentment that was irresistible. They watched the movie, ate popcorn, whispered, and laughed; and when Maggs dropped her off, she knew Delaine had nothing as special in her life as Melody. Or her other three grandchildren. She wouldn't trade a single hug for any amount of Hollywood glamour—so why this gnawing feeling of discontent? The question made her uneasy, and she hastily put it out of her mind.

As she flew through the rest of her schedule, the vague restlessness stayed with her, as it often did these days. She arrived home exhausted, reapplied her makeup, and changed clothes before starting dinner. She made a pitcher of ice-cold martinis, just the way Stephen preferred them, and sat down to go through the mail.

There was a letter from Greg, which she eagerly opened. It was the first in several weeks, and though she never worried about Greg, she had begun to wonder why she hadn't heard from him. His letter was newsy, filled with details he knew would interest them. His interest in his job had not wavered since he arrived in Oklahoma two years ago. Greg was more like Maggs than her other children. Responsible, dedicated, and on track with his life, he had finished college in the top of his class and immediately landed a job as a geologist with a major oil company. Maggs felt the miles between them keenly, but his strong sense of who he was and what he wanted always reassured her.

She slid the letter back into the envelope as the clock struck seven. Stephen wasn't home. That wasn't uncommon lately, but he usually called when he was delayed. She phoned his office, but the switchboard had been turned off. She waited another half-hour and then ate her dinner standing up while she made Stephen a plate to warm in the microwave and put the food away.

She closed the pantry door and jumped as the phone rang, expecting to hear Stephen's voice. It was Leah.

"Mom, can you possibly watch Jason tomorrow? He came home this afternoon with a bug, and I can't take him to day care until he's over it. I've got a hectic day tomorrow, and I can't stay home with him. Matt has an important interview, and he can't keep him either. I hate to ask you so late, but I'm really in a jam."

"Of course I will. Don't give it another thought. I don't have anything scheduled that can't be changed, and you know how I love to keep him. What time are you bringing him?"

"We'll be there around seven-thirty. And if I can get him an appointment with his pediatrician, would you mind running him over?"

"Just let me know what time, dear. I'll see you tomorrow," Maggs said as she hung up the phone. She checked her calendar to see what would have to be rearranged.

She climbed the stairs, tired and generally dissatisfied, and started running a bath, hoping it would restore her spirits. She laid out a pretty nightgown, poured bath oil into the running water, and lit some candles. She went into the small study off their bedroom and poured a snifter of brandy. She put some soft music on the stereo, turned off the lights, and lowered herself into the scented water, sighing with pleasure. The rich aroma of the brandy mingled with the scent of the bath oil and floated up to her.

She luxuriated in the warmth of the tub much longer than she realized. Her peace was interrupted by the sound of the front door closing. Sassie called out, "I'm home, Mom. Do we have any leftovers?" Maggs looked at the clock on the vanity and saw that it was ten-thirty. *Where could Stephen be?*

The bathwater had grown tepid. The bubbles had fizzled, and the candles burned low and flickered when she stepped from the tub. As she toweled off, she looked at her body in the full-length mirror behind the bathroom door. *Not too bad for fifty-two,* she thought. She had been a tall girl, slender and graceful, with a face that was appealing more than it was pretty; and she had been very popular. She had dark blonde hair, tons of it, the color that some called sandy and some called blonde. Her driver's license said blonde, and it still was, mostly. A little longer than shoulder length, it curled easily into whatever style she chose. Next to her smile, which showed her perfect teeth and which was always close to surfacing, it was her best feature.

She had retained her youthful appearance for the most part. She was one of those fortunate women whose loveliness increases with the experience of living. She weighed a few pounds more than she wished, but with her height she carried them well. She had never been vain about her appearance but knew she used to occasionally turn heads when she passed. She wondered what it would be like to experience that again, unaware that it still happened with a regularity that would have surprised her. Critical of her reflection, she failed to realize she was comparing herself to the carefully cultivated glamour that was Delaine's.

Shrugging her shoulders dismissively, she put on her gown and sat down at her vanity. She began to brush her hair, slowly and rhythmically—the habit of a lifetime of never going to bed until she had brushed her hair a hundred strokes. When she finished, she rubbed lotion on her arms and legs. Finally, she turned back the covers, fluffed up the pillows, and got into bed with her book, intending to read until Stephen came home.

She was almost instantly asleep.

Chapter 2

*M*aggs was in the kitchen trying to get organized before Jason arrived when Stephen came downstairs. He hugged Maggs perfunctorily and reached for the coffeepot.

"More coffee, hon?" he asked with a smile.

"Please. Jason will be here soon, and I won't have time for anything until he's gone again. Stephen, what happened to you last night? And why didn't you call? I was so worried." Maggs exchanged the cup he handed her for the breakfast plate she had prepared for him.

"All in good time, Maggs. First things first. Why are we expecting Jason?"

"He can't go to day care today, he's got a virus or something. Leah called last night to ask if I'd keep him. It's nothing serious. He just can't go to day care with a temperature. Stephen, will you please tell me where you were last night?" Maggs sat down across from him and waited.

"I'm sorry I didn't call, Maggs, honestly. The time just got away from me. And when I realized how late it was, I didn't want to wake you. Terry Matthews wants to invest some capital in a venture that has good potential, and a friend recommended me. This could be the solution to expanding the company.

"Anyway, we went to have a drink after work to discuss the possibility. The discussion got pretty involved. I didn't realize what time it was until we started to leave. I'm sorry I worried you, but this may be the answer to my prayers. At the very least, it's worth investigating. We're going to discuss it further today."

They were interrupted by Leah bustling Jason through the door, his fat mouth in a smile, holding his arms out for Maggs to take him.

Leah deposited the load of paraphernalia that always accompanied Jason onto the kitchen table and said, "He seems to feel better this morning, Mom, but I'm going to get in touch with the doctor's office as soon as it opens and get him checked anyway. I'll call you as soon as I have an appointment. He's already had breakfast." Her voice trailed behind her as she made her way out the door, her arrival and departure seeming to be accomplished in one continuous circuit of the kitchen.

Maggs cuddled Jason against her, breathing in his delicious baby smell while he wiggled protestingly to get free. She put him on the floor; and he headed straight for Stephen, who gave him a bear hug, set him back on the floor, and kissed Maggs as he put on his coat and took his car keys from the hook beside the garage door.

"I won't be late tonight, and I'll tell you all about it when I get home. You be a good boy, Jason, and I'll bring you a surprise tonight."

"Come on, Jason, let's have some juice and then we'll go outside and feed the birds," Maggs said to Jason as she ruffled his dark ringlets.

The doctor confirmed that Jason would be fine by the next day. Maggs gave him lunch, coaxed him into taking a short nap, and in return was entertained by him the rest of the day. When Leah arrived to pick him up, Maggs gave her the doctor's report and kissed Jason soundly before returning him to his mother. Maggs watched them depart, feeling an almost painful surge of love for this precious baby. "Thank God, whatever differences Leah and Matt have, they haven't allowed them to affect Jason or Melody," she said to the empty driveway.

The phone was ringing when she went back into the kitchen.

"Hi, honey, how's it going out there?" Stephen asked.

She laughed. "Leah and Jason just left, and the house feels so empty now that he's gone. He can go back to day care tomorrow. What's up with you," she asked.

"Well, I know you must be tired, and I hate to put you on the spot, but I really need you to come into town and meet me for dinner. Can you manage?"

"I don't know, Stephen. I'm a wreck after today, and I'll have to start from scratch just to get ready. What's so important?" she asked, trying to keep the exasperation from her voice.

"Terry wants to continue our discussion at dinner. I'd like to include you in the discussion, and this would be a good opportunity for the two of you to meet. I have reservations for eight o'clock at the club. Say you'll come?"

"Stephen that's not but two hours from now, and it takes half an hour just to get into town. I'll give it my best shot, but if I look like a bag lady when I get there, don't be surprised. Is Terry bringing his wife?"

"Well, he isn't a . . . hold, on a minute, there's a call on the other line. Come on, Maggs, you couldn't look like a bag lady if you tried. See you at eight, okay?"

As she hung up and began mentally going through her closet, Maggs wondered irritably if it ever occurred to anyone in this family that she might need some time just for herself. She tried to shrug it off as she went upstairs to get ready. *Of course, I'll go,* she thought. *Of course. I always do what they ask me to. One of these days, I'm just not going to* anymore. *I wonder what they'll do then.*

At precisely eight o'clock, she drove into the parking lot, handed her keys to the attendant, and hurried inside to meet Stephen. She spotted his dark head above the rest of the crowd as the headwaiter ushered her to his table. He was listening attentively to a spectacular-looking woman.

Stephen stood up and put his arm around Maggs. The woman remained seated, extended her hand to Maggs, and said, "Hi, I'm Terry Matthews. I'm so pleased to meet Stephen's wife. He's told me a lot about you, all very complimentary. I'm glad you could join us. I know Stephen didn't want another long evening with me, but last night just sort of set the stage, so to speak, and we really need to get some of the details out of the way. Please sit down."

She assumed the role of Stephen's hostess with an ease and a presumption that immediately irked Maggs and set off warning signals in the female part of her brain. As she spoke, Terry's eyes appraised Maggs from top to toe while her smile suggested that another long evening with her would not have been disagreeable to Stephen, no matter what her words said.

She crossed her slim legs and said, "Stephen, be an angel and order me another glass of champagne. And order Maggs one too. I hope we'll have something to celebrate before the evening ends."

My god, thought Maggs, *I probably really do look like a bag lady compared to her. How could he not warn me? This lady is a piranha, and unless I miss my guess, Stephen is swimming straight for trouble and doesn't even know it.* She couldn't tell whether she was more annoyed with Stephen or Terry Matthews.

Maggs allowed her annoyance to disconcert her only momentarily however. She could hold her own against this kind of blatant encroachment. She recognized this kind of woman, and she wasn't intimidated. She just hadn't expected "Terry" to be a woman.

As Stephen seated Maggs, she sat back, leisurely crossed her own shapely legs and said, "Darling, I don't think I'm in the mood for champagne, it's so dull, don't you think? Order me a martini, if you would."

She smiled directly into Terry's eyes and saw a flash of understanding register, followed by a cool reappraisal of Maggs as a potential opponent, and followed immediately after that by a mask dropping into place in a too-late attempt to disguise her obvious interest in Stephen.

Maggs turned her attention to Terry. "Well, I must say your interest is most appreciated, Terry. Details do make the difference, of course, and certainly have to be ironed out. It's so gracious of you to include me at this stage of discussion and to understand that Stephen and I really do function as a team. I look forward to our association." Maggs gave her a dazzling smile and waited to see what her next move would be.

Terry seemed to understand that she had not only tipped her hand but grossly underestimated Maggs as well as her influence with Stephen, and the remainder of the evening was impersonal and businesslike.

*No further challenge—tonight, anyway—*thought Maggs with grim satisfaction. *But I'm sure this isn't over yet.*

Dinner seemed interminable. They discussed the prospect of expanding the market, not only statewide but eventually throughout the southeast, how much capital it would require, and what the options were for getting the ball rolling. Maggs was exhausted but attentive and offered pertinent comments and shrewd suggestions.

At length they finished their coffee, and Maggs was relieved that the evening was finally over. The parking attendant brought Terry's car around first—a shiny, expensive sports model—followed by Maggs's luxury family car. The contrast between the two vehicles was obvious to Maggs, but she wondered if the symbolism was lost on Stephen. She felt sure it was.

She beat Stephen home by several minutes and was getting ready for bed when he came upstairs. He talked all the time he was preparing for bed, and Maggs realized he hadn't been so enthusiastic in years. She also realized that he was clearly unaware that Terry Matthews's interest was anything more than business.

Maggs kept her part of the conversation light, supportive, and interested. But *not* unaware of the real motivation behind Terry's proposal, she reminded herself as she kissed him good night and turned out the light.

Chapter 3

Maggs awoke the next morning feeling groggy, disoriented, and vaguely ill. Nothing specific, mostly a sense of not being up to the demands of the day. But she put on her robe and washed her face, gave her hair a quick brush out, put on a trace of lipstick, and went downstairs.

She called to Sassie on the way downstairs, took Stephen's breakfast order, and made morning conversation while he ate his grapefruit and toast. After Stephen and Sassie were gone and she had straightened the kitchen, she still felt in the grip of something slightly evocative of an impending crisis.

She went to her desk and checked her calendar. Not too bad, just bridge and a manicure. Not feeling up to the girls today, and needing a breather worse than a manicure, she made phone calls to cancel both. Thankful that all the arrangements for the upcoming weekend at the club had been made, she made a pot of tea, put some fruit and toast on a plate, and went upstairs. She selected some magazines she had not looked though yet and climbed into bed.

She poured a cup of tea, picked up a magazine, and settled down for a little self-indulgence. She read for about an hour before drifting off to sleep and was dozing peacefully when the telephone ringing right next to her jolted her rudely back into the day.

"Maggs, it's Larry. I'm afraid I'm the bearer of some unhappy news, and I don't know any easy way to tell you. Aunt Eleanor died suddenly last night of a massive stroke while she was getting ready for bed. Molly was bringing her a glass of warm milk when she found her in distress. It was over almost instantly, if it's any comfort to know she didn't suffer. The doctor said there was nothing that could have prevented it. I've been here with her for the past several days, and she was fine right up to the time it happened. I'm really sorry to break it to you this way, Maggs."

"Oh, Larry, how awful! I can't believe it," Maggs exclaimed, struggling to sit up in bed. "I just talked to her last week. Oh, poor Aunt Eleanor! And poor Molly! Is she okay, Larry? She's so devoted to Aunt Eleanor. Oh dear, this seems like a bad dream." Maggs was trembling, and her lungs seemed unable to take in any air.

"Yes, I know what you mean. I'm rather in shock myself. Visitation has been set for four o'clock tomorrow afternoon, and the funeral will be Sunday afternoon. She'll be buried in the family cemetery on the grounds, of course. It's rather short notice, but you know Aunt Eleanor. She knew exactly what she wanted when her time came, and she's had the arrangements made for years, right down to the last detail. Will you and Stephen be able to make it?"

"Yes, of course we will," Maggs answered, already making mental arrangements. "I'll check the airline schedules as soon as I get off the phone, and we'll take the first flight out tomorrow. Is there anything else I need to know—or anything I need to do?"

"I don't think so. Oh yes, Aunt Eleanor specified that the reading of the will take place immediately after the funeral. Her attorney will meet with us in the library. Shall I arrange for Tom to pick you up at the airport tomorrow?"

"Yes, that will help. Will you be at the house when we get there?"

"No, I have to go to Columbia tomorrow. I can't get out of it, but I'll be back in time for the funeral. And I'd better tell you also that I have to leave Sunday night. I have an appointment Monday with my publisher in New York. I can't postpone it, but I'll take care of my business as quickly as I can. Can you manage until I get back?"

"Certainly. Take as long as you need," Maggs replied, her mind still running in high gear. "We'll see you Sunday then."

Maggs's hands shook as she hung up the phone. She was stunned and incredulous. Two weeks ago, Aunt Eleanor was in good health and good spirits, wanting Maggs and Stephen to come for a visit before the spring weather turned into the steamy summer heat of coastal South Carolina. Summers could be a real torture—even at Myrtlewood, Aunt Eleanor's breezy home on the banks of the Ashley River, about half an hour's drive outside of Charleston.

Eleanor Betford was actually Maggs's great-aunt, the twin sister of Maggs's maternal grandmother; and—with the exception of Maggs and her cousin, Lawrence Betford—she was the last of the Betford line.

Eleanor and Patrice (who was Maggs's grandmother) had been inseparable as girls. They had made a commitment to their papa, Charles Oliver Betford, III, to keep Myrtlewood in a condition befitting a gracious southern estate and to keep it in the family. He had left a large part of his considerable fortune in a trust for that purpose.

When the sisters were nineteen, Patrice met and married a young engineer who was just out of Virginia Military Institute, and they moved to Mobile to begin his career. Maggs's mother was their only child, and Maggs their only grandchild.

Aunt Eleanor was destined never to leave Myrtlewood. She became the unchallenged belle of the surrounding counties, not just because of who she was, but because she was a genuinely charming young woman—lovely, gracious, and generous of nature, a perfect example of a well-born young lady of the time. She had any number of interested suitors but didn't entrust her heart to any of them until she met a handsome young man from Boston who was less than honorable or honest. After the true nature of the gentleman was revealed and her papa expeditiously dispatched him back to Boston, Eleanor never again took any young man to be exactly what he claimed to be. In spite of her resistance to any further romantic involvement, she led an active social life. She flirted and laughed with her numerous admirers and genuinely enjoyed their company, but she kept them all at a distance and held on to her heartstrings. The guest without whom no party was complete, she became an established, well-loved fixture in her world.

She proved to be extremely clever—well up to the task of preserving the family home. Her wise stewardship actually added to the financial security of Myrtlewood as well as her own.

She and her sister visited back and forth through the years, and when Patrice gave birth to Martha Rose, Maggs's mother, Aunt Eleanor found an outlet for any frustrated maternal feelings she may have still felt. When in turn, Martha Rose married and Maggs came along, the situation perpetuated itself, and Maggs spent many memorable summers with her adoring aunt. Eleanor was never to anyone's knowledge bitter over not having a family of her own; rather her energy, devotion, and imagination were lavished on Myrtlewood and its extended family, always believing that they belonged to Myrtlewood and not the reverse. Teas, dances, graduations, engagements, weddings, christenings—all were celebrated grandly and joyously at Myrtlewood; and there was even an occasional retreat to mend a broken heart or recover from a bout of bad health.

Aunt Eleanor had lived alone at Myrtlewood for many years now, cared for by Molly Bridges, her devoted housekeeper and friend who had been with her since they were both girls. Molly's husband, Tom, took care of the grounds and the vehicles and drove Aunt Eleanor where she needed to go.

Myrtlewood had always been as much a part of Maggs's history as the home she and Stephen had shared in Mobile for so many years. Through the years, she had a multitude of friends at Myrtlewood and later on, not a few interested young men. Sleepovers and barbecues and parties at Myrtlewood were as much a part of her youth as those in her own hometown.

Maggs was Aunt Eleanor's only surviving relative, with the exception of Lawrence, who was not really a Betford by blood. Aunt Eleanor's father had had a younger brother who had been lured away in his teens by an adventurous nature and a desire to see the western half of his country. He had roamed happily for years, sending word occasionally of his whereabouts, finally settling in northern Montana with a young widow and her two-year-old son. He married the widow, adopted the child, and spent the remainder of his years in Montana, never once returning to his native South Carolina. He had no children of his own. Lawrence's father was that adopted child, and Lawrence himself was the only remaining member of that branch of the Betford family. As a boy he was always welcomed at Myrtlewood and always accepted as one of their own.

Lawrence was a noted Civil War historian and author who had never married and never seemed, as far as anyone could tell, to have a permanent residence anywhere. Over the years, he spent much time with Aunt Eleanor when he was in the South for some project or research. South Carolina's significant role in Civil War history had captivated Larry when he was still a boy spending most of his summers at Myrtlewood. He never tired of stories of the battles and visits to the battle sites, and he poured over the rich history of Charleston and Fort Sumter and the fall of Beaufort and Port Royal while his boyhood friends were playing sports and fishing. That early interest was the determining influence in his choice of professions. When he occasionally returned to teach courses on Civil War history at the College of Charleston, he was the happiest. He had an apartment in New York, and though he could rarely be found there, his agent could generally be prevailed upon to locate him if there was a need.

Maggs and Larry had grown up knowing that Aunt Eleanor's will provided for the house, her possessions, and her fortune to be left to Maggs with the exception of some bequests to favorite charities and institutions. Myrtlewood's fine collection of Civil War relics, weapons, and personal correspondence from Aunt Eleanor's great-grandfather were promised to Larry along with a generous legacy from Aunt Eleanor. It was all he wanted—besides the assurance that Myrtlewood would be preserved. The trust would see to that.

So as Maggs stood in her bedroom in a patch of dappled sunshine on this late April morning, she was overwhelmed by the realization that something she had always understood in the abstract had become an unhappy reality and required immediate action on her part.

As she mentally ticked off the things she needed to do, Maggs remembered with a jolt the husband-and-wife golf tournament and dinner dance this weekend at the club. It was a major charity fundraiser, and she and Stephen were hosting it this year. It had been months in the planning, and they couldn't just bow out now. They were responsible for seeing that it came off successfully.

What am I going to do? She ran her fingers through her hair, thinking frantically. I have to go to Charleston. But I have a responsibility here too. She sat down at her desk and dialed Stephen's number. She felt the tears begin to slide down her face as she heard the phone ring. She needed to share her grief with Stephen. She needed him to comfort her, and she needed him to tell her how they were going to manage being in two places at once.

She stood and paced the floor behind her desk. After what seemed a very long time, Stephen came to the telephone, his voice distracted and rather impatient.

"Oh, Stephen, the most terrible thing has happened. Aunt Eleanor has died. Larry just called and told me. And the funeral is Sunday. We have to be there, but I don't know what to do about the tournament this weekend. Stephen, I just can't believe she's gone. She was so full of life, and she had so many plans for this spring. It just doesn't seem possible."

The tears burned in her eyes as she tried to control herself, and Stephen said, "Now just take a deep breath, Maggs. Why don't you check the airline schedule, and I'll see if I can figure something out before I get home. I'll be there in a little while, and we'll make some arrangements then, okay?"

Maggs was a little calmer as she hung up the phone. She called the airport and got flight information. She got out her luggage but couldn't decide what to pack. She went back to her desk and telephoned a few close friends. She called Larry back to see if he had arranged for flowers. She called her older son, Mike, in Tuscaloosa and talked to his wife. She called Leah last.

When she had done all she could think to do, she sat on the chaise at her bedroom window and tried to collect her thoughts. She looked down into her garden without any perception of the color and pattern she had so carefully planned and tended while unbidden memories of Aunt Eleanor presented themselves for silent examination.

She had realized Aunt Eleanor was eighty-four years old, but somehow her age had always seemed to be mere information about her, like the place of her birth or the color of her eyes, and had no relevance to the living, breathing Aunt Eleanor. Maggs had never considered that Aunt Eleanor wouldn't always be at Myrtlewood because she simply always had been. But it had happened. She was gone. And in her place there remained a heartrending sense of loss.

As the reality of it invaded Maggs's soul, a small thunderhead erased the sunny patterns on the floor, and raindrops began to fall as if in silent partnership to the tears that overflowed from her eyes. Just as unexpectedly, the cloud gave up its final drops and passed on its way, allowing the sun's rhythmic dance to resume. Maggs knew Aunt Eleanor would have appreciated the symbolism. She would have found it interesting and appropriate and would have thought it an eminently satisfying parallel to her departure from this world. It had been one of her most ennobling qualities that she steadfastly believed life was for the living and mourning the inevitable was an unconscionable waste of time. As Maggs dried her eyes and went to wash her face, she whispered her silent thanks to Aunt Eleanor, whose spirit felt very close at that moment.

Maggs was downstairs mixing martinis when she heard Stephen's car pull into the garage. He came in, looked at her sad face, and hugged her to him tenderly. He could be unexpectedly sensitive to her feelings sometimes, and she was grateful that this was one of those times.

"I'm sorry, Maggs, I truly am. I know how this must hurt. I loved her too. She was a wonderful part of our lives, and we'll all miss her." His drawn face reflected the depth of his own sorrow.

"I think I have a solution to the problem of the tournament. It's not ideal, but it is workable. Suppose we find a substitute hostess for you, and I'll stay here and take care of the tournament while you go on to the funeral. I'll fly out to join you on the first flight I can get

Monday, and we'll fly home together later in the week. I hate like hell to send you off alone to deal with this, but we can't just excuse ourselves from the tournament at this point."

"Who could we ask to stand in for me? It's awfully short notice."

"I haven't got that far yet, but I'm sure almost any of your friends would fill in for you. Better yet, Sassie can take your place. She's a good golfer, and she can handle the receiving line. Anyway, I don't want you to worry. I'll take care of all that. You just get ready to leave, and I'll join you as soon as I can get there," he said.

Maggs poured their drinks, and they walked arm in arm out onto the terrace. It was late afternoon now; the birds were winding down their evening concert, and it was peaceful in the garden. It was Maggs's favorite time of day, but there was little serenity in her heart right now.

"Sassie has evening classes," Maggs said. "She doesn't know about any of this. We'll have to tell her when she gets in tonight."

"Have you talked to Leah?"

"Yes, she won't be able to come to the funeral. Jason doesn't seem quite back to normal yet, and she doesn't want to leave him. And I don't think she's comfortable leaving the children with Matt. She and Matt aren't on very solid ground right now. Anyway, Leah's never been as close to Aunt Eleanor as Sassie was. Sassie will miss being there, but I'm sure she'll agree to be your hostess."

"What about Greg?" And as an afterthought, "And Mike?"

"I called Greg earlier and left a message on his answering machine, but I'm sure there's no way he can come home. Mike was at the library when I called, but I talked to Meredith. She told me he's studying for finals next week. His acceptance to law school depends on these grades. He has to hit the books really hard this weekend. They're optimistic that he'll make it."

Stephen's jaw tensed and he snapped, "He should have been this serious six years ago, and he'd be studying for the bar by now. He probably wouldn't have come anyway."

Stephen's refusal to forgive Mike's cavalier attitude about his education was the cause of much ill will between them. Mike had played his way through three years at the University of Alabama and finally had to drop out because his grades were unacceptable. Stephen angrily refused to pay his expenses any longer, so after working for two years in a job he hated, Mike went back to school on his own. He had worked hard and was about to graduate, but at twenty-six, he still had law school ahead of him.

Maggs felt as though Mike had finally realized what he wanted out of life and was earning it on his own. She was proud of him. But Stephen couldn't overlook Mike's mistakes and would give him no credit for trying to rectify them. Maggs rarely talked to Stephen about Mike because they invariably argued when they discussed him. Maggs grieved deeply over the distance that existed between her second child and his father, but she grieved in private because there was no reasoning with either of them. Neither would give an inch; and she was stuck in the middle, understanding much about each of them that the other wouldn't concede, and loving them both. At times she was as angry at the two of them as they were with each other.

Mike had married during his second year in college; and his wife, Meredith, who was two years older than he, was already practicing law in Tuscaloosa while he continued in school. Meredith was a responsible young woman who loved Mike devotedly and had been willing to encourage him, defend him, and support him while he was floundering for direction. She juggled the multiple roles of rising young attorney, mother of four-year-old Jennifer, homemaker, and breadwinner in an admirable, uncomplaining way. She was very much like Maggs and even bore a striking resemblance to Maggs as she had looked in her twenties. One of the qualities they shared was unfailing loyalty toward those they cared about. Meredith and Maggs appreciated each other, and both were concerned about the immense distance that separated father and son.

Maggs had believed all along that Meredith's patience with Mike would ultimately prove worthwhile though it was understandably wearing a little thin by the time he decided to go back to college. It looked as though Mike had finally found the purpose Maggs had prayed for, but he and Stephen were still miles apart.

Maggs put her drink on the table and walked to the edge of the terrace to keep Stephen from seeing the telltale shine of the tears that came unbidden to her eyes. Mike seemed to always come between them, no matter what the occasion.

"Well, I guess your plan will have to do. There's not much choice. But I don't see any point in your having to fly all the way to Charleston just to escort me home. I can manage fine. Molly and Tom are there, and Larry will be there during the funeral and the reading of the will. We'll discuss what we need to do about settling the estate before he leaves. I'll spend the night Sunday and fly home Monday morning. I just hate that Sassie won't be there."

Maggs turned resolutely back to face Stephen, her emotions under control now that a plan had been decided upon. If he realized the pain their exchange about Mike had caused, he showed no sign of it. She gave him a quick hug as she went inside and dialed the airport.

She hung up the phone and said, "The only flight out tomorrow leaves early. I need to call Molly and make sure Tom knows what time to meet my plane. I'll finish packing after we eat. I haven't given dinner much thought. Does an omelet and salad suit you?"

"Why don't you let me take you out to get something to eat instead?" he said as he followed her inside. "We'll go somewhere quiet, and you can finish packing when we get home."

Maggs shook her head. She took the eggs from the refrigerator and said, "I don't really feel like going anywhere. I'd rather just finish packing and go to bed, if you don't mind."

As she cracked the eggs into the bowl and whisked them briskly, the tears began their slow descent down her face again. She thought she was crying for Aunt Eleanor, but she wasn't entirely certain.

Chapter 4

The flight from Mobile to Charleston was uneventful except for the omnipresent ill-behaved toddler with the permissive mother who seemed to be a part of every flight Maggs had taken in the last ten years. She was glad when they deplaned, and she spotted Tom's lanky form in the crowd. She waved to him as he headed toward her with his familiar loping gait. To look at Tom, one would never suspect the strength contained in the wiry body which looked so frail and brittle to her now in her fresh awareness that age can rob you so cruelly of your loved ones. He must be very close in age to Aunt Eleanor though he had not slowed down one whit in his chosen mission to protect and care for her and for his own Molly. His loyalty to Aunt Eleanor and those she loved was unchallenged.

Maggs had known Tom Bridges all her life. He was almost as much a fixture at Myrtlewood as Aunt Eleanor had been. He had walked Maggs around the grounds when she was first able to toddle and patiently answered her never-ending questions when she was learning to talk. He had driven her to parties and movies and was tactfully out of sight but never very far away when she was old enough to sit in the swing under the willow tree with a young man.

Maggs greeted him with a warm hug, which he accepted stiffly and then said gruffly, "I'll get your luggage, and we'll be settin' out, Ms. Maggs." He efficiently accomplished this, settled her in the car and they were soon on their way out of Charleston, bound for Old

Ashley River Road and Myrtlewood. Huge, moss-laden oak trees shaded dignified old streets and farther along as they left the city and neared Myrtlewood, more live oaks lined winding country roads that were a fond and familiar part of her childhood. The smell of honeysuckle and the hum of honeybees at work filled the air. Charmed by the countryside, she caught her breath in anticipation when they turned through the whitewashed gates and started up the long, tree-lined drive to the house.

Myrtlewood was early Carolina architecture at its finest. Built in the late 1700s, it had been in the Betford family for seven generations. It stood as elegantly in its surrounding acreage as a perfect diamond in a custom mounting, and as they approached the house, Maggs took in the four white Doric columns that supported a semi-circular front porch. Wide steps led from the circular driveway up to the porch. Leaded-glass doors, framed by similarly patterned sidelights, opened into a large marble-floored entry hall. In the center of the hall a large round pedestal table sat on a very old Persian rug. An ancient hall tree and a dignified grandfather clock faced each other from opposing walls. On the table, Aunt Eleanor always kept a large arrangement of freshly cut flowers from her gardens. Maggs wondered if she would find any there now.

The main body of the house was offset from the entry hall on both sides, and double pocket-doors of carved oak fitted with their original brass hardware led into the drawing room on the left and the library on the right. A massive fireplace dominated the end wall of each room, and floor-to-ceiling windows looked out onto the front lawn.

A smaller hall led from the foyer to the back of the house, which contained the kitchen, breakfast room, dining room and butler's pantry, a downstairs bathroom, and a laundry room.

An elegant double staircase curved gracefully up to a spacious upstairs sitting area where lamps glowed softly night and day. A Queen Anne library table contained books and magazines and, always, fresh flowers in porcelain vases. A small desk held writing materials. Two large front bedrooms opened into this area. Overlooking the back lawn and the river was an upstairs powder room for guests and the former nursery at Myrtlewood, which presently served as the fifth bedroom. The two rooms separated Aunt Eleanor's bedroom on one end and what had long been referred to as Maggs's bedroom on the other.

On the back of the house, six wooden columns supported a balcony that ran the entire length of the second floor and covered a porch below. Wooden railings bordered both balcony and porch, and colorful baskets of fragrant flowers hung between the columns in the warm months of the year. Wicker and wrought iron furniture provided seating for the back porch, and a glass-topped table and server for outside dining allowed Aunt Eleanor to take her meals there whenever the weather permitted. The formal dining room opened onto the back porch, and Maggs remembered many dinners with the double doors opened to the soft night sounds and the summer breezes from the river.

Stone steps led from the porch to the lawn, and an irregular flagstone path curved down to a small pier that protruded a slight distance out into the Ashley River.

When the car was clear of the trees, Maggs caught her first unobstructed view of the house, and the love she felt for this place came back in a rush of emotion. Myrtlewood rose, clean and white and evenly proportioned, in perfect placement amid lush beds of scented white flowers of every variety adaptable to growing in the climate of coastal South Carolina. Aunt Eleanor had been partial to white flowers, believing them to lend a style and grace to their surroundings that promised both peace and serenity. Crepe myrtles abounded, often as centerpieces for symmetrical beds of clipped ivy. The glossy foliage that would eventually give way to an impressive floral show when the heat of the deep summer brought forth the lacy blossoms and bent the branches near to the ground with their weight was now just barely visible. The azaleas—spectacular in their vibrancy and variety of color—were scattered everywhere among majestic old trees and provided the only glimpses of color this early in the spring. The grandeur of the ancient live oaks gave a dignity to the grounds that couldn't have been equaled by a lesser species. Squirrels frolicked along the gnarled branches as if certain they couldn't have found a better playground. The grass was already thick and vividly green and in its customary manicured state. Robins picked their way among the lushness, looking for midmorning snacks, ignoring the mockingbirds that chattered and quarreled as they chased each other through the trees in an attempt to settle territorial disputes and get on with their nesting. The brilliant red of a cardinal's wing could be glimpsed as twigs were brought to a favorite nesting site. Maggs wondered if they would nest again this year in the gardenia bushes around the gazebo. There had been a new generation of baby cardinals there every spring that she could remember.

Tom pulled the car up to the front of the house, and as he came around to open the door, Molly came quickly down the steps and held out her arms. Her eyes were swollen, and her face was puffy. She embraced Maggs, and they cried together while Tom shifted from one foot to the other in uncomfortable witness to more emotion than he liked to deal with.

Molly finally released Maggs and said, "Come on inside, dear, I've prepared lunch, and then I'm sure you'll be wanting to rest a bit and freshen up. Would you care to eat on the back porch where your dear aunt, God rest her soul, preferred her lunch this time of year? Blessed Jesus, I don't know what I'm to do, not having her to look after anymore." Her voice rose as she spoke, and her words ended in a fresh outbreak of tears; she struggled hard to regain control and then said to Tom: "Well, don't just stand there. Bring her things in, man."

Molly was slightly younger than Aunt Eleanor was, but she spoke as if Aunt Eleanor had been her child. Eighteen-year-old Molly O'Flynn had come to Myrtlewood to be Eleanor's personal maid when Eleanor was barely twenty and had remained ever since. The daughter of Irish immigrants, Molly was smart and funny and energetic, and she and Eleanor soon became fast friends, much more than mistress and servant. Molly was eventually promoted to housekeeper, a duty she assumed with pride while refusing to relinquish her duties as Eleanor's personal maid. When Molly married Tom Bridges, an energetic young gardener employed by Eleanor's father, there was never any question but that they would be given the caretaker's cottage on the grounds to set up housekeeping. For over sixty years, Molly had seen to Eleanor's every need. They were confidantes and friends; they grieved over each other's losses, laughed together over life's vicissitudes, and had had more than one rousing disagreement.

The lustrous red hair of Molly's youth had long ago turned white, but though the color had faded, its abundance was still something she was inordinately proud of. Her beautiful Irish complexion had softened with age but lost none of its glow. She had remained a small woman, a little rounder now—soft-looking but very strong, and the twinkle in her eyes that had so captivated everyone when she was young was still very much a part of her charm. Today the twinkle was replaced by despair.

I'll bet it never occurred to either Molly or Aunt Eleanor that the other might not always be here, Maggs thought as they climbed the steps and walked into the foyer.

"The porch sounds fine, Molly, but I'm not really hungry. I hope you didn't go to a lot of trouble. I could use a rest though."

"I've put your things in your room, Ms. Maggs," said Tom as he came downstairs. "Can I do anything else for you before I put the car away?"

"No, Tom, you've been very helpful. Thank you for coming to get me. I'll be fine with Molly."

He stood there awkwardly, red faced, twisting his hat in his rough hands, and finally blurted out, "I just want to say how bad I feel about this, Ms. Maggs. Ms. Eleanor was the salt of the earth, and there won't be nobody can take her place in my book." In one swift movement, he jammed his hat on his head and went swiftly across the foyer. Molly stared as the door slammed behind him.

"Well, I never! Well, let me get back to the kitchen. Lunch is almost ready," said Molly, still gazing at the front door. "Why don't you go in the library and prop your feet up while I finish. I'll come for you when it's ready." She paused briefly and then continued, "Ms. Maggs, I'm really glad you're here. It's been so awful. I feel like it's my life ending as well as hers. And I almost wish it was!" She burst into tears again and rushed to the back of the house, leaving Maggs staring after her helplessly.

Maggs looked around at the familiar surroundings with a heavy heart—the beauty of the marble floor; the fine grain of the wooden banisters on the hand-carved staircase, its intricate design polished to a high gloss with beeswax which left its well-remembered scent floating faintly on the air; the rich fabric of the draperies; the detail of the fine old moldings on ceilings, baseboards, and door casings; and the priceless crystal chandeliers hanging from their original plaster medallions. She gazed at it all as if she'd never seen it before, astonished that she had always taken such beauty for granted. In the days ahead serious decisions would have to be made concerning its future. Much of importance would be determined by the decisions she would make, and she wasn't sure she was prepared to make them.

The house was strangely silent as if it, too, mourned Aunt Eleanor. It had always been so filled with sound: laughter, telephones ringing, people coming and going, good music in the drawing room, the clink of china and crystal in the dining room, the drone of the lawn mower outside. It was almost as if the house, like Molly, was waiting to see what its fate would be.

She was surprised at how hungrily she took in every feature of her surroundings—how lonesome she had been for the peace and serenity this place never failed to impart. Even the faintly dusty smell that emanates from rare old things was remembered and welcomed. She went into the library, a favorite hideaway when she was a child, and slid her fingers over the rich leather on the wingback chairs, buttery soft and shiny from years of use. She looked at the multitude of books, the accumulation of forgotten generations of literate ancestors: leather-bound volumes, many of them irreplaceable, behind the glass doors of custom-made bookcases, and more books methodically catalogued on shelves that reached all the way to the fourteen-foot ceiling. Mahogany ladders reached to the top of the highest shelves and slid on brass rails along two sides of the room. As a child, the ladders had always enticed her because she was forbidden to climb on them. Now they were hers. Now it was *all* hers.

The impact of that single fact was sudden and powerful, and for the first time, she truly understood that her ownership of this place was an irrefutable reality. It wasn't just a question of deciding in the abstract what she would do with inherited property and possessions—this was all a part of her, and now it belonged to her with all the rewards and responsibilities that went along with ownership. She felt behind her for a chair and sank quickly into its reassuring depths. She drew her legs up under her and tried to put some order to all the feelings she was experiencing.

Foremost in her mind was the awareness that Aunt Eleanor would never again stand in the foyer or come down the staircase with welcoming arms. She would never again enter this library where she had so often found Maggs curled up with a book in front of the huge fireplace and say, "Come, dear, it's time to change for dinner. Put your book away for now." Maggs ached from the sense of loss, her pain sharp and new each time the thought recurred. Next to the awful finality of those thoughts, everything else just jumbled and spun around in her head—gratitude that Myrtlewood had been part of her family history for so many generations, anxiety over whether she would choose wisely about its disposal, concern about its future if she didn't choose wisely, nostalgia for the good times of the past. The thought of Myrtlewood no longer belonging to her family—of strangers wandering through its familiar rooms— was intolerable. She didn't think she could part with it.

And surely she must sell it! How could she keep it? She certainly couldn't live in it. Her life was in Mobile with Stephen and her family and her own home. Keeping Myrtlewood open for occasional visits wasn't practical. She would have to explore the options and take the necessary time to make the best decision.

For now she just wanted to be still and relax a few minutes before lunch. She watched the prisms of the chandelier move gently in the breeze from the open windows and felt some of the stress begin to dissipate. When lunch was ready, Maggs discovered she had an appetite after all. Molly seemed to have regained some of her composure as well. As she cleared the table, she said, "Now, Ms. Maggs, you just go right upstairs and have yourself a little nap. You'll find everything unpacked and your bed turned down. I know you're tired. Visitation's not until four o'clock. You just go on up there and rest, and everything will seem better when you come down."

"I think I'll do that. Thanks for lunch, Molly. You certainly haven't lost your touch in the kitchen."

She rose from the table and went through the dim, cool interior of the house and up to her bedroom. It had always been her bedroom even when she was a little girl, and it had been decorated in little-girl prints. It was a huge room, dominated by a tremendous four-poster bed with an elaborate canopy and side panels that were pulled back and tied with satin chords. The bed was very old as were the other pieces of furniture, all massive and dark and crafted of some unfamiliar highly polished wood. The room was saved from being gloomy by its generous size, which more than adequately accommodated the heavy furnishings and by the abundance of light that flowed into it.

The window draperies and the canopy over the bed were made of purple brocade lined with ivory satin. The bed linens were edged with handmade lace, and the pillowcases were monogrammed. The loveseat and chairs were upholstered in pale lilac and complimented the wallpaper above the chair rail. The hardwood floor was mellowed to a fine patina by much use and lots of wax. A large Aubusson rug was centered under the bed, and smaller rugs were scattered about the room like bright bouquets. An intricately carved marble mantelpiece surrounded the fireplace.

Molly had laid a fire against the chill of an early spring evening. In front of the hearth, an overstuffed chair sat beside a delicate Victorian table. Maggs had fallen asleep in the chair many times as she read late into the night; and Aunt Eleanor or Molly would find her there, close her book, and lead her to bed.

Maggs opened the balcony doors and went outside, filling her lungs with the familiar smells of the river. A chaise lounge sat directly outside the balcony doors, and she noticed that Molly had put the thick purple and cream striped cushions on the old wicker furniture and laid an afghan across the foot of the chaise.

Wrought iron tables held hurricane lamps, and the latest issues of several magazines were on the table next to the chaise. A pitcher of ice water and a bonbon dish filled with Maggs's favorite lemon drops gave further evidence of Molly's loving solicitude.

The balcony was long and shady. At the far end, a second set of French doors opened from Aunt Eleanor's bedroom. A porch swing was suspended from the ceiling facing another wicker seating group. Maggs noticed with a pang that no cushions were on the furniture at that end of the balcony and the swing was sadly still. It was impossible not to recall the many times she had been lulled to sleep in that swing by Aunt Eleanor's soft lullabies.

Turning her eyes quickly away, Maggs looked toward the river. The back lawn sloped gradually to the water's edge. A little rowboat, weathered but intact, lay upside down on the grass beside the small pier. Flowerbeds abounded here too, carefully planned so as not to detract from the view of the river. These beds were not restricted to white flowers, and later in the summer, they would provide colorful contrast to the green of the spacious backyard.

Maggs noticed someone had also put cushions in the gazebo that sat halfway between the porch and the river. Wisteria twined pale lilac blooms around the posts, and eaves and wafted its delicate perfume aloft to the river breezes. Gardenia bushes surrounded the gazebo and promised their almost overpowering scent by early June, and large pots of geraniums on the steps awaited the sun's enticement to bloom. The sight of the gazebo brought to mind long summer hours spent reading, gossiping with friends, or sitting in the moonlight with a sweetheart while the ceiling fan whirred drowsily. Later she had spent many hours there with Stephen, dreaming and making plans for their future.

Maggs's deep feeling of contentment was tinged with guilt over how she could feel so much pleasure in her surroundings at the same time she felt so much pain over her loss. As she stood there, she suddenly realized Aunt Eleanor would not only understand— she would heartily approve of Maggs's acute awareness of all the beauty she had worked so lovingly to create, and she was comforted by the thought.

Reluctant to give up the view, Maggs sat down on the chaise and pulled the afghan over her legs. The gentle flow of the river soothed her bruised heart, and she fell asleep.

When she awoke, it was nearly three o'clock. She bathed, dressed, and went downstairs to find Molly waiting, dressed in her Sunday best.

"Tom has brought the car around, Ms. Maggs. We're ready when you are." Maggs nodded her head in acknowledgment but didn't speak as they went out to the car. Molly was uncharacteristically quiet on the drive into Charleston, and Tom said nothing at all. They were all preparing themselves for the next few hours and the next few days. When visitation was over at last and she had been hugged and patted and consoled by the seemingly endless stream of Aunt Eleanor's friends and admirers, Maggs was exhausted. The drive home found the three of them even more subdued.

When Tom let them out at the front door, Maggs went to change out of the black dress and the shoes that had been pinching her toes for hours, and Molly went straight to the kitchen to put the teakettle on, her timeworn antidote for troubled spirits. Maggs washed her face, put on a pleated linen skirt and a lightweight summer sweater, and was slipping on some flat shoes when there was a knock on her door.

"Come in, Molly."

"Ms. Maggs, you have a visitor. Mr. Huntingdon is downstairs. Will you see him?"

"Of course. Show him into the drawing room and give him a drink. Say I'll join him right away."

"Shall I bring your tea to the drawing room, dear?"

"Yes, please, Molly."

Maggs combed her hair, applied a little lipstick, put on her earrings, and went down to meet her guest.

Entering the drawing room, Maggs had an opportunity to observe George Huntingdon before he realized she was in the room. He was tall and slender and elegantly turned out. He had the unpretentious dignity of someone completely sure of his place in his world and thoroughly comfortable with that place. He owned the adjoining property, an antebellum style plantation estate called Riverside, which had a rich history of its own though neither quite as lengthy nor as distinguished as Myrtlewood's.

Riverside was separated from Myrtlewood by acres of dense hardwood forest through which a maze of creeks twisted like veins of marble before spilling into the dark waters of the river. Marshy areas bordered by bald cypress, live oaks, and willows created a marked contrast between the tranquility of the forest and the wild and beautiful if somewhat sinister feel of the marshes.

Maggs had played in the edges of this forest as a child, venturing at times farther than she was allowed because the wildness of the place found an answering wildness in her fearless young heart. Its appeal was irresistible in spite of the many warnings she received from her elders to stay away.

Once she had wandered far into the vivid maze of color and scent and sound and had eventually lost her way. A bright autumn sun had shone through bare spots on the trees where they were beginning to shed their vivid fall coats. Brilliant orange and bloodred and yellow and gold leaves floated in the air, driven by a brisk breeze that carried the promise of cooler days to come. Birds of every sort sang out into the brightness. Some were strident and raucous and others sweet and lilting, and they all mingled in a powerful melody that filled the forest with sound before rising high above the tops of the tall trees. She imagined the beauty of their song reaching all the way to God in his heaven. The scent of the rich verdant soil which lay just underneath the coating of glistening leaves filled the air; and she breathed deeply of it, filling her lungs until they felt as if they would burst while the magic of the sights and sounds and smells surrounded her and spurred her on ever deeper into the enchanted forest. It had rained the night before, and the glistening droplets remaining on the leaves that had not yet fallen gave a sparkling, crystalline brilliance to everything the sunbeams touched. The leaves on the ground were damp and shiny, and as she walked, they made soft swishing sounds which she found very pleasant.

She had wandered for hours, never afraid, never thinking she was lost; and when she finally came out again, she had somehow made her way through the entire width of the forest and found herself on the grounds of Riverside. George Huntingdon was supervising the gardeners in the planting of a new rose bed and was delighted when he looked up to see her gazing at him with a precocious smile and shining eyes. That was the beginning of their friendship. He had given her milk and cookies after letting Aunt Eleanor know that Maggs was with him and drove her home in his antiquated touring car, which seemed to her very grand. Aunt Eleanor was so relieved to see her that she only scolded her mildly. Maggs always suspected that Uncle George (as he asked her to call him that day) had privately interceded on her behalf, and she and George Huntingdon were fast friends from that day on although she had to promise that her visits would not be the result of wandering through the woods again. The wild beauty of the forest was dangerous to the unwary traverser, he said, and she mustn't take chances. She didn't know what a traverser was, but she promised dutifully. After that, he would send the car for her, and they visited often.

As he turned to greet her now, Maggs's pleasure in seeing him was as great as his when he had looked up from his roses to find her smiling at him on that day so long ago.

"Hello again, my dear. I've come to take you to dinner. I know you must be exhausted, and you surely must feel as if you've seen enough people for one day, but I don't want you to spend the evening alone. We'll have a quiet dinner, and I'll bring you home right afterward so you can get some rest. Say you'll come."

Maggs responded to the sincerity that radiated from his dear face and the genuine affection she could hear in his voice, and as she considered his invitation, she realized she had dreaded the long hours of the evening that remained ahead of her.

"That sounds wonderful, Uncle George. Let me tell Molly and get a sweater, and I'll take you up on your offer. We need to catch up on each other's news, and this will give us a chance to do that." She gave him a quick hug as she went to find Molly.

They were driven to Riverside in the same grand touring car he had owned since the day she had met him. It was very old now; but its surface was polished, its chrome sparkled, and the rich leather of the interior still had its wonderful cared-for feel. *This car suits him*, she thought. They are both of another era but still elegant and gracious and handsome. And irreplaceable.

As Maggs gave her hand to Uncle George's driver to help her from the car, she glanced up and saw a very tall man standing at the front door. Uncle George took her elbow as they climbed the steps; the tall man stood at ease, smiling.

"My dear, I'd like you to meet my nephew, Christopher Allendale. Chris, this is Eleanor's niece and my very dear friend, Mary Margaret Masters."

He turned to Maggs and said, "Chris is the son of my only sister, who lived in Maine until her death several years ago. I don't believe the two of you have ever met, and it's high time you did. Chris is staying with me for a while. You aren't going out, are you Chris? I had hoped you could join us for dinner."

As Maggs extended her hand, she looked into the most interesting face she had seen in a long time. Still smiling, he took her hand.

"I'm delighted to meet you, Mrs. Masters. And I'll be happy to join you and your guest for dinner, Uncle George," he said, turning to his uncle.

Maggs found herself almost uncomfortable. "Please call me Maggs. Everyone does. I'm so glad to meet you after all this time. Uncle George has always talked about you, and I can't believe none of our visits ever coincided. I'm glad you can join us."

She sounded to herself as if she was babbling, and it embarrassed and irritated her. She felt self-conscious and awkward and struggled to regain her poise.

When she looked up, he was smiling directly into her eyes, still holding her hand. His gaze was friendly and open and in no way inappropriate; nevertheless she removed her hand hastily enough that she knew it showed her discomfort. Uncle George assumed command of the situation, much to her relief, asking his nephew about his day and making polite conversation as he ushered them into the drawing room.

"Will you have some sherry, my dear? Or would you prefer a martini?" A sharp memory for details was only one of the things that made him special, and Maggs was not surprised that he remembered her drink preference.

"Sherry, I think, Uncle George."

As she accepted the glass, she looked around and said, "This is such a beautiful room. I feel so comfortable here—I always have since I was a little girl. It feels wonderful to be back again. I'm glad you came for me tonight, Uncle George. It's been a tiring day, and I think I really needed this."

"My dear, you know you're always welcome here. I have long felt as if you were a part of my family, and I'm always happy when you are in my home. I'm only sorry the occasion of your visit is such a sad one. But let's not dwell on that tonight. Shall we go in to dinner?"

The draperies were open, and an evening breeze ruffled the panels at the dining room windows. The table was beautifully set, candles glowing softly, and somewhere in the distance, she could hear the gentle strains of Chopin.

During dinner, Maggs shed her awkward feelings for the most part, but once or twice, she looked up and found Christopher smiling across the table at her and felt strangely unsettled, somehow vulnerable. She wasn't sure why she was reacting this way. It wasn't simply because he was attractive. He was also educated, interesting, and exuded an air of quiet sophistication; but none of those things accounted for her confusion. She wasn't inexperienced in the art of casual flirting, but this didn't feel like flirtation, either. His behavior was well within the boundaries of accepted social exchanges, and she knew it. It could only be that it had more to do with her than with him.

She discovered that Christopher was engaged in research for the detection and prevention of genetic birth defects. Uncle George supplied that he was an eminently respected physician in the field. He was taking a yearlong sabbatical to offer a series of lectures at the Medical University of South Carolina in Charleston. He had been in Charleston about eight months and planned to return to Maine at the end of the summer.

Maggs was thoroughly enjoying herself as they lingered over brandy in the drawing room when the mantle clock struck eleven.

Rising from her chair, she said, "Uncle George, this has been a great pleasure. I can't tell you how much it has meant to me. But tomorrow is going to be another long day, and I really should be leaving. Will you ask Anthony to bring the car around?"

"Yes, of course, my dear, I'll see you home at once. My apologies for keeping you so late; but you have given us a welcome break from our solitary dinners, and it has been wonderful to have you here again." He rose from his chair and went to the telephone to send for the car.

"It's not necessary for you to see me home, Uncle George. I'll be fine with Anthony. Please don't bother," she said as she collected her purse and her sweater.

Uncle George helped her on with her sweater. "It's out of the question. I wouldn't dream of sending you home unescorted," he said.

"I agree, Uncle George, but let me do the honors," Christopher said, taking Maggs's arm. "You look tired yourself, and I'll be glad to see Maggs home."

"Very well, Chris, if Maggs has no objection. I am rather tired, at that, so I won't wait up for you. I'll see you at breakfast. My dear, please let me know if I can be of assistance while you are here. You have given me a most enjoyable evening."

He placed his hands on her shoulders and kissed her lightly on the forehead. They walked into the foyer together, and Uncle George started up the stairs as Christopher steered Maggs to the waiting car.

They were companionably quiet on the short drive home. When he walked her to the front door, he said, "I've really enjoyed meeting you, Maggs. It's a shame we haven't met before. How long will you be at Myrtlewood?

"I'm leaving Monday morning. I'll have to come back later to tend to some of the details of settling the estate, but I'm not sure when that will be. I'm sure I'll see you and Uncle George when I return. Thank you for a lovely evening. I understand why Uncle George has always spoken so fondly of you."

She extended her hand and felt a warm, friendly pressure before he released it and walked toward the car. She started inside, then, on impulse, turned and called after him softly.

"Christopher?"

He turned back to her with an inquiring look.

"There was a time when I thought Aunt Eleanor would always be here whenever I found time to be with her. I'm glad you're spending this time with Uncle George while he's still here. And thanks for bringing me home."

She went inside, feeling rather warm and fuzzy from the brandy and the good company, and went straight upstairs. She knew Tom was around somewhere, in the kitchen probably, waiting to secure everything for the night after making sure she was home safely. It felt strange to be looked after in this way. But comforting. It had been a long time since someone else waited up and locked up and made sure everyone was in for the night. In fact, she had felt protected and cared for and appreciated ever since Tom picked her up at the airport that morning.

Her bed was turned back and a small fire glowed in the fireplace. She went into the bathroom and washed her face and brushed her teeth before changing into her gown and robe. She was tired, but somewhat restless, and the breeze coming through the windows was tempting. She picked up her brush, turned out the light on the bedside table, and went out onto the balcony to brush her hair and unwind a little in the quiet of the late hour.

She wondered why Stephen hadn't called. She had left a message on their answering machine that she had arrived safely and had asked him to let her know how the tournament was going. Molly would have left a note if he had called.

She gazed down into the gauzy mist floating low over the river and reflected on the evening. She had been flattered by Christopher's interest, his warm, admiring manner. His interest wasn't personal, of course, merely the ordinary courtesy he would extend to any friend of the family; but she wasn't sure her response had been quite so impersonal. Had it been that long since a charming man had admired her? Maybe she felt so compelled by this one because there seemed to be nothing shallow or superficial about him. And she had indisputably found him compelling.

She finished brushing her hair and still wasn't sleepy, but realizing that tomorrow and its sad responsibilities would be upon her in a few short hours, she went reluctantly inside, leaving the balcony doors open to the night breezes, and climbed into the large, empty bed.

Chapter 5

he next morning while Maggs was having breakfast on the sunny back porch, Molly bustled through the screened door to announce the return of Lawrence Betford, who followed close on her heels.

"Good morning, Maggs," he said. "It looks like it's going to be a beautiful day for Aunt Eleanor's funeral. If there's any such thing as a beautiful day for a funeral. Is everything going okay? I feel like a rat for abandoning you yesterday and having to leave again tonight, but these arrangements were made a long time ago, and they're very hard to reschedule. I'm really sorry."

He kissed the top of her head and then collapsed disjointedly into a wicker armchair as Molly placed a cup of steaming coffee in front of him. "Will you be wanting something to eat, Mr. Larry?" she said. "The grapefruits are nice just now. Or I can whip you up some eggs if you'd prefer."

"No thanks, Molly, I grabbed a bite at the airport in Columbia before I left. Just keep the coffee coming. I'll get a shower and shave as soon as I catch my breath."

Larry was tall and bone-thin. He had a head full of wiry hair, salt-and-pepper now, Maggs noticed, and a thick handlebar mustache of the sort commonly worn by soldiers in the Civil War. He might have appeared quite ludicrous except for mischief-filled dark eyes that signaled immediately that he didn't take himself too seriously and didn't want anyone else to either.

He was exactly what he appeared to be; he was secure and happy just as he was and had no time for anyone who wanted to change him. His reputation was that he was honest and intelligent and ethical in his profession as well as his personal affairs, and all who dealt with him held him in high regard. His work was his passion. He found it endlessly inspiring and absorbing and seemed to need nothing else in his life. He was boyish in his enthusiasm with the few people he bothered to be close to.

Maggs loved him dearly and always had. Aunt Eleanor had understood from the time he was very young what a special person he was and had wisely encouraged his interest and nourished his talent. She had also helped enormously with his education, and Larry was very grateful for all she had done. He would miss her as deeply as Maggs would.

Maggs smiled her forgiveness at him and said, "Don't give it a thought. Everything went fine. I'm glad you're here though. Today will be harder to get through."

Folding her napkin and pushing her chair back, she said, "I'm going upstairs to get ready for the funeral. Tom will drive us all in together when we're ready. He and Molly will sit with us in the family pew, of course."

On the way into Charleston, Larry raised the glass between them and the front seat and said, "Maggs, we've known about Aunt Eleanor's will for a long time. I just want you to know I wholeheartedly agree with its terms. She was generous to me beyond measure, all my life. She gave me love and family and support, and those are things that can't be measured. I want nothing more. Do you understand?"

"Of course, I do. I've always known Myrtlewood would be mine some day. I guess I just never considered what the reality of it would be. Now it's here, and I'm not prepared for the responsibility that goes along with it. But the real importance of Aunt Eleanor in my life was the same as in yours, Larry, and that loss seems monumental right now. I'll deal with what follows as it comes.

"Fortunately, I know a little about settling an estate because of the years I worked for Patrick Delaney. Since Aunt Eleanor's personal finances were always kept separate from the trust, everything should be pretty straightforward. I don't think there will be anything I can't manage. Her attorney has managed her affairs as long as I can remember, and he'll help us through the process. Go on with your plans. I insist. Just stay close today, okay? I really need Stephen, and it just isn't possible for him to be here."

"Thanks, Maggs. I knew you'd understand. My flight doesn't leave until ten o'clock tonight, and after that I'm as close as the nearest phone. If I need to come back, it won't be a problem."

He patted her hand; and they fell silent, each thinking about the grand lady they were laying to rest, all she had meant to their lives, and all her absence would signify.

The funeral was dignified and brief, planned long ago to be as painless for relatives and friends as possible. Aunt Eleanor was as painstaking in the matter of her departure from the world as she had been in the everyday living of her life. Afterward, the line of cars returning to Myrtlewood seemed endless and reminded Maggs again of how beloved her aunt had been.

Eleanor Betford was laid to rest in the small family cemetery in a quiet grove of ancient oaks separated from the rest of the grounds by a freshly painted white picket fence. Weathered benches were scattered among the moss-laden trees, and grave markers ranging from simple headstones to elaborate monuments testified to the longevity of the Betford family. Eleanor had valued the serenity and harmony of this place, often coming here to read and think when she had a rare free hour. The gnarled old trees she had loved so well stood guard now as if they too were paying their final respects.

In the time-honored tradition of the South, mourners were invited back to the house for refreshment. When Maggs thought she couldn't remain standing one minute longer, the last condolence was offered, and the last neighbor departed.

There remained in the sudden stillness of the house only Maggs and Larry, Molly and Tom, and John Grover Houston III, Eleanor's attorney. It was late afternoon, and the last rays of sun sprayed the floor in front of the windows. Maggs led the way to the library where they seated themselves and waited for Mr. Houston to begin.

He placed his briefcase on the desk, took out a folder, cleared his throat, and—after again expressing his condolences—read the last will and testament of Eleanor Betford.

When he was finished, they sat as before, in silence, while he offered any assistance he might provide and gathered his papers into his briefcase, declared his intention to see himself out, and quietly departed.

There were, as expected, no surprises. Eleanor had provided generously for Molly and Tom Bridges, left the precious Civil War papers and relics to Larry, and made provision for some personal bequests. The remainder of her estate would pass to Maggs. There was a sealed letter for Maggs, which Grover Houston gave her to open later, when she was alone. Maggs numbly placed it on the desk as she rose from her chair, summoning what energy she had left to decide what to do next.

As the sad group walked out of the library, the day was drawing to a close and dusk was settling in. The sounds of the birds finding their perches were becoming fainter and farther apart as they waged their nightly battle for position. Evening breezes from the river ushered in the light fragrance of wisteria. *Strange*, thought Maggs, *how everyday life goes on regardless of the arrival or departure of frail humanity as though in confirmation that birth and death don't really alter things in any significant way. Nothing is the same, and yet everything is the same.*

Molly was the first to regain her sense of purpose. "I'll just make a fresh pot of coffee and lay some supper out for you and Mr. Larry. He'll need something to eat before he leaves. Tom, you come help me."

She hurried off into her familiar kitchen, almost as if she were grabbing a lifeline. She knew what to do when someone needed feeding or caring for. Maggs understood Molly's need for some connection to keep her going; she wondered what her own would be.

She turned to Larry and said, "I need a breath of air. Let's go for a walk."

They walked through the great front doors and down the steps into the soft evening. Larry put his arm around her and said, "Is there anything we need to discuss, anything I can help you with before I go?"

"I can't think of anything, Larry. You've been a great comfort, and I can't tell you how grateful I am for your support today. The rest is just a matter of getting everything started, and I think it will help to have something to do. Please don't worry about me, I'll be fine."

They walked in silence for a while, and Maggs felt some of her strength return. As they approached the house, Molly was standing at the top of the steps, beckoning them in.

"Before we go in, Larry, I want you to understand that Myrtlewood will be as much your home as it has always been. I'm sure you must understand that, but I wanted to say it anyway. I don't know what I'll finally do with the house, but as long as it belongs to me, it's also yours."

"It never occurred to me that it would be otherwise, Maggs."

They ate in the breakfast room and took their coffee to the library. When it was time for Larry to leave, Maggs hugged him fiercely and then stood outside the front door and watched Tom take him down the drive and out of sight, feeling a good deal more uncertain than she had let on.

When she came back inside, her exhaustion seemed to be exerting some sort of paralysis on her body. She went in search of Molly and found her in the kitchen. Molly took one look at her face and held out her arms. Maggs walked into Molly's comforting embrace and stood for a long time without moving.

Finally she said, "I'm going upstairs to have a hot bath and then go to bed, Molly. I'll see you in the morning."

"Go right on up, dear. I'll bring you a brandy. You'll sleep better afterward. Things will look brighter to us all tomorrow, I'm sure."

Maggs was halfway up the stairs when she remembered the letter from Aunt Eleanor and went back to the library to get it. In her bedroom, the fire was burning brightly, the lamps were glowing, and her bed was turned down. She marveled at Molly's resourcefulness, wondering where she found the time to do all she did for this family in the space of one short day.

Maggs ran the tub as hot as she could stand it while she undressed. She pinned her hair up and slipped down into the steamy water. She closed her eyes and immediately felt some of the weariness begin to dissipate. After a few minutes, she opened her eyes and reached for the letter. It was addressed simply "Maggs." The writing paper was familiar—cream colored, monogrammed in deep red—the same familiar stationery Aunt Eleanor had used all her life. Inside the envelope were several sheets, written in Eleanor's old-fashioned script. It felt very odd to be here in these familiar surroundings reading a letter from someone who should be sleeping in her own bedroom just down the hall. As Maggs read, her thoughts were like a kaleidoscope, changing constantly as the words of the letter surprised her, consoled her, and ultimately offered an unexpected alternative to the routine of her life that intrigued her even as it challenged her.

My Dearest Maggs,

When you read this letter I have no doubt you will be in an emotional state. I regret that this request will befall you at a time when you are not prepared for it, and I apologize most sincerely for presenting it to you in this way. It has, however, been given a great deal of thought, and I pray you will understand why I have chosen this way.

From your first visit to Myrtlewood as an infant, I felt your destiny was here. You have exhibited a strong sense of belonging here all your life, and I have been thrilled that you felt so. You have always known Myrtlewood would be yours one day, but unless I am mistaken, have given little thought to exactly what that would mean.

You are aware of the trust that was established by Papa to provide for the preservation of Myrtlewood. If Grover Houston has not explained the mechanics of the trust by now, I am sure he will soon. This trust will apply—unless you decide to sell Myrtlewood. My dearest wish is that you will find a way to keep it in our family. I understand exactly what that would entail. Your own home is dear to you, as it should be, and it would be most difficult for you to oversee the operation of Myrtlewood from such a distance.

It goes without saying, my dear, that it is yours to do with as you choose. I trust you will believe I mean that most sincerely. I know your decision will be made with careful consideration of all options. That is all I can ask. God has blessed me with a long and full life here, for which I am truly grateful.

Dearest Maggs, here is my request. I am asking you to spend one uninterrupted month as chatelaine of Myrtlewood before making your final decision. As I write this, I appreciate the enormity of my request and anticipate the amazement with which you will surely receive it. But if ultimately you decide to part with Myrtlewood, you will have experienced for a short while the joy that belonging here has given me. You will have that memory always.

Molly and Tom are provided for regardless of what happens to Myrtlewood. I long ago deeded them the caretaker's cottage and the acre of land it rests upon. They will want for nothing. But I feel sure they would be delighted to look after you at Myrtlewood should you find you can stay.

I have prided myself in attempting to live my life as unselfishly as I could, and it is no casual matter that I set aside that commitment to make a request of such magnitude of someone to whom I wish only the best life has to offer.

I have told no one that I would ask this of you, and if you cannot find a way to grant my wish, no one need ever know. I can only say in closing that sometimes we are faced with a choice that can make a difference in our lives; and I speak from experience when I say that security is a fair sacrifice for great love. I have always treasured your love and believe you know how greatly I have loved you in return. You are the child my heart would have chosen had my life taken a different course. Always follow your heart, my darling. Be brave, and be happy. Above all, be happy.

Aunt Eleanor

Maggs laid the letter aside; although the bathwater had grown cold, she felt very warm inside. Very stunned and very shaken, but very warm indeed. It was as if somehow Aunt Eleanor's love had reached out and wrapped her in a warm, cozy blanket.

She dried herself slowly, pulled on a thick robe, and sat down at her dressing table to brush her hair. One hundred strokes later, her mind was still doing a fast spin over the unexpected contents of the letter. She picked up the snifter of brandy Molly had left, turned off the lamps, and went outside. She stood on the balcony, lost in thoughts that were erratic and confused. After a few minutes, she sat back on the chaise and covered herself with the afghan.

There was no way Myrtlewood could become their permanent home. Stephen would never be willing to leave his business. He had worked long and hard and was enjoying the resulting success. It wouldn't be fair to ask him. As she thought of Stephen, she was reminded that he had still not returned her messages. It was unlike him not to be in touch when he knew she was upset. Had there been a problem at the tournament? In any case, it was too late to call him now. She would try to catch him in the morning before he left for work.

Her thoughts returned to the question at hand. She fully understood the twin impracticalities of keeping the house always ready for occupancy or the alternative of closing it for long periods of time. Myrtlewood needed to be alive, all the time, filled with people who wanted to be there, not waiting for dry rot and deterioration to set in during long periods of vacancy.

But selling it outright was something she couldn't bear to consider. And anyway, who would buy it? Someone who might tear it down for the property on which it sat? Someone who wanted to buy someone else's history? The cost of the upkeep alone, without the trust established for that purpose, would deter almost anyone who wanted to buy it even if she could tolerate the thought of parting with it.

No, the historical register sounded like the best plan, by far. Grover Houston could put her in contact with people who could tell her how to go about it. She believed the process was quite lengthy, requiring a proposal and various stages of approvals by divergent boards and commissions; financial arrangements would have to be made to convert the trust, and God knows what else. She thought it could be set up so she could either retain ownership and allow the house to be maintained and operated by the historical society or relinquish ownership of the entire property, trust fund and all, and sever all ties.

She couldn't make such a complicated decision until she had more information, but she could get started. She determined to get as much information as possible, present it to Stephen, and see what he thought she should do. A month should give them plenty of time to decide.

For she realized as she stared out at the mist-laced river that she would do as her aunt had asked. How could she not? She also realized, with a bit of surprise, that she wanted to do this. Stephen wouldn't like it, and she had conflicting feelings about his disapproval; but she had been in the doldrums over the ordinariness of her life for a long time, and a month away might allow her to figure out what the problem was.

She had intended to write a book ever since she had finished college, but the demands of her life had never quite allowed her time. At least she thought that was the reason. This would be a good time to find out whether writing was something she might be able to do or just something she used to daydream away her frustrations.

She would do it. There was no valid reason why she couldn't or why she shouldn't. She would talk to Grover Houston tomorrow morning first thing and then catch her flight to Mobile. She would explain all this to Stephen and make arrangements to return to Myrtlewood.

The relief that followed her decision finally translated into drowsiness. As she rose to go inside, she saw a canoe gliding silently down the river in the moonlight. Her impression of its solitary occupant was not one of loneliness—she sensed rather that he was filled with peace by his late night's journeying, that it filled a need and was in no way random or impulsive. His contentment was oddly reassuring. She wondered idly who the man might be and why he chose this hour. Maybe I'm starting a journey of my own—a journey in search of me. *About time*, she thought, as she folded herself into the soft enveloping bed.

It had been a long, tiring day, sad in so many ways, but ultimately positive somehow, leaving her inspired and challenged. She had a strange sensation that Aunt Eleanor knew what she had decided and approved. Stephen would be a different story.

Chapter 6

The overflow of sunshine and a soft morning breeze coaxed Maggs awake the next morning. She stretched and snuggled deeper under the bedcovers and began to plan her day. It was a long-standing habit and persisted even when she was away from home. The first thing she needed to do was call Stephen and tell him what time to meet her flight. The second was make sure Molly and Tom could stay with her another month.

She dialed the number and got the answering machine again. It was far too early for Stephen to be at work. She dialed the code to get the messages from the machine and found that there were a great many, including all the ones she had left for him and one from Sassie saying she was sleeping over with a girlfriend.

Either Stephen hadn't been home, or he hadn't bothered to check the messages. She left another message saying she had missed him again and telling him what time to pick her up at the airport. She called his office on the chance that he had gone in early but reached his answering machine there too.

She was surprised but not concerned as she turned back the covers and reached for her robe and slippers. She walked outside and inspected the view from her balcony with a proprietary perspective. She was eager to get on with the plan she had tentatively worked out.

As she crossed her bedroom to go find Molly, there was a knock and Molly came into the room with a tray that held steaming coffee, an old-fashioned country breakfast and a small bouquet of daffodils.

The morning paper was neatly folded beside the plate, and a small white envelope lay on top of it.

"Ms. Maggs, I heard you up and thought you might like to have your breakfast up here this morning. Here's the paper. Ms. Eleanor's obituary is written up very nicely. Oh, and Mr. Allendale sent this note over first thing this morning. Shall I pour you some coffee?" She placed the tray on the small table beside the fireplace. "I'll just rekindle this fire a little to take the chill off the morning," she said as she bent down to stir the coals and add some logs.

"This looks wonderful, Molly, but you shouldn't have gone to so much trouble. I usually have a light breakfast. Toast and coffee would have been fine."

"It's no bother at all. It's soon enough that I won't be having the opportunity to do for you anymore. Now you sit right down here and eat your breakfast." She picked up the napkin and held it as she waited for Maggs to be seated. *No getting around this*, Maggs thought and did as Molly asked.

"Molly, I want to speak to you for a moment if you aren't too rushed right now. Please sit with me and have some coffee." She poured another cup as Molly sat down at the desk.

"In the letter Grover Houston gave me yesterday, Aunt Eleanor asked me to spend a month at Myrtlewood before I decide what to do with it. I've decided to do that, but I'll need someone here to help me. Do you and Tom have any immediate plans that would prevent your staying on and running the house through the end of May? If you do, perhaps you can recommend someone to come in for a few weeks."

Molly's beaming face expressed her pleasure. "Of course we'll stay, Ms. Maggs. You should know that. I was dreading the closing of the house. It makes everything so final. And Tom will be relieved to have something to keep him busy a while longer. I know he's been worrying about how he'll occupy himself after we have no more responsibilities here."

"Well, that sounds perfect, Molly. I'll go home today as I planned and make arrangements to be away for a while. I'll probably return next Sunday. I'll call and let you know for sure. I need to talk to Grover Houston before I leave. I'll call him as soon as I finish breakfast."

She picked up one of Molly's fat biscuits, broke it open, and spread it with homemade preserves. "I can't get in the habit of doing *this* every morning, Molly, but I'm certainly going to enjoy it today."

Molly rose and said, "I'll be downstairs if you need anything else. I'm going to tell Tom the grand news. Ms. Maggs, you don't know how much lighter my heart is than when I thought I was bringing you your last meal in this house." She squeezed Maggs's shoulders as she passed behind her.

"Oh, Molly, will you ask Tom to bring the car around at ten-thirty to drive me into Charleston?" she asked as Molly left the room.

Maggs finished her breakfast and took the telephone and a second cup of coffee out to the balcony, breathing in the pungent smell of the river mixed with the milder scent of the early blooms that already flavored the air. She called Grover Houston, outlined her intentions, and made her request and then prepared to go home and break the news to Stephen.

As Tom eased the car down the driveway, she turned and looked out the back window at Myrtlewood, comforted that she would soon return and that it would all be here when she did, just as it had always been.

On the flight home, she thought about the coming month, and more immediately, about what would happen when she told Stephen what she planned to do. Maybe he would be able to take a few days away from the office and spend some time with her at Myrtlewood. With no outside intrusions, maybe they could rekindle the intimacy in their marriage that seemed to have gone by the wayside. Myrtlewood would certainly be an opportune place to try, and the season couldn't be more ideal. She could hope anyway.

She was on the ground again before she knew it, and Stephen was nowhere in sight. Maggs took a cab home.

She unlocked the door and found the house dark and quiet. It seemed to emanate a feeling of emptiness. She turned on some lamps, opened the draperies, and raised the windows. The sun was shining, and it was several degrees warmer in Mobile than it had been in Charleston.

She went upstairs to her bedroom and knew immediately that Stephen hadn't been home last night. She didn't know quite how she knew, she just did. There were definite signs of occupancy. Socks on the floor, rumpled towels in the bathroom, closet door half-open, all indicated his presence there; but she knew it hadn't been last night. She picked up the telephone and called his office. When he came on the line, his voice was a bit unnatural, not enough so that anyone else would notice, but she did.

"Hi, honey. I'm glad you're home. Did you have a decent flight? Did you manage okay without me? I really hated not being there with you. Damn, it's good to hear your voice. Did you just get home?"

It was totally unlike Stephen to be so loquacious.

"Yes, I just got home. Yes, my flight was fine. Yes, I managed okay, but it was very sad, and I'm glad to be home too." She laughed and said, "So how are you?"

"I'm fine too, just missed you. The weekend went fine though there was a slight change in arrangements. Sassie came down with a viral infection—one of those twenty-four-hour ones. She's perfectly all right now—and couldn't fill in for you, but fortunately Terry Matthews volunteered. Wasn't that lucky? She was a big hit, and everything turned out okay. I'll tell you all about it at dinner tonight."

"That sounds great, Stephen. Will you also tell me why you didn't sleep here last night and where you were?" She recognized the icy inflection in her voice and realized she was jumping to conclusions, but she knew absolutely that *lucky* wasn't the correct word.

After the barest of pauses, he said, "Of course. The dance was late ending, and I had to stay until everyone left to settle up with the manager. So when I finally got Terry home, it was pretty late.

She offered to make breakfast, and to tell you the truth, I had just a tad over my limit to drink and knew I had to get to work early this morning, so I took her up on her offer. I must have fallen asleep while she was cooking because I woke up on her couch this morning and it was already nine o'clock. I didn't have time to go home and shower and change, so I came straight here. Thank goodness Terry is such a good sport. I practically flew out of her house this morning, and I'm not sure I even thanked her properly."

"Yes, thank goodness! But I'm sure you'll find a way to thank her later," she replied. She couldn't manage to keep the anger and suspicion out of her voice. And she was angry, she realized. *And* suspicious. *And* hurt.

"What does that mean, Maggs? I can't believe you would have any objection to Terry filling in for you. You should be grateful that she was willing to do it. After all, these were our friends, not hers. She didn't know anyone there except me. And she helped make the weekend a success. I would have thought you'd appreciate her efforts."

"Well, I guess my perspective differs a little from yours. We probably should discuss this later. I have something else to discuss with you anyway."

She took a deep breath and, goaded by her anger, plunged right in. "Aunt Eleanor left me a letter requesting that I stay for a month at Myrtlewood before deciding what to do with it. I've decided to do it—because it was her final request and because I need a break. I've been thinking a lot lately about the book I've always wanted to write. This will give me a chance to start it. I don't know what to do about Myrtlewood yet, and this will give me some time to explore the possibilities. My plan is to spend this week making arrangements and tying up loose ends so that I can leave on Sunday. I hope you'll support me in this, Stephen, but I intend to go either way. Give it some thought, and we'll talk about it tonight."

She knew she sounded stiff and distant, knew he could feel her anger, and probably thought she was making this decision because of it; but she was very tired and not much inclined to care what he thought right now.

His response was also stiff but patronizing as well. "Why don't you lie down and rest until I get home and we'll talk this through. I think you're being a bit hasty, but we'll see. I'll be home in a couple of hours. I'll take you to dinner, and we can figure it out later. Okay?"

"Sure. I'll see you when you get here."

She hung up the phone, angrier than she was before. How dare he patronize her? After all these years, he should know she wouldn't make a decision as important at this simply because she was angry about someone as insignificant as Terry Matthews. Maggs had never been a spiteful person, and she didn't have a jealous bone in her body. But she knew exactly what Terry Matthews had in mind, even if Stephen didn't yet. Or maybe he did. She had assumed that he was unaware of any ulterior motives in Terry's attentions; in point of fact, he would be the last to recognize any deviousness there, but now Maggs wondered if something had happened last night which changed their relationship in some way. Knowing Stephen to be an honorable man, she didn't really believe there had been anything more involved than just what he said. After she calmed down enough to think about what he said, she regretted that she had overreacted like a threatened female. She had projected her own feelings about Terry into an imagined situation that she believed Stephen should somehow have prevented.

She unpacked her suitcase, gathered some laundry, and went downstairs. She started the washing machine and then glanced at the clock. It was too late in the day to make any plans about returning to Charleston.

She walked out onto the terrace. The warmth of the day was beginning to be replaced by a chill in the air, but her garden offered the serenity she needed just now.

Recognizing her share of the responsibility for the impending quarrel, Maggs decided to make Stephen a special dinner. Afterward they would talk. It was the right thing to do. She would make Stephen understand about Myrtlewood and give him a chance to make her understand about Terry.

She and Stephen had always resolved their problems through calm discussion and a willingness to consider the other's point of view. It had worked for minor disagreements as well as major decisions, and it would work this time too.

She went inside to get her car keys, feeling much better. Everything would soon fit back into neat, manageable little compartments. *Manageable, yes, but oh, so dull!* was the thought that insinuated its unwelcome way into her mind. But she had no time to examine that now; there were things to do. Although it nagged at her somewhere in the back of her head, the fact eluded her that she had not only sublimated but also justified in this exact way every thought she'd ever had that challenged the status quo of her existence. One of these days she would have to figure it all out but not today.

She rushed to the grocery store and flew down the aisles collecting the ingredients for Stephen's favorite dinner. She bought a good bottle of wine and some steamed shrimp for appetizers. She bought tangerine jellybeans to put under Stephen's pillow because he loved surprises, dashed to the florist to get flowers for the table, and then headed home to get everything ready. She remembered a nightgown she had been saving for a special occasion and decided to wear it later tonight. She had mixed the martinis before she left, and they were chilling.

The answering machine was flashing when she brought the groceries into the kitchen. She pressed the button, and Sassie's voice said, "Hope you got home okay, Mom. I've got a lecture tonight, and Jeff is taking me to get a burger before I come home. I'll see you in the morning." Maggs received the news with a smile. *So much the better,* she thought.

The second message was from Stephen. "Sorry, I missed you, but something important has come up, and I won't be able to make dinner after all. I don't expect to be too late, but don't wait up for me. I know you're tired. We'll talk in the morning."

He sounded impersonal, distracted, and disinterested. She put the groceries away, poured the martinis down the drain, left the flowers in the sink, and went upstairs to bed. She had no idea when he came in.

Chapter 7

Stephen was in the shower the next morning when Maggs came downstairs to make coffee. She was still feeling the sting of last night's anger, and when Stephen attempted to kiss her, she turned her face aside.

"Uh-oh," he said. "I can explain about last night, Maggs, if you'll listen to me. I have some wonderful news."

"I'm really not interested in your evening, Stephen. I spent mine alone, something I do a lot of lately, and I've decided that since it doesn't seem to matter very much anymore whether I'm here or not, I'll return to Charleston at once—tonight if I can take care of a few things today. If not, I'll leave tomorrow. I'll talk to Sassie and Leah today. The two of them can look out for you around here. Sassie is gone most of the time now, except to sleep, and I'm sure my absence won't be a problem for her. You probably won't be here much of the time either. I'll be back around the first of June. You know how to reach me."

She handed him a cup of coffee and asked, "What would you like for breakfast?"

"I don't want anything. Come on, Maggs, I know you're angry, but it's not like you to be spiteful. You haven't given me a chance to explain. Terry was able to set up a meeting between our lawyers at the last minute yesterday. It was running so late, we decided to grab a quick bite and then come back and finish up. When we were done, I had to go back to my office and get some figures they would need first thing this morning. It was so late when I finally finished that I didn't call because I thought you'd probably already gone to bed."

He took her hand and pulled her to him and said, "I'm really sorry not to have been here on your first night home, but, Maggs, listen, it looks like the merger is really going through. It looks great on paper, and we're supposed to get the final word today. I'm having a hard time believing it's really going to work out. If it does, we're going to have the freedom to do anything we want from here on. Don't you understand how important this is?"

She withdrew her hand and walked over and looked out the window above the sink, her back to him.

"Congratulations, Stephen. I'm very happy for you. I do think it's wonderful—it's something you've worked a long time for. You'll have to forgive my lack of enthusiasm, but we have so little time together as it is that I imagine this will only worsen an already-bad situation. I hope the merger turns out to be as worthwhile as you anticipate. I really do. And I'm sure you'll find it easier to attend to all the details with me gone. You probably won't even notice."

Stephen came up behind her, placed his hands on her shoulders, and turned her around to face him.

"I thought you would be as excited about this as I am. I can't believe you're so angry over one evening alone that you can't even share this with me. I need you here to support me. This is no time for you to be responding to some half-baked whim of Aunt Eleanor's. This is our future we're talking about here."

As was his habit when cajolery didn't work for him, he resorted to manipulation to accomplish his purpose, usually managing to gain her sympathy while negating the importance of what she wanted. Except for his unfortunate remark about Aunt Eleanor, he might have succeeded this time too.

She removed his hands from her shoulders. Her eyes flashing, she said in a cold, very controlled voice, "Aunt Eleanor never had a half-baked whim, as you so ungraciously put it, in her life. If you had shown the slightest interest in what she has asked me to do, or if you had even been here to discuss it, for that matter, you would never have made that remark. And furthermore, this is something that I need to do for me, Stephen, though you don't seem to be aware that I have any needs of my own."

She knew she was saying more than she wanted to right now, but it was as if a dam had burst, and she couldn't contain her fury. She sat down at the kitchen table and looked up at him.

"I spend most of my time providing for your comfort and happiness and that of the kids, and no one in a very long time has paid any attention to mine. It's like I don't exist except as an extension of someone else. You may be shocked to learn that I'm tired of it. Very tired of it. I want to find out what *I* think—and what *I* feel and—what *I* want. Not what someone else wants me to be.

"Aunt Eleanor's request has come at a time when I need to figure out some of these things. Your plans will go forward just as successfully without my presence. You don't need me for this. You don't really need me for much of anything, anymore."

She saw the rigid set of his jaw but continued, undaunted. "Don't you understand? I need to do this for me. I had hoped to go with your blessing, but as I already told you, I've made up my mind."

Stephen stood before her, his anger obvious. It was the tense, unyielding kind of anger that so often held sway when he dealt with Mike. She knew it well, and though she hadn't often been the recipient of it, she wasn't intimidated by it.

"I have a meeting at ten o'clock this morning with the attorneys, Maggs," he said coldly. "I don't want to leave this situation up in the air, but the meeting is important. Wait until I get home tonight, and we'll see if we can't deal with this a little more reasonably. If you feel you just have to go, maybe we can work it out so you can spend a few days there. Maybe you do need a change. We'll settle it tonight. I've got to go."

She hated the imperious tone of voice and his high-handed manner; he might as well have said aloud what he really meant: "this is finished." He picked up his jacket and his briefcase and turned to leave. She followed him to the door.

She took a deep breath and said, "Stephen, apparently you don't yet understand. I'm not asking your permission. I'm not asking you to understand. I am telling you I am going to Myrtlewood, either tonight or tomorrow. Period. I'll leave word at your office if I don't see you before I go. Good luck with your merger."

She closed the door firmly, resisting the urge to slam it. She was shaking inside, but she squared her shoulders and went upstairs. She was upset at the turn their discussion had taken but determined to abide by her decision. She would talk to Sassie before she left for school and tell Leah later. Leah wouldn't like her leaving any more than Stephen did, but sooner or later, Leah had to learn to be responsible for Leah. Sassie, on the other hand, would understand that Maggs felt an obligation to Aunt Eleanor and would support Maggs's decision to go. Sassie had always seemed to appreciate that Maggs was more than just mother, wife, and homemaker.

Maggs went to the desk in her bedroom and made a list of things she needed to take care of before she could leave: call the vice president of the garden club and ask her to take over for the coming month, cancel an appointment with her hairdresser, go by the bank and get some cash, go to the grocery store, and stock up on a few items for Stephen and Sassie . . .

She caught herself even as she had the thought. They can make a list and shop for what they need. They probably won't be eating here much anyway, and the maid will be here every Wednesday to clean and do the laundry. She crossed the grocery store off her list.

She called a few close friends and told them her plans, canceled her commitments, rescheduled some others, and finally called the airport. There was a flight out at seven o'clock this evening, and she booked it without hesitation.

She called Molly and told her she would need Tom to pick her up at the airport at eleven o'clock tonight, apologizing that he would have to come into Charleston so late. Molly was elated that she was returning so soon and assured her that although Tom might grumble, he wouldn't really mind.

As Maggs hung up the phone, she wondered momentarily if she was being too hasty and then realized that waiting overnight would only postpone the inevitable. Another conversation with

Stephen would resolve nothing, and she really didn't want to put herself through it. This way, she would already be at Myrtlewood when she woke up tomorrow.

She went to her closet and selected clothes that were casual and comfortable, a few dresses for business appointments, and one or two for evening wear, just in case, and the accessories to go with them. She packed a lot of jeans and sweaters and sneakers and socks. She packed two oversized suitcases and a garment bag and decided that would have to do. She was a compulsive packer, Stephen always said, and reminded herself that she wasn't going away for good.

She opened the wall safe and took out the diamond cross Aunt Eleanor had given her for her sixteenth birthday. She wouldn't need anything more elaborate than that. She took the worn leather volume of her favorite poetry from the bookcase, got her journal and address book from her desk, picked up the novel she was reading from her bedside table, and put them in a carry-on bag, along with her makeup case. She looked around and decided anything more would require a moving van. There was some element of truth in Stephen's accusation about her packing.

As she stood in the midst of her luggage, she was overcome by a feeling she couldn't identify. This departure felt more permanent than she had expected it to. This pretty bedroom that she and Stephen had laughed and planned and made love in for so many years didn't feel like her room anymore. She and Stephen had made a pact when they first built the house that they would never quarrel in their bedroom, and they had honored that pact all through the years. *I'm just having second thoughts,* she mused. *I always do when I'm tempted to do something Stephen or the children don't like. This is silly. I'm doing something I believe is the right thing to do; I'm not running out on anyone.*

Sassie's shower cut off, and a few minutes later, she knocked on Maggs's door. She came in with her hair wrapped in a towel and gave Maggs a fierce hug. Maggs inhaled the warm, fresh fragrance of her, and hugged her back, laughing with pleasure at seeing her.

Sassie looked around the room, taking in the luggage. "Mom, why are you packing? You just got home. Where are you going?" She removed the towel and climbed into the middle of Maggs's still unmade bed. Her incredible eyes, so like her father's, widened, and she gave Maggs a questioning, no-nonsense look.

"What gives, Mom?"

"I want to talk to you about that, darling. Why don't you go dry your hair and then come downstairs? I'll fix some breakfast and tell you all about it."

When Sassie came down, Maggs was frying bacon and slicing fresh peaches. She put bread in the toaster and poured them some coffee and then turned to meet her daughter's puzzled countenance.

"Sassie, Aunt Eleanor left Myrtlewood to me. That comes as no surprise. We've always known that would happen. What I didn't expect was that I would have so much conflict about what to do with it once it was mine. To complicate things, Aunt Eleanor left a letter to be given to me at the reading of the will asking that I spend a month at Myrtlewood before I make a decision."

As she talked, Maggs set the table, drained the bacon, and put the fruit and toast on the table. Sassie was still looking at her expectantly.

"I've decided to do as she asked. I plan to leave tonight. I've made most of the arrangements already, and I'll tie up a few loose ends sometime today. I'm going to stay at Myrtlewood through the end of May.

"I'll talk to Leah later this morning and ask her to help you see that Stephen eats regularly. He's very busy right now. His long-awaited expansion may finally become a reality. There's a merger in the works, and he'll be working long hours. He's likely to forget all about eating. Can I depend on you to remind him?"

"Of course, you can, Mom. We'll manage fine. But a month is a long time for you to be gone. I'll miss you terribly, and I know Dad will. I can't believe he's letting you go without a battle—especially since you just got home yesterday."

"Well, to be honest with you, he's not overjoyed about it. In fact, he doesn't want me to go at all. But I have to do this, Sass. I can't exactly explain, but it's as if Aunt Eleanor's request has freed me to do something I've needed to do for a long time. I need some time to myself. I'm afraid it all sounds dreadfully dramatic, and it really isn't at all."

Sassie laid her fork down and reached across the table to take Maggs's hand.

"You and Dad aren't having some kind of crisis, are you? I understand what you're saying, Mom. I just don't see what the rush is all about. You've put us first for years, and you deserve this. I think it's wonderful for you. You know I do. I just hope you're not avoiding something that needs working out between you and Dad."

She looked directly at Maggs and continued, "If you're going to do this, it ought to be something that brings you joy, and somehow joy isn't what I'm picking up on here. Am I wrong? Because if I am, I'll be relieved to hear it."

Maggs sighed as she looked into her daughter's concerned face and said gently, "I should have known your intuition would be working over time. You're more tuned in to me than any of my children. I won't tell you I have the most charitable feelings toward your father at this particular moment, but I can honestly tell you that I had made my mind up about this before I left Charleston. This is about me, Sass, and not your father. For once, it really is only about me. Our differences right now are very insignificant, and I'm sure we'll work them out. There's nothing for you to be concerned about."

She pushed her chair back and came around the table. Sassie stood too, and Maggs took her in her arms and held her close.

"I'll miss you dreadfully," Maggs said as she released her and began clearing the table. "I will probably miss you most of all."

"Okay, I'm going to take you at your word," Sassie said. "I'll miss having you here to talk to, and I'll probably run up a terrible telephone bill, but I'm glad you're going if it will make you happy."

Bless your generous heart, Maggs breathed in silent thanks to this child who was so like her.

Sassie carried the dishes to the sink and began rinsing them. "My lab begins in about an hour, so I guess I'd better get dressed. Will you be here when I get home?"

"No, I'll get a cab to the airport when I'm ready. Give me another hug, and go get ready for school. I won't get to Myrtlewood until around midnight, and I won't call that late, but I'll talk to you very soon. Maybe you can come up for a long weekend before I come home, and we'll do something special, just the two of us. And I'll be back before you know it. Now, run along."

One down and one to go, she thought as Sassie headed upstairs. *Leah isn't going to take this nearly so calmly. She finished up what she was doing, turned out the kitchen light, and went upstairs to call Leah.*

To say that Leah didn't take the news calmly was an understatement. She wailed, she argued, she pleaded, and she pouted. But finally she had to give in because she couldn't budge Maggs.

"Well, I don't understand how you can just abandon Melody and Jason," was her final pitch. Finding her weak spot was a talent Leah inherited from her father, but just as it didn't work for him this time, it didn't work for Leah either. It was high time Leah learned to shoulder her own responsibilities.

"I'm sorry, darling, but I'm not abandoning them. I'll call them often. A month isn't very long when you're their age. I'll be home before they realize I'm gone. I'll miss them terribly and you too, but I'm not changing my plans. I just called to ask you to help Sassie look out for Stephen and to tell you good-bye."

Maggs walked back and forth in front of her bedroom windows as she talked. As she looked down into her garden, she realized that most of it would come into full bloom while she was away, and there would be no one to tend it. She felt a pang of regret and countered it with thoughts of how beautiful the grounds at Myrtlewood would be in the coming month.

"Well, if you're determined to do this, I guess nothing I can say is going to make a difference, but honestly, Mother, sometimes I just don't understand you," Leah said.

"Well, maybe someday you will, but until then, you'll just have to accept me as I am—just the way I've always accepted you. I'll call the children in a few days. Don't forget to check on your dad."

She hung up before Leah could register any more protests. She walked across the room and picked up a picture of Stephen and the kids from her bedside table and a snapshot of Melody and Jason and Jennifer taken when they were together last Christmas and tucked them into one of the suitcases. She did a quick mental run-through of anything else she might need to take care of, and while she was making a few more calls, Sassie stuck her head in and mouthed good-bye. Everything was arranged.

But when she heard Sassie's car pull out of the driveway a few minutes later, Maggs felt strangely adrift. Maybe her life wasn't as complicated as imagined, if she could put it all on hold with just a morning's worth of phone calls and canceled commitments. The idea was very disconcerting and totally unexpected. Maybe her problem was more basic than an overloaded schedule.

She stifled this train of thought quickly by getting up and laying out a pair of plum-colored silk slacks, a matching jacket, and a soft silk shirt in a bright coordinating print, leather flats, some dangling earrings Sassie had given her just for fun, and a scarf to tie her hair back from her face. It was totally different from the tailored look she usually chose, and she was pleased with the casual effect. *In fact*, she thought, *casual is what I'm going to be for the next four weeks.*

When she had showered and dressed, she carried her bags to the front door and walked through the house to see that everything was in order. She took last night's flowers from the sink, found a vase, and arranged them. She put them on the desk in the study. She considered writing Stephen a note, but she had said all she wanted to say this morning, and he hadn't called at all. It was early, but she called and ordered a cab. She would stop by the day care center to say good-bye to Melody and Jason, and she could get a drink at the airport lounge to pass the time until her flight left. She didn't want to wait here.

She went back upstairs to get her shoulder bag and take one last look to see if she had forgotten anything. She opened her bag to get her keys out and found the note from Christopher that Molly had given her at breakfast yesterday. She had intended to read it on the plane coming home but had forgotten about it. She opened it now. He had written to say how much he had enjoyed her company, that he knew some great restaurants in Charleston, and hoped they would be able to have dinner when she returned. He asked her to telephone when she got back. He had drawn a smiley face under his signature, and it brought a smile to her face as well. He really is a charming man, she thought as she slipped the note back into its envelope and dropped it in her bag. Maybe I'll take him up on his offer.

She felt a pang of something unidentified as she heard the cab turn into the driveway, but she walked resolutely downstairs and out the door without a backward look. There was something momentous about this solitary leave-taking. She didn't know what it was, but she understood that she was on the verge of finding out, and she was excited at the prospect.

Chapter 8

When she awoke the next morning, it took her a few minutes to realize where she was. The events of the two previous days replayed themselves as if part of some videotape that had nothing to do with her personally. The words and feelings that had passed between her and Stephen didn't evoke pain or anger or regret. She wasn't affected by them at all.

She had arrived in Charleston on schedule and found the faithful Tom waiting for her. She had apologized for the lateness of the hour, and although he did grumble, he gathered her luggage and drove her home.

Home.

She was aware of the meaning her use of the word implied, as if, in some unexplained way, she was indeed home. Last night's strange frame of mind persisted this morning.

In the past five days she had been bombarded by intense emotions. She had been deeply saddened by Aunt Eleanor's death and its surrounding events. Anger, hurt, and concern for Stephen had followed each other in rapid succession once she had returned to Mobile. Last night on the plane she had felt excited as she embraced this chance to contemplate her life and consider her future.

Coming fully awake in this beautiful room, she felt a deep contentment and a delicious tingle of anticipation for the adventure ahead. Because she *would* make it an adventure. She was committed to making the most of this brief opportunity. And she hadn't felt this free in a very long while.

She hoped Molly had one of those outrageous Southern breakfasts waiting downstairs. Today she was in the mood for it. She looked at the clock and was astonished to see that it was ten o'clock. She couldn't remember the last time she had slept this late.

She turned back the covers and reached for her robe and slippers. She went into the bathroom and washed her face. She found a pair of faded jeans and a favorite worn cotton pullover and put on canvas tennis shoes with no socks. The only makeup she applied was a little lipstick and mascara. She pulled her hair back in a ponytail and went downstairs, unaware of how young she looked this morning.

Downstairs, the sunshine was brilliant. She heard the sounds of Molly's bustling even before she got close to the kitchen. She smelled the coffee and the delicious aroma of bacon frying, almost as if Molly had anticipated her appetite this morning. Evidently it wasn't too late for breakfast.

She was ravenous—not just for Molly's breakfast but for the day that lay ahead and all the choices it held. And the days and days and days of choices after this one. She felt young and free and cherished. She felt like singing or skipping or engaging in some kind of boisterousness to express her joy. She wondered what Molly would say if she did, laughed out loud at the thought, and gave Molly a hug as she came into the kitchen.

"Gracious me, child, but you've made an amazing recovery from the bedraggled little creature that made its way home in the middle of the night last night!"

Molly continued her preparations, pouring orange juice and handing a glass to Maggs.

"Where would like your breakfast this morning?"

"Right here, where I can talk to you while I eat. Where is Tom?"

"He's about somewhere, seeing to something that needs doing. You know he can't be idle. Do you want him for something?"

"No, I just wanted to thank him again for coming to get me so late last night. Molly, I'm so happy to be right where I am this minute that I can hardly contain myself. I'm going to take it easy for a few days and do absolutely nothing but sleep and eat and read and sleep some more. Don't tell anyone I'm here yet. I'd like to just be a hermit for a little while."

"Bless your heart, if it's privacy you'll be wanting, it's privacy you'll be having. Mum's the word, I promise."

She set a heaping plate of food in front of Maggs that looked every bit as delicious as it smelled. Maggs ate every bite and poured herself another cup of coffee. She wondered why coffee always smelled so much better here than anywhere else. She had always thought so.

Molly was tending to some chore elsewhere while Maggs sat looking out the open kitchen windows, thrilled by the beauty of the morning. The fresh air was as tempting as the breakfast smells had been and lured her just as effectively.

She gave in to the temptation, took an old sweater from the rack beside the back door, and strolled down to the river's edge. A small painted bench stood under the drooping branches of the aging willow tree, which was putting forth bright new foliage just the way she remembered it had when it was a young tree and she was a young girl. She sat down and watched the river gurgle and swirl its impatient way to the sea.

The sun was getting warmer now, and sated by the good meal she had just eaten and the steady drone of the bees, she felt more content than she had imagined possible. She decided to go for a walk to forestall the drowsiness she was feeling.

She found the old path along the river, and when she approached the edge of the woods, she continued to walk, following the bank as it rose and fell in gentle elevations and curved in and out. The silence was broken only by the call of birds in search of their own breakfast and the occasional scramble of a forest inhabitant disturbed by her presence. The woods beside the river became thicker as Maggs went on, and she had to slow down at times to make her way through a tangle of vines or a thicket of dense hardwood trees. She hadn't dressed in anticipation of spending her morning in the woods; thorns and sticks snagged her clothing and scratched her bare ankles, and her hair kept getting caught by vines and low-hanging limbs, but she didn't mind.

She entered a large clearing that was part of a sandbank that sloped down to the water's edge, and she stopped to rest. The water was shallow here, and she could see small pebbles on the sandy bottom. She sat down on a large flat stone and watched the river. A soft breeze blew and cooled her cheeks, which had grown pink from the exertion of her morning ramble. The Ashley River was swift in places but not usually treacherous, and its gurgle and splash as it flowed over and around projections of worn rocks and other, more temporary obstacles were reassuring sounds. She thought of bringing a picnic basket and a book and coming here to eat lunch. *It won't be today*, she thought, *but I'm definitely going to come back.*

She got up reluctantly, aware that Molly would be wondering where she had been for so long, and stretched her protesting muscles before starting back, refreshed and exhilarated. As she was leaving, she noticed the remains of a campfire that had been carefully extinguished. Footprints led to the water's edge. It hadn't been too long since someone else had the same idea. These woods were private property, and she wondered about the camper who broke his journey here. Maybe it was the man in the midnight canoe she had seen from her balcony a few nights ago.

It was well past noon when she came again to the edge of the lawn and made her way past the little bench and up to the back porch. The early morning's coolness had given way to the warmer temperatures common in the middle of the day this time of year, and she was hot and tired. She was hungry again too, much to her surprise. Molly wasn't in the kitchen. Maggs went to the refrigerator and found cheese and some large red grapes and put them on a plate. There was a bottle of wine chilling, and she took it out too and went to the pantry in search of crackers. Instead, she found a loaf of Molly's crusty homemade bread and cut off a large chunk. She got a glass from the cupboard, opened the wine, put everything on a tray, and went out to the porch, which was shady and inviting. She put her tray on the table beside the glider, took her shoes off, and poured the wine. She drank the first glass quickly because she was thirsty and then refilled the glass, savoring the second one.

She removed the rubber band and shook her hair loose with her fingers. She curled her bare feet under her, greedily anticipating her feast. The exercise had left her empty, and the wine went to her head. She relished the sensation. When she had finished eating, she leaned back against the soft cushions, content and relaxed. She could hear Molly moving around in the house now, probably preparing dinner. She wondered what they were having tonight and couldn't believe she was thinking of food again.

Soon the cooler temperatures of the approaching evening were replacing the warmth of midday. She loved this time of day best, wherever she happened to be, and she found this particular moment unequaled by anything she had experienced recently.

Inside the house, the telephone rang. She heard Molly's measured tread approaching the back porch and guessed it was probably Stephen. When Molly came out onto the porch, however, she explained, "Ms. Maggs, it's George Huntingdon on the line. He called to ask if I had heard from you as to when you might be getting back, and I didn't think you'd mind, so I told him you got in early this morning. I hope I'm not talking out of school, but it's done now."

She looked concerned, and Maggs quickly reassured her, "Of course not, Molly. It's not a secret that I'm back. I just wanted a chance to catch my breath before everybody finds out."

"Do you want the phone out here?"

"No, I'll take it in the library," she said, getting to her feet. In the library, she lifted the receiver and said, "Hello, Uncle George. How nice to hear from you."

"Hello, Maggs. I didn't expect to find you back already. I was merely inquiring as to when you might be returning because I've had an inquiry from someone who may be interested in purchasing Myrtlewood—if you should decide to sell it. I know it's a bit premature, but I thought you might want to be aware of an interested party, to add to your other options. I must say I'm delighted you've come back so soon."

"How thoughtful of you, Uncle George. I plan to stay here a few weeks while I make a decision about what to do with Myrtlewood, and I intend to consider all possibilities. I appreciate your letting me know about this."

"Well, I won't keep you, my dear, but when you have had time to get settled in over there, I would love to give a small dinner party for you. What do you think?"

"Sounds lovely, and I'd be honored. Just give me a couple of days, and I'm all yours."

They rang off with a promise to be in touch. Maggs went back to the kitchen.

"Did Stephen call while I was out, Molly?"

"No, he didn't, and by the way, where in the world did you wander off to for so long? Off in those woods, I'll bet. Ms. Maggs, you've been knowing all your life that you shouldn't be wandering around out there all by yourself. Something could happen to you, and it would be hours before anyone even knew anything was wrong."

She stood in the center of the kitchen floor, frowning and waving a long wooden spoon. Maggs went to her and gave her a quick hug as she laughed and said,

"Molly, you know I love to walk in the woods. I've done it as long as I can remember, and I've no intention of stopping now. I'm always careful, I promise. Don't worry so much! The exercise did me a world of good. I feel fabulous. I'm going upstairs and take a shower before dinner."

She started toward the door and remembered the campfire she had seen on the sandbar and turned back.

"Oh, by the way, I found evidence of a recent campfire while I was in the woods today. And when I was here last weekend, I saw a man in a canoe paddle by late in the night. Do you have any idea who might have built a fire in the woods? It's kind of strange, don't you think?"

"As a matter of fact, I know exactly who it was," Molly said as she removed a pan from the oven. "It was Mr. Huntingdon's nephew, that's who. He's always out on the river in his canoe, and I seem to remember Tom's mentioning that he ran into him in the woods hunting wild turkey several times. He's quite an outdoorsman, so Tom says. So you don't have to worry about any transients in the woods. Just the bogs and the critters. Lord knows, that's enough to worry about if you're determined to traipse about out there. Now go on up and get your bath before dinner is ready. I'm making a nice roasted chicken." She turned back to the stove to baste the chicken, her disapproval of Maggs's willfulness evident in every line of her body. Maggs took a long shower and could almost feel her muscles relaxing under the stream of hot water. She dried her hair and brushed it until it shone and then put on a long-sleeved caftan against the chill of the evening. She approved of the sun-kissed glow on her cheeks as she looked in the mirror and added a touch of lipstick. As she went downstairs, she made a mental note to talk to Molly about a light menu. She would have to stick to it, no matter how tempting Molly's culinary productions were.

Maggs was perfectly content to sit alone in the dining room with the candles burning softly while she ate her dinner. Afterward, she went into the library and read until she found herself nodding. She reluctantly got out of her chair and went to the kitchen, thanked Molly again for dinner, and went upstairs.

Glancing at the clock, she was surprised to find that it was only a little after nine o'clock. She picked up the phone and called Stephen. One of them had to be the first to call. He wasn't home, and she wasn't in the mood to talk to the answering machine. She hung up, wondering where he was. A fire was burning softly in the grate and she considered reading a while longer, but she was so thoroughly relaxed she would be asleep in the chair before she turned a page. She didn't want the television on. She walked out on the balcony to look at the stars; and as she filled her lungs with the crisp night air, she wondered where the solitary canoer was tonight. Christopher, huh? Very interesting.

She climbed into bed, and as she went to sleep, her thoughts were not of Stephen but of Christopher Allendale and his late-night journeying.

Chapter 9

She awoke early the next morning. She didn't hear Molly downstairs yet. Maggs knew immediately how she wanted to spend this day. She performed her morning routine hurriedly, pulled on a pair of jeans, tucked a short-sleeved shirt under a heavier sweatshirt, put on socks and sneakers, brushed her hair, and headed downstairs.

She turned on the coffee maker, and while she waited for the coffee to perk, she went to the library and foraged through Aunt Eleanor's desk for paper, pens, a notebook, a sketchbook, and some colored pencils. Clutching her treasures, she went back to the kitchen where Molly was in the process of starting breakfast. Maggs kissed her on the cheek, dropped her collection on the kitchen counter, and went into the pantry in search of an old knapsack she remembered seeing there once. She found it hanging on a nail and took it back into the kitchen.

"Why are you up so early, dear? I was going to bring you breakfast in bed," said Molly as she took eggs and bacon and juice from the refrigerator. "I've got a lovely cantaloupe that will hold you until I get the rest of your breakfast ready. If I'd known you'd be up this early, I would have come over before now."

"Molly, come sit down. I want to talk to you a minute. And I don't want a big breakfast every morning, as tempting as it is. I normally just have juice and toast or maybe an English muffin and jam. I'll be perfectly happy to see to it myself. There's no need for you to get up so early every morning to make my breakfast.

"What I would like you to do is make me a light picnic lunch. I'm going to be out by the river most of the day, and I don't want to come all the way back for lunch."

Maggs removed the orange juice from the refrigerator and poured a glass of juice for herself and then handed Molly one. Molly promptly set hers down, placed her hands on her hips, and looked at Maggs in dismay. *Here it comes*, Maggs thought.

"And just what will you be doing out by the river all day, if I might ask? I told you yesterday, that's not somewhere you need to be wandering around alone. And furthermore, making breakfast is my job around here. I made your Aunt Eleanor's every morning of her life, and if you don't want a big breakfast, that's fine with me, but I'll be making breakfast of some sort every morning. You just let me know what time you like to eat."

Maggs could see that Molly was getting all prickly, so she said, "Okay, fine, make my breakfast if you want to, but put away the heavy stuff and just let me have a slice of melon and a piece of toast with my coffee. But first I want to tell you something."

She sat down at the table and took Molly's hand. "Molly, I've decided that I'm going to use the month I'm here to see if I have the talent or the persistence to write a novel. I've had some ideas for a long time, but I've never had the chance to see if I can actually put anything down on paper. I'm going to take this stuff down to that little sandbar I found yesterday and sit in the sunshine while I try to get started. If I have a good feeling about it, I want to devote some time to writing every day. I'm not telling anybody else about this. Will you keep my secret?"

"Why, Ms. Maggs, you know I will. Of course I will. I just don't see why it's necessary to lug all this stuff down to some riverbank when there's a perfectly good library here that you can use—and be a lot safer into the bargain."

She turned away with a long-suffering sigh and said, "Let me see what I can put together for your lunch and then if you're determined to go off down there. I'll have it ready shortly. It's too early to be out yet anyway; it's still chilly out there. You'll catch a cold, sure as I'm standing here. You just sit here and eat your breakfast, and by the time you're ready to go, it should be a sight warmer."

She went into the pantry, mumbling under her breath. Maggs poured another cup of coffee and ate her cantaloupe and toast without tasting them, swallowing her impulse to argue with Molly about being a grown woman. She was too excited and too full of ideas to waste her precious time.

Soon she was headed out the back door with the picnic hamper packed so full she supposed Molly was expecting her to wander in the wilderness for forty days and nights. She blew Molly a kiss as she started off, secretly pleased to have someone worried about her, even if having to explain her actions was going to be a nuisance.

Molly had insisted she wear a scarf, and the breeze blew the ends of it merrily behind her as she went. She walked swiftly to the spot from which she hoped to entice her muse. She picked a place where the ground was dappled with sun-posies, spread her blanket, and sat down in the middle of it to unpack her writing materials.

It was still a little chilly, and the stone ring where Christopher Allendale had conscientiously extinguished his recent fire inspired her to build one of her own. She found some seasoned limbs and twigs that would quickly catch fire and put them in the circle and touched a match to them. Soon the fire was sizzling and popping.

She lay down on her stomach and began making notes. She wrote rapidly, but it was impossible for her hand to keep up with the pace of her thoughts as ideas tumbled spontaneously over each other. She tried to get them down on paper clearly enough to elaborate on them later. Unaware of the fountain of inspiration that existed just below the surface of her ordinary existence, she occasionally paused long enough to gather more wood to keep the fire going, but even that didn't interrupt the ideas that practically erupted from her fertile imagination.

At some point she noticed that the sun was directly overhead, and later that, it had started on its downhill arc. She looked at her watch and was amazed to find that it was almost two o'clock. She was suddenly starving. She added more wood to the fire, stretched her cramped muscles, and sat down to eat.

As predicted, Molly had packed enough food for a three-day camping trip and included a bottle of red wine. China, cutlery, linen, and even wineglasses were in the hamper as well; and Maggs laughed as she unpacked them. Molly never half-did anything.

Maggs ate leisurely, savoring it all—the smoke from the fire adding its flavor to the food; the feel of the river breeze and the sunshine on her face and arms; and the wonderful, fruity scent of the wine and its full-bodied taste on her tongue.

When she had demolished her picnic, she packed the remains back into the hamper and sipped at another glass of wine as she sat cross-legged on the blanket evaluating what she had accomplished in this first effort. The words had come easily. She felt as if she had discovered a vein of pure gold in an abandoned mine and had only to find the tools to excavate it. She had loved writing the words, and it felt very natural to express herself this way. She might actually have been right to trust the long-dormant belief that she could write. Tonight, before she went to bed, she would reread what she had written, and if she still thought it had any merit, she would begin to work seriously tomorrow to develop her story.

She raised her glass to the trees and said, "To Mary Margaret Masters and whatever her efforts may bring. Cheers, Mary Margaret." She chuckled as she emptied the glass and then lay back on the blanket, drowsy from the warmth of the wine and the food and the sun. Pleased about what the possibilities her morning's work suggested, she drifted off to sleep.

She was startled into awareness by sound and motion and a voice calling out her name. She was disoriented and a little frightened. As she blinked her eyes and tried to clear her head, she recognized the voice.

Christopher Allendale walked up from the river's edge and stood (or rather, towered, she thought, irrelevantly) over her blanket. She sat up with a jolt, brushed her hair back into place, and adjusted her clothes self-consciously, acutely aware she couldn't possibly have presented a worse appearance. *Damn, damn, damn.*

But he was grinning down at her, obviously delighted to find her here.

"Hello, there. I saw the smoke from your fire and thought maybe we had some trespassers in our woods. I stopped to send them on their way, and instead of trespassers, I find Sleeping Beauty. I won't tell you how tempted I was to waken you in the traditional way. But sadly, although you certainly qualify for the title, I'm not a prince. Still," he said, his eyes twinkling with good-natured delight at her obvious discomfort, "I can't help thinking I missed a golden opportunity. Is there no reward for overcoming one's less honorable impulses?"

Maggs still had said nothing. She was embarrassed and more than a little inclined to say something ungracious about his interruption of a perfectly peaceful afternoon nap. But her irritation was tempered by amusement at the imp that challenged her from behind his eyes, and finally she capitulated and laughed back at him.

Her neck was getting uncomfortable staring up for such a distance. She moved to one side of the blanket and smiled at him.

"Doing the honorable thing usually brings its own reward, I have found. Won't you sit down, Mr. Allendale? I was just resting after a good morning's work and one of Molly's incomparable lunches. Will you join me in a glass of wine?"

He nodded. She took another glass from the hamper, poured the wine, and offered it to him. He was still standing.

"Oh, for goodness sake, Christopher, do please sit down. You're giving me a pain in the neck. Literally."

The smile on his full well-shaped mouth turned into laughter, and he obligingly folded his remarkable length into a seated position on the blanket beside her, holding out his hand for the glass.

"My apologies, Ms. Beauty, I certainly wouldn't want to cause you any distress."

He looked at her directly from eyes that were intensely blue and filled with amusement under a mop of dark hair that was thick and slightly curly, which he wore full and well cut. He had very long eyelashes, a straight nose, and a small scar above his left eyebrow, which should have detracted from the perfection of his face but actually gave him an appealing, roguish look. He wore jeans and a red sweater that made his eyes appear even bluer.

They sipped their wine in silence, and after she overcame her initial discomfort about her appearance, Maggs realized she was as comfortable with him now as she had been the night they met.

He leaned back on one elbow and said, "What kind of work have you been engaged in, if you don't mind my curiosity?"

She thought about avoiding a direct reply, but the evidence was all around her. She impulsively told him what she had been doing. And before she knew it, she also told him why. And how long she had wanted to write. And how good she felt about it. She told him of her plans for the coming month and explained briefly about Aunt Eleanor's letter. She was surprised at how easy he was to talk to. She didn't share her feelings often or easily, and here she was, pouring out hopes and dreams she had never discussed with anyone.

He was interested in what she said. She sensed that he understood and, more, approved of her effort. He wasn't patronizing or dismissive as Stephen was prone to be, and she found herself growing more enthusiastic about her subject. Without intending to, she even told him her story idea.

He poured another glass of wine, and they continued to talk, absorbed in their conversation and unaware that the daylight was waning. Maggs was stimulated by the exchange of ideas. He listened as she expressed her doubts, and instead of meaningless reassurances, he told her that the only way she would ever know for sure was just to get started and see where it went.

"I have a few contacts in publishing circles, Maggs, and I'd be glad to arrange for someone to take a look at what you come up with if you want me to. I've dabbled some in the writing field myself, and I understand your desire to capture on paper what goes around in your head. I'm aware also that it's much easier said than done. Writing gets pretty personal, and it can leave you very vulnerable. But it can also be one of the most rewarding things you'll ever do because ultimately it's all about you—your passion, your commitment, your imagination, your energy, and your words. And that's just for starters."

"Are you an author, Christopher? Have you had something published?"

"Well, I've written a few medical texts over the years, and a few years ago I wrote a spy novel that was modestly successful." He seemed uncomfortable disclosing this last bit of information.

Maggs was captivated by the revelation. "Why a spy novel?"

He shrugged his shoulders self-consciously.

"I have a passion for them. Started reading them when I was in medical school to give my brain a rest from the tedium of all the other stuff I had to cram into it. I got hooked on them, and I've been a fan of the genre ever since. I still read every one I get my hands on, good, bad, or indifferent.

"I was sort of like you are about this effort you're making, I guess. I had always secretly believed I could write a novel—at least do as well as some of the ones I read—and one day, I decided if I didn't get started, I'd never find out.

"I had lost my wife shortly before that, and I was going through an evaluation process of sorts, trying to figure out where I wanted to go with my life, and I decided to plunge in and see what happened.

"I had a lot of fun with it. I took my time, didn't pressure myself, and just let it go where it wanted to. I didn't think it was very good, him though I was pleased that I finished it. I let a friend read it, only because he insisted. He liked it a lot and insisted on giving it to someone he knew who was an editor in a small publishing company. The publisher liked it too, and the rest, as they say, is history. It wasn't a raging success, but it was well received and I think one reviewer even deemed me 'a very promising newcomer to cloak-and-dagger fiction.'"

He had been tracing designs in the sand with his finger as he talked. Now he brushed his hands off and turned to her.

"So you see, you never can tell. You may be the next 'promising newcomer.' You just have to go for it."

"Why, Christopher, that's fascinating. I had no idea. Did you write under another name or your own?"

He laughed disparagingly and said, "Believe me, I considered using a pen name. I was scared to death I'd be a laughingstock. But I finally decided to use my own name. The book is on the shelves of the libraries in town, and you might even find an odd copy in a bookstore if you were really looking for it."

"Well, is that the end of it? Don't you intend to write any more?"

"As a matter of fact, the publisher gave me an advance for an idea I have for another book, but since I came down here on sabbatical, I really have been too busy to start it. I probably will, at some point. The main thing with me was always to discover whether I was capable of writing fiction. Having proved that, I'll probably pursue my idea someday, but it's no longer a driving force. I might get back to it in the fall, after I'm back home. Winters are harsh, and people stay in a lot in Maine, so I may start it then."

He paused briefly and then said, "The important thing for you to remember about writing is this: If you think you can, you probably can, and if you probably can, you definitely should."

He looked up at the trees, and she followed his line of vision. It wouldn't be long before it was completely dark. He stood up, brushed the sand off his jeans, and held out his hand to her.

"I had better take you home in the canoe. You'll never get back before dark if you walk. Molly will be sending out the search parties, if I know her. Tom's probably already been sent to look for you."

He helped her gather her writing materials and covered the fire with sand while she put away the wineglasses and the empty bottle and shook the blanket and folded it. They carried her things to the canoe, and he packed them neatly inside and then held out his hand to steady her.

As she took his hand and prepared to step into the canoe, it rocked slightly and she lost her balance. He caught her in his arms to prevent her fall, and for just a second, she thought she felt his arms tighten around her. Impossible to know for sure. They laughed at her attempts to get to her seat while the canoe continued to rock, and if the involuntary embrace was anything more than her imagination, he certainly didn't act like it.

The canoe ride back to the small pier at Myrtlewood was accomplished with practiced, efficient strokes. It was clear that Christopher was skilled at handling his craft. Maggs also noticed the way rowing showed off his powerful body. She focused her attention on the view from the river, to keep from watching him.

After a while, he smiled at her and said, "Obviously, Pocahontas you're not, but if you think you might enjoy it, I'd like to take you canoeing some afternoon. I find it relaxes me in a way few things do any more. This is a very beautiful river. How about it? Would you like to come out with me sometime?"

She laughed. "I'm surprised you asked, but if you're willing to put up with such a hopeless landlubber, I'd like to very much. I saw you on the river late one night before I went back to Mobile. Do you go out often at night?"

"Sometimes. When I need to clear the cobwebs."

He was assisting her out of the canoe as he spoke, and his hold on her arm was very firm. Still, she almost lost her balance again, and they had another laugh as he steadied her. He handed her the blanket and picked up the hamper and knapsack. They crossed the lawn and walked up to the back porch as darkness settled in.

"I'll turn you over to Molly before I leave. I'm sure she'll give me a tongue-lashing for keeping you out so late, but maybe she'll get it out of her system on me and let you off easy."

They went through the kitchen door, and Molly was there with the expected scowling face. Christopher laughed at her and whirled her around the kitchen in a demented semblance of an Irish jig until she ordered him to stop.

She collapsed in a chair, out of breath, laughing, and red-faced. She wiped her face with her apron and said, "Don't think for a minute I don't know what you're doing. You're lucky I don't take my broom to you. What the two of you could be thinking, out in those woods so late, is beyond me. I was fair worried to distraction. But I do appreciate your seeing Ms. Maggs home safely, so I'll be holding my tongue. I don't know what I'm going to do with her, headstrong as she is."

Christopher patted her shoulder placatingly and said, "Now, Molly, you worry too much. I guess I'd better be on my way. Uncle George will be wondering what's keeping me too. Let me know, Maggs, when you'd like to see the river, and I'll show you some scenes that will take your breath away."

As he opened the door, Molly said, "Mr. Chris, you're welcome to stay for dinner if you'd like. I'm sure Ms. Maggs would enjoy the company. It doesn't hardly seem right for her to sit in that grand dining room and eat her dinner alone."

Maggs felt her face redden at Molly's audacity, and Christopher understood immediately.

"Thanks, Molly, but I'll take a rain check. Uncle George is expecting me for dinner tonight, and I shouldn't disappoint him this late. But I'll take you up on your offer another time. Ask me again, will you? Talk to you soon, Maggs?"

Maggs got up to see him out.

"Yes. And thanks, Christopher. For the encouragement, I mean. Good night."

She closed the door after him and gave Molly a stern look. "Molly, I can't believe what I just heard you say. I'm not exactly desperate for company, you know. And I'm not exactly unattached either. You embarrassed me and probably Christopher too."

"I'm sorry, Ms. Maggs. I didn't think. It just doesn't seem right for you to be eating all by yourself. You should have someone to talk to. I didn't mean to embarrass either of you. I'll apologize to Mr. Chris next time he comes around."

"I think it's best to leave it as it is. Just do me a favor and don't play matchmaker, okay? It's not appropriate."

Maggs knew this wouldn't be the end of it. Molly may have capitulated, but she wasn't convinced.

"How well do you know Christopher Allendale anyway?" Maggs asked casually. "You seem to be on pretty familiar terms."

Molly gave her a swift look. "Well, for someone who isn't interested, I'd say you are pretty interested. I happen to think he's a fine man. Sometimes when he's out rowing he comes by for a piece of pie or whatever I might have fresh baked. He would check on Ms. Eleanor from time to time to see if there was anything he could do for her while he was in town, and sometimes he'd stay and eat dinner with her. Ms. Eleanor was very fond of him, as we are. *She* always enjoyed eating with him," she said pointedly before warming to her subject.

"Mr. Huntingdon's housekeeper is my good friend, Nell, and she told me Mr. Chris's wife died rather suddenly about five years ago. She said their marriage was one of convenience mostly, but they seemed content with it as it was; and although he wasn't devastated by her loss, he had to readjust his life. They had one child. An officer in the army now, stationed somewhere in Europe, I believe. Nell says Mr. Chris is devoted to his son.

"That's about all I really know. He's been staying with Mr. Huntingdon since last fall, teaching some kind of course at the Medical University in town. I think Nell said he's going home after summer is over. He lives in Maine, you know. Now why are you so curious?"

Maggs shrugged her shoulders indifferently. "I'm not. I just wasn't aware you knew him, and when he was here, you seemed to be accustomed to his teasing. I just wondered why."

"I'm not very hungry tonight, Molly. Maybe just a salad. I'll have it in my room, I think. I'm going to take a bath and go to bed early and go over what I wrote today. I think I made a good start."

She gave Molly a hug as she started from the room. "By the way, did Stephen call this afternoon?"

"No, dear, he still hasn't called."

"Well, maybe I'll give him a call later."

Maggs went upstairs and turned the shower on as hot as she could bear it and stepped in. Muscles she had used trekking through the woods the past two days were protesting, and the hot water felt wonderful. She relished the soothing steam and the clean, fresh scent of the soap. Her mind wandered contentedly over the day she had just spent, and she found herself thinking of Christopher. She wondered what his life had been like since his wife died. He hadn't struck her as being lonely. *Some people were sufficient unto themselves,* she thought enviously. Another person was never a cure for loneliness anyway. She was often lonely when she was with Stephen.

When she had lost her balance getting out of the canoe and Christopher caught her in his arms, she had thought she sensed more than just a steadying hand, something he hadn't meant to do. But it had happened so quickly she couldn't be sure she hadn't imagined it. She must have.

She turned off the shower, put on her robe, and wrapped a towel around her hair. Molly had left her dinner tray on the desk.

Maggs took the notebook from her knapsack and began reading while she ate her salad. After she finished eating, she dried her hair and brushed it, put on her gown, and climbed into bed to finish reading what she had written. She liked it. She really did. She was tired, but it was a wonderful-feeling tiredness, eased by warmth and happiness and freedom from care. She didn't know when Molly came in and took the notebook from her hand, turned off the light, and took the tray out.

She hadn't thought again about calling Stephen.

Chapter 10

uphoric was the word that Maggs would later use to describe the beginning of this period of transition in her life. The days were spent relaxing and dreaming or planning and writing her novel; it was all interchangeable and all meant the same thing to her: peace. She gloried in the freedom to choose from each day's possibilities the activities which enticed her and to reject those which did not. She was completely happy.

Old friends soon discovered her presence among them and included her in all the activities of the Old Ashley River Road community. Maggs and Christopher Allendale attended many of the same gatherings. They were often paired by hostesses because they were unattached and because they were obviously compatible, and after a while, they were invited as a couple. It was comfortable for them both, and they laughed about it sometimes; but gradually Maggs realized that not only had she begun to look forward to being escorted by Christopher, she took for granted that she would be.

She enjoyed his attentions and his admiration more than just casually and knew that at some point she would have to consider exactly where this was leading and whether it was a path she wanted to follow; but in the beginning, she was content to let their friendship take its course.

She knew that any change in their relationship would be her decision, and Christopher's behavior never caused her any anxiety in that regard. After a while, she also understood that he was ready for the relationship to deepen into something more than occasional embraces and self-conscious kisses that left them both unsatisfied. She was ready too, just not yet willing to deal with the complications of anything more serious.

She was surprised by the intensity of her feelings. Their friendship had progressed so naturally that she was unaware of any emotional attachment until it was too late.

When she talked with Stephen, which she did regularly at first but much less often as time went on, their conversations were mostly informational. He was busy with the merger, said he missed her, but not very convincingly, gave her the neighborhood news, and said he was fine. Leah and the kids were fine. Maggs talked more often to Sassie than to Stephen.

He was unquestionably distracted. At first Maggs thought it was business; but lately, she wondered if he was getting his emotional needs, if not his physical ones, met by the obliging and conniving Terry Matthews. He was often unreachable, uncommunicative, and impersonal, vague about his plans. Their "I love you and I miss you" reassurances became less frequent and less and less convincing. His anger over her arbitrary decision still festered although he denied it, but Maggs felt there was more going on with him than just his anger.

Rather than disturbing her, the distance she felt when she talked with Stephen interested her in a curiously abstract way. It also, implicitly at least, gave her permission to continue her relationship with Christopher as long as she wasn't technically unfaithful. She didn't believe Stephen was observing the same restriction, but for now she was comfortable with her behavior and wasn't too interested in Stephen's.

Her writing was another issue. She had faith now in her talent, her feeling for it, and her commitment to doing it. But most of all, the writing was pure joy. Christopher shared her enthusiasm, supported her, and encouraged her to continue. He brought her a computer and then respected her schedule scrupulously.

And that was another thing.

Christopher's interest meant a lot, but more important to Maggs was that he never questioned her commitment or the likelihood that she would finish the book. He truly appreciated her desire to write, and his primary interest was helping her achieve that desire. He knew firsthand the effort required to keep going when she was discouraged and the sense of accomplishment she would experience when she did. He was never too tired to discuss the details and progress of her day's work, but only if she brought it up. He was willing to help; but he never pushed, never led, never intruded.

On the other hand, Stephen's patronizing attitude showed clearly his doubt that she could do anything as productive as writing a novel. He had always, as he did now, laughed good-naturedly whenever the subject came up, questioning where she would find the time between bridge games and art classes. Wouldn't she be happier without taking on something else? Didn't she want to have any free time at all? Before she had retired, the obstacles seemed to be her job and her growing family. Later, her intention just sort of got lost.

At Myrtlewood she confronted a suspicion she had never been willing to examine: Stephen had actually not wanted her to try. Why? Perhaps because he was happier with all her efforts directed toward his comfort and happiness? Perhaps. Probably, she finally concluded, but right now it didn't really matter.

Her days had developed naturally into a routine. She arose early every morning. She ate breakfast on the balcony when the weather was nice, at her desk when it wasn't. When Molly came for the breakfast tray, she left a fresh pot of coffee and unplugged the telephone in Maggs's bedroom. By eight o'clock every weekday morning, Maggs was at work, and Molly allowed no interruption until noon. Maggs was impatient to begin each day, thrilled at how easily the words came. She no longer doubted herself; she believed now that if she worked diligently, there was a decent chance of getting published.

After her morning's work was completed, she would have lunch (sometimes with Christopher on days when he had only morning classes) and then rest a while. Sometimes she would fall asleep, and sometimes she would just lie on the chaise or sit in the swing outside Aunt Eleanor's bedroom and plan the next part of her story. She usually worked another hour or two and then changed for dinner. Many times Christopher would be waiting in the library for her to join him for a drink.

Sometimes she and Christopher spent the evening with Uncle George at Riverside. Maggs thought George Huntingdon was probably aware of the growing attachment between her and Christopher, but since he neither meddled nor judged, it was unlikely he would let on if he had any concern about where their friendship might be going. The easiness of her life in Charleston was irresistible to Maggs after the hectic pace of Mobile. Maggs easily grew accustomed to playing hostess at Riverside. Drinks would often turn into dinner, and it wasn't unusual to spend the entire evening at Riverside. Sometimes she and Christopher would wander along the river and talk for hours, not coming in until they realized how late it was or until their embraces became too intense.

Other evenings they might go to the symphony, the ballet, the theater, or simply a movie. Dinner might be at one of Charleston's many wonderful restaurants or an out-of-the-way Italian place they both loved, where they would dine on pasta and red wine and breadsticks and come away stuffed and reeking of garlic.

There were fund-raisers for the museum, dress parades at the Citadel, afternoons spent in the serenity of Charleston's beautiful Cypress Gardens. They drove to Aiken for a polo match, which one of the directors of the Spoleto Festival arranged for them to attend after learning that Maggs had never seen a polo match. They had breakfast at the City Market in the early hours of the morning after they had danced the night away and then browsed in the stalls of the Flea Market in their evening clothes before going home to sleep all day.

The children were living their own lives. Stephen appeared to be unconcerned about what she was doing, and Maggs rationalized her absence with the thought that for the first time in her life, she wasn't essential to anyone's well-being but her own. She called her grandchildren once a week, not because she thought they needed her but because she missed them.

Sassie came for a weekend visit. Maggs and Christopher and Uncle George took her to a ball at the Citadel, where the cadets made her evening an unqualified success. Sassie understood Myrtlewood's appeal. She made one attempt to discuss the situation between Stephen and Maggs, but Maggs pleaded that they shouldn't spend any of their precious time on something that was a problem only in Sassie's mind. Maggs didn't fool her, but she did succeed in avoiding the conversation. When she put Sassie on the plane for home, she realized she had missed her a great deal.

But the next day found her occupied with the perils of her heroine again and plans for the evening with Christopher.

As the days went by, she thought of Stephen less and less often, and when she did think of him, it was usually with a feeling of regret. She was sorry he wasn't a part of this time when her life was so full and so rewarding. She knew Stephen's life was moving very fast too, and she had no clearer idea about what was going on with him than he did about what was happening to her. She knew his merger was working out, and he knew she was excited over the progress of her book. After thirty years of marriage, there should be more to say than that. Their lack of communication was something she didn't allow herself to analyze.

She knew it was only a matter of time before it all jumped up to confront her. But for the present, she was truly happy with things as they stood, and she would do just as the old South's most famous heroine had done before her—she would "think about that tomorrow." She understood for the first time in her life what living in the moment really meant.

Chapter 11

beautiful day in mid-May found her hopelessly stuck. She had written her character into a situation she had worked long and hard to devise, and having put her there, she didn't know where to take her next. She worried it around in her mind all morning, littering the floor with paper, starting and restarting. She finally conceded the futility of wasting any more time, and looked around for something else to do.

Molly told her when she went downstairs that Grover Houston had some information about the historical register and could be reached in his office all afternoon, but Maggs wasn't in the mood to deal with that subject right now.

She wandered aimlessly through the house for a while until it occurred to her that she hadn't been in the attic since she was a little girl. She really should see what was up there. Sooner or later she would have to sort it all out.

She got the key from Molly and went up to the dim, quiet repository of so much of Myrtlewood's history. There was wonderful old furniture, priceless pieces that had been replaced rather than repaired, and a virtual treasure trove of lamps, trunks, old toys. Maggs made a mental note to have Tom bring down a beautiful old case clock she found in a corner. She would see about having it repaired. True to her nature, Aunt Eleanor had kept the contents of the attic as organized and uncluttered as she did every other part of Myrtlewood, keeping what was of value and disposing of the things most people cart to the attic and forget forever.

In another area of the attic, dusty wardrobes filled with carefully sealed dresses and gowns revealed the fashions of Betford ladies since the 1700s. Maggs browsed through the old wardrobes in fascination. Some were elaborate, towering armoires whose shelves of hatboxes held bonnets that matched the gowns. A few boxes even contained the gloves and shoes that had been worn with the gown. Some of the wardrobes were very primitive and contained clothing so old and fragile she couldn't begin to guess its age.

In one of the wardrobes she found what she believed to be her grandmother's wedding dress. She would ask Molly about it when she went downstairs. The dress was handmade and hand embroidered, elaborately detailed. Her grandmother would have married sometime in the early 1920s; but this dress must have belonged to *her* mother before her because the style dated the dress from somewhere around the turn of the century.

The dress had been carefully packed and was only slightly discolored. The waist was so small it seemed only a child could have fit into it. Maggs was almost sure she had a faded photograph somewhere in her own attic of her diminutive Gramma Patrice wearing this dress. Maggs's mother had often remarked about the strong resemblance between Gramma Patrice and Sassie. Maggs could visualize it now too, especially in their sizes. This dress would fit Sassie almost perfectly.

Maggs decided to have the dress restored by a textile restoration expert. Wouldn't it be something if Sassie not only wanted to wear the gown some day, but also chose to have her wedding at Myrtlewood? She would be a picture coming down the stairway in this dress. Assuming, of course, that Myrtlewood is still in our possession, Maggs thought with a stab of anxiety.

She lifted the hanger to remove the dress from the wardrobe, but the bottom of the garment bag caught on a splintered panel in the back. As she burrowed inside to free it, she noticed that the panel had been removed and replaced, and that it bulged slightly, as if something kept it from fitting back into place. Delighted with her discovery and certain she was on the verge of discovering a secret, Maggs carefully freed the dress and hung it on a peg close to the attic door. Holding her breath, she went back to the wardrobe and pushed the remaining garments to one side so that she could get a better look. She caught the panel by a corner and worked it from side to side, trying to dislodge it. It was wedged tightly in its fitting. When it finally came loose, she lost her balance and fell backward onto the floor, but she had her answer in her hands. The panel had concealed what appeared to be a lady's journal and a small packet of letters tied with a slender faded ribbon.

Maggs picked herself up and looked around for a place to read them, too excited to wait until she went downstairs. She removed the dust cover from an old Victorian sofa that was close to the attic window and sat down.

It was very quiet as she opened the journal. She could hear faint summer noises in the distance, and an occasional sound from the house below signified that Molly was about her business. Maggs could never, in her wildest imagination, have believed what she was about to discover; and two hours later, tears streaming down her face as she put the last letter back into its envelope, she sat stunned, her mind racing, her heart aching for Eleanor Betford.

The journal and the letters told the story of a heartbreaking love affair between Aunt Eleanor and a prominent married man in the community. He was an honorable and decent man trapped in an unfortunate, unhappy marriage. He and Eleanor had never expected to fall in love, but they did. His love for Eleanor was deep and abiding, and she loved him with all the passion of her young heart. They became lovers, even considered flaunting the conventional moral strictures of their day. They would declare their love; he would get a divorce, and they would go away and begin a new life somewhere, together. She was afraid. He was unsuccessful in overcoming her fears and persuading her to take the only chance that could bring them happiness. In the end he stayed in his unhappy marriage and moved to another state. Eleanor continued her solitary life, filled with parties and activities, but no one to share them with.

She remained aware of his whereabouts and the general circumstances of his life though she never made a conscious effort to know; she even met him socially when he occasionally visited relatives who still lived nearby; and when he died many years later, Eleanor grieved privately but deeply over all she had given up.

Molly cared for her during this period of debilitating grief. No one knew of her devastation except Molly, and Molly guarded her fiercely until she was able to go out again. Friends thought she had a virulent influenza that took a long time to recover from.

Her journal revealed that she felt she had made the only acceptable choice, the only one which would allow her to live with herself, but that later she came to believe not being brave enough to take her destiny into her own hands was the biggest mistake she would ever make.

When enough time had passed and she began to heal a little, Eleanor closed her journal and sealed it away forever, just as she closed that agonizing chapter in her life. She would never again speak of it to anyone, even to Molly. It would be as if it had never happened. The final entry attested to her resolve to advise anyone agonizing over a choice that might change the course of one's life to be bold and seize the opportunity, regardless of what it cost. To do otherwise cost so much more, in the long run. She vowed to live her life in as exemplary a manner as her standards dictated, but her chance for personal fulfillment was lost, and she knew it. The last words she wrote expressed her deep regret that she hadn't understood that when it mattered.

Maggs closed the journal, tears streaming from her eyes. How sad that a yellowed journal and a few tattered letters were all that remained of a great passion.

Maggs finally understood the mystery of Aunt Eleanor's solitude. She never loved again. Everyone thought the reason she remained single was the faithless young man from Boston whom her papa had sent packing. Only Eleanor and Molly knew the truth. The enigmatic encouragement in her letter to Maggs to take risks and follow her heart was explained. And Maggs fully grasped for the first time that she had known, in some indiscernible way, that the choice to come here despite Stephen's displeasure might alter her life. She had been apprehensive, but she had taken the risk.

Had her aunt sensed something lacking in Maggs's life? Because it was certain to her now, whether Aunt Eleanor had seen it or not, that something was definitely missing. She thought the something might be herself.

Maggs put the journal and the letters in her pocket. She absently replaced the dust cover on the sofa, took the dress from its hanger beside the door, and quietly left the attic. She needed time to reflect on this startling revelation. She didn't even want to talk to Molly until she could think about what she had discovered.

As luck would have it, Molly was putting laundry away when Maggs entered her bedroom. She took one look at the tearstains on Maggs's face, and exclaimed, "Whatever is the matter, Ms. Maggs?"

"Nothing, Molly, I'm just slightly unsettled. It's nothing, really. I don't want to talk about it just now, if you don't mind."

She attempted to change the subject by holding up the dress. "Look what I found in the attic. It's Gramma Patrice's wedding dress, isn't it? I'm going to have it restored and take it with me when I go back to Mobile. Maybe Sassie will wear it one day. Isn't it beautiful?"

"It's no good you're trying to change the subject on me. I know you better than that. Something happened in that attic that upset you, and I want to know what it was. I'll not be budging from this spot until you tell me."

The stubborn streak in Molly's Irish soul was operating at full strength. Maggs hesitated a moment and then, realizing Molly wasn't going to be put off, said, "Molly, I found Aunt Eleanor's journal behind a panel in the back of the armoire where this dress was stored. What I read touched me deeply, but more than that, it upset me terribly to learn that there was this overwhelming love and passion in her life, followed by what must have been almost unendurable heartbreak; and through it all, she never let on to anyone. What she had to overcome just to keep going would have been impossible for most people. To rebuild her life in such an admirable way was a truly formidable accomplishment."

Molly had an indescribable expression on her face. She looked at Maggs and said, "Well, sure it was a bad time for her, but it would have been worse if her father hadn't discovered the scoundrel for what he really was and sent him packing. She got over it in due time."

There was an almost hopeful tone in her voice which suggested that she hoped this explanation would satisfy Maggs and end the discussion.

Maggs looked at her levelly and said, "Molly, I'm not talking about the scoundrel, as you put it. I'm referring to the man Aunt Eleanor truly loved, and you know it. If you don't want to discuss it, I understand, but let's don't pretend we're talking about something that didn't happen. Her account was too heartbreaking."

A suspicious shine in Molly's eyes showed she understood that what she had feared was true. Maggs had discovered the most closely guarded secret of Molly and Eleanor's long history. Molly hung her head in despair.

"She would have been so mortified to know you had found out about this," Molly said. "She hid that journal away so many years ago, rather than destroying it as I begged her to. Years later when we thought about it, we searched and searched for it, but neither of us could remember where she had hidden it, and after a while we just had to give up. I promised her I'd keep looking for it, and I have, but without any luck."

"Molly, surely you know I'm not judging her in any way. I just find it tragic that she gave up the one person who could have made her happy. In her letter, she urged me to follow my dreams, and I wasn't sure what she meant. I understand now. She regretted her decision for the rest of her life. It makes my heart ache.

"But I would never breathe a word of this to anyone else. Not even Stephen. In fact, I'm not sure I would have told you I found the journal if you hadn't insisted on knowing what upset me. Please don't worry that her secret is no longer safe because it's as safe with me as it is with you. It just explains a lot, that's all."

Relief flooded Molly's earnest countenance. "I beg your pardon, Ms. Maggs. I should've known you'd guard her past the same way

I always have. I was just shocked that the journal had at last come to light. I'm grateful that you found it instead of someone who wouldn't understand."

She put her cheek against Maggs's dusty, tear-streaked one, and they stood silently in each other's arms.

After several moments, Maggs gently released herself from Molly's embrace and said, "What should we do with the damned thing, Molly? I can't bear the thought of destroying it. It was part of her, after all, and it's a treasure to me just because of that. But we must be sure no one else ever sees it and the only way I know to be sure of that is to destroy it. What do you think we should do?"

Molly wiped the tears from her cheek and said, "I think we should burn it at once. Her secret will be safe forever if we do that, and we won't have to worry about it ever again. She should never have written about it all in the first place. But I'm not sure she'd have survived if she hadn't been able to. And I didn't have the heart to scold her. For a long time, it was all she had left of him, and she desperately needed something to cling to. Her darling papa had been gone for several years by then, and Ms. Patrice was busy with her own life. I think it was the only thing in her life she didn't share with Ms. Patrice. Ms. Eleanor had no one but me to share her pain. I just wasn't enough. Sure it was a terrible thing to watch, believe me. She would shut herself up in her room and write for hours, day after day. Then one day, she just put it away. It was like she put him away too, like she was finally able to seal that part of her life away forever. She recovered, bit by bit, after that, and she never spoke of him again though I knew well enough she hadn't forgotten—just gone forward as she had always been taught to do.

"When he died, she remembered about the journal, and that's when we started looking for it. She was as concerned that it might come to light one day and be an embarrassment to his family as she was about guarding her own privacy. But we never found it."

Molly was crying quietly again, and Maggs put her arms around her.

"We'll take it downstairs right now and burn it. It's the right thing to do. She can rest in peace, and you can stop worrying too.

You guarded her loyally all her life, Molly, and you have done no less after her death."

Maggs found a box of tissues and gave Molly a handful.

"Come on, let's do it right now, and then we'll have a nice cup of tea. I think we could both use one. Maybe even with a touch of something to strengthen it a bit, what do you say?"

They went downstairs and together they closed the chapter on Eleanor Betford's lost love forever. Before Tom came in from his evening chores, the journal had been reduced to ashes, and he found them drinking tea in what he might have described as a conspiratorial mood if he had been an articulate man. If he suspected something eventful had just taken place, he couldn't have any idea what it was, and they offered no enlightenment. He accepted the tea they offered, patted Molly awkwardly on the shoulder, sat down at the table, and studied his teacup, obviously relieved to be uninformed.

Chapter 12

When Maggs awoke the next morning, she felt in her bones that something momentous was impending. The feeling persisted as she went about her morning routine. She had wrestled with Aunt Eleanor's story in her dreams, and the night had left her exhausted and pensive. She felt strongly that the message of the journal and the admonition in Eleanor's letter was pertinent to the choices imminent in her own life. She had postponed them successfully so far, but it wouldn't be possible much longer. She dreaded coming to terms with what she felt *obligated to do* as opposed to what she *wanted to do*; not ready to accept the consequences of either choice. This emotional quandary alternately goaded and pacified her, leaving her at times eager to meet her dilemma head-on and at others, paralyzed, praying unrealistically that time would resolve her indecision without any necessary participation on her part.

She ate her breakfast on the balcony. The morning seemed sweeter, every sensation heightened and intensified. When she turned on the computer, the words spilled forth like bullets as if they were missiles of the machine rather than her mind. Yesterday's block no longer existed. Perhaps this was merely a temporary respite—a blessing to be accepted and not analyzed. Or perhaps writing would be easier from now on. Whatever the significance, it didn't matter now. Her coffee grew cold. She had no awareness of time or place until Molly knocked and came into the room.

"Aren't you going to stop for lunch today?" Without waiting for an answer, she went on, "Mr. Allendale has called twice, but he said not to interrupt you. He wants you to meet him at seven o'clock for cocktails and dinner. Some kind of faculty presentation, he said, in the president's dining room. He said it will be a dreadful bore, but they're honoring him, so his attendance is mandatory. If you don't want to come, he'll understand, he said, and he'll call you later."

She busied herself removing the coffee service and straightening the room. She said, "I really think you should eat a bite of something, dear, to keep you going. How about some fruit salad? I just made a fresh poppy seed dressing. Let me bring you some and a nice cup of tea."

Maggs reluctantly pushed her chair back from the desk, detached herself mentally from what she was doing, and tuned in to what Molly was coaxing her about.

"All right, but I'll come down for it. I need a break, I guess. I didn't realize how long I've been sitting here. Molly, my writing is going so well right now that I'm afraid to stop for fear I'll get stuck again."

"Of course you won't, dear. But you do have to eat. And you have to rest. Come along, now. Oh, and will you be wanting Tom to take you into town later?" Molly asked as she juggled the tray and ushered Maggs out of the room at the same time.

"Well, I'd about as soon go to the dentist as a faculty dinner with Dr. Satterfield, but I don't see how I can refuse," Maggs grumbled. "Tell Tom I'll be ready at six-fifteen."

She followed Molly downstairs and ate her lunch on the back porch. Bees were working the new blossoms and butterflies flitted busily in the breeze. The willow branches swayed invitingly over the bench facing the river. The buds on the gardenia bushes around the gazebo were on the verge of bursting open. She imagined she knew how that felt.

She wished Christopher would come home and take her out in the canoe. Instead, she had to get dressed and go into town.

She rested a while and then sat in the middle of her bed and telephoned Stephen at the office. His secretary said he was out for a meeting, and she wasn't sure he'd return. Maggs called the house, but he wasn't at home. She told his answering machine that she was fine, hoped he was fine, would be out for the evening, and would catch him later. Mechanical communication with Stephen was no longer unusual or uncomfortable.

Christopher waited for her outside the administrative building, and when she caught her first glimpse of him, her breath caught in her throat. To others, she knew, he seemed reserved; his bearing was dignified and his manners were elegant. He was indisputably all those things, but there was another side of him. Maggs knew how he loved old sweaters and khakis and deck shoes and canoes and roasting marshmallows on the sandbar, reading poetry as the sun went down, talking for hours while lying on his back on a blanket, or making ridiculous toasts about the glow in her eyes while she sat laughing down at him.

His blue eyes often belied the humor, and he sometimes caught her to him abruptly and fiercely, kissing her until she was as dizzy as a schoolgirl before letting her go and apologizing for his impulsiveness. Affectionate and demonstrative, he smiled often, laughed easily, teased mercilessly, but always kindly.

She realized she was taking inventory in a very proprietary way. But she really did feel that he was hers, in some indefinable way, and the feeling made her happy, even if it was only a temporary ownership. He responded in kind, keeping everything light and fun, but she knew he felt the same incontestable connection.

He walked down the steps and took her hand, leaning down to speak to Tom. "I'll bring her home, Tom. Thanks for driving her in."

"What is this all about, Christopher?" she asked as they walked down the marble hall. "It sounds so ceremonial."

"I'm sorry if I made it sound that way. It's not at all, and I really didn't intend to bore you with this. It's just that I'm being recognized at a president's dinner and Dr. Satterfield insisted that you be invited. Do you mind terribly? I'll try to get us away as early as possible, and I promise to make it up to you."

"Of course I don't mind. I'm pleased you wanted me here. I think it's wonderful that you're appreciated, and I'm sure it will be fun."

He shook his head in denial as he ushered her into the somber dining room. Dinner was typical—nourishing, but unimaginative. When coffee was finally brought around, Dr. Madison Satterfield stood up.

"It gives me great pleasure tonight to recognize our eminent colleague, Dr. Christopher Allendale, who has spent the past eight months as a temporary member of our faculty. We have benefited enormously from his dedication and commitment. Most of you are aware that Dr. Allendale is widely renowned for his achievements in genetic research. Most of you don't know yet that he has been offered a permanent position on our staff. Obviously, we hope he decides in our favor. Ladies and gentlemen, our friend and colleague, Dr. Christopher Allendale," he said.

Maggs felt Christopher's body tense. He recovered instantly, arose, and said, "I thank you all sincerely for honoring me tonight. I have enjoyed my time here with you immensely.

"I also thank Dr. Satterfield for the offer to join the staff. I'm more than a little fond of this part of the country, but I hadn't considered staying here. There are excellent research facilities here, and there is no reason I couldn't continue my work somewhere other than Maine. But I will have to give serious thought to leaving my home there. I have until the end of the summer quarter before my contract here is completed, and I will certainly have an answer for you by that time. I thank you again."

After a few toasts and some superficial conversation, Christopher repeated his gratitude to his hosts, and he and Maggs were able to leave.

Outside in the soft evening air, Christopher said, "Let's walk a while, okay?"

She nodded. He took her hand and led her across the street to a small park. They walked in silence until they came to a bench that faced a small pond. The moonlight wrapped them in a silvery glow, and the scent of wisteria was faintly detectable from where it had wound its way to the top of a very old live oak beside the pond. They sat down wordlessly. Christopher took her in his arms and kissed her with unusual urgency. She returned his kiss and clung to him with the same feeling of disquiet, understanding somehow that what had happened tonight would change things between them.

Christopher took her face in his hands and said, "Maggs, I don't understand everything I'm feeling right now, but I do know that I find the possibility of remaining in Charleston appealing. But I wouldn't want to stay unless you stayed too.

"I promised myself I would make no demands on you, that I would enjoy what we have and give you all the time you need to figure out how you feel about us. I understand the conflict you must be feeling, and I haven't wanted to influence you.

"But this job offer changes things. It makes my return to Maine a choice now, rather than a given. And that choice will depend on you." He removed his hands and shrugged his shoulders.

"I love you, Maggs. It's as simple as that. I have for a while now. Maybe not long enough to compete with the history you and Stephen have, but long enough to be sure of what I feel. I've never discussed my relationship with Katherine except in the most general way, but I need to tell you about our marriage so you'll understand why you have become so important to me."

Maggs put her fingers over his lips gently. "Christopher, you don't have to do this. I respect your reticence about your marriage. That's in the past, and I'm content to let it remain there. Please don't think you have to tell me about it."

"I don't feel I have to. I want you to know. I met Katherine while I was in medical school at Harvard. She was a nurse in the Boston hospital where I did my internship and later my residency in pediatrics. I was very serious back then, totally absorbed in my work. She was serious about her work too, but she had a wonderful spontaneity that attracted me, and I had forgotten how to have fun. I had spent years absorbed in the pursuit of my education and training, and I knew little about people—particularly women.

"At first, I didn't realize Kate was so needy—she disguised it very well, even, I know now, from herself. I came to understand much later that she tried to save herself by saving others. She had a very unstable childhood, and because she was powerless to change any of the things that made her miserable as a child, she had developed an overpowering need to save others. Nursing satisfied that need at first. Later, I became the focus. My single-mindedness triggered her need to rescue. She thought I was lost, incomplete somehow, and she set out to save me from myself—to make me a whole person.

"We were fairly happy at first. I believed she completely supported my goals and understood my desire not to be distracted by things of a less than serious nature. She believed I subconsciously wanted someone to distract me from such monotonous dedication. I don't think either of us intentionally misled the other. It was just an unfortunate misunderstanding on both of our parts. After a while she felt excluded by my interest in my work, and her attempts to divert me and amuse me lost their attraction for me. But we were congenial enough—and not yet unhappy enough—to make any changes.

"In due time, Kate became pregnant and our son was born. Prentiss was the pride of my life. He still is. Katherine's devotion surpassed mine. She had a justification for her existence at last, and if I had secretly worried during her pregnancy that she would become obsessive about him, I soon came to understand that he added balance to her life in a completely healthy way. She was a wonderful mother. She had very good instincts, and she adored him.

"When Prentiss was four years old, Katherine wanted another baby. I didn't, particularly, but our life had proceeded smoothly since Prentiss's birth, so I agreed.

"I don't know what happened, but the pregnancy was trouble-filled from the onset, and when our daughter was born, she wasn't only premature, she was born with multiple congenital birth defects. The doctors in the neonatal unit advised against keeping her on life support and I agreed with them, but Katherine couldn't live with that choice, so I conceded, knowing it was a mistake.

"The baby managed to survive, but her health would never be anything but risky at best, and once she was well enough to take home, which was many months after she was born, she required constant attention. She was blind, her heart was very weak, and her lungs would sometimes just stop breathing. There were numerous trips to the emergency room. Our home resembled a hospital ward more than anything else.

"Katherine was untiring and uncomplaining in her care of this doomed little girl. We all suffered from her relentless determination to save this child—especially Prentiss. He had been the focus of all Kate's devotion, and although she pushed herself to the point of exhaustion in trying to care for both children, Prentiss suffered the most because of the tragedy in our lives. I finally insisted on hiring a housekeeper, which may be the only thing that saved Prentiss.

"I had understood from the beginning that the baby couldn't overcome the formidable problems she had, and I tried to keep myself from becoming too emotionally attached to her. I spent all the time I could manage with Prentiss in an attempt to alleviate some of the bewilderment I could see in his face.

"Just shy of her first birthday, the baby developed a respiratory infection that went straight into pneumonia, and with her heart in its weakened state, she didn't have the strength to fight the infection. She made a gallant attempt, but it was futile. She spent three weeks in the hospital connected to every conceivable means of life support before she died.

"Katherine was devastated. I had tried to prepare her for the eventuality, but with her customary refusal to consider anything she couldn't accept, she was completely unprepared for the loss of this baby she had fought so hard to save. To her mind, she had failed again to save someone she loved.

"By this time, I had realized that my intention of remaining emotionally uninvolved had failed miserably. Even so, I was unprepared for the depth of my own grief. I had known she couldn't live, but I was desolate when she died."

His eyes were filled with anguish. Maggs put her arms around him and said, "Christopher, please don't go on with this. I can't bear to see you in this much pain."

He stood up and took her hand. "Let's walk some more. I need to finish this, Maggs. I've never discussed it with anyone. I need to do it. For my sake, but I also want you to know everything. I want you to be a permanent part of my life, and I can't ask you to do that unless you know what my life was before."

Maggs knew where this was leading and had no idea what to do about it, but what most concerned her was Christopher's obvious distress. It had grown late. The bell in the tower chimed midnight. The night was very still; the breeze seemed to be holding its breath until this sad story was finished.

They walked a while in silence. Finally, Christopher went on, "After the baby died, Katherine was never the same. She suffered from severe depressions that would incapacitate her for days on end, sometimes weeks. She had psychiatric care, the best in Boston. She was hospitalized on several occasions, and she honestly tried to help herself. But she had been so severely damaged by what happened that she just couldn't pull herself together.

"There were long periods when she seemed able to resume her life, and we made the most of those times—for Prentiss's sake. She no longer turned to me for anything she needed, emotionally or otherwise. I didn't know how to help her, so I concentrated my attention on Prentiss, in an attempt to make up for what his mother could no longer give him. For the next ten years her condition deteriorated, and she spent more and more time in institutions.

"When Prentiss was fifteen, Katherine had enjoyed a fairly consistent period of stability and had been at home for almost a year. We all thought she was making progress. Then Prentiss came home from school one afternoon to discover her in the garage, under the exhaust pipe of the car. She was dead when the paramedics arrived—finally out of her misery. A one-line note, unaddressed, said simply, 'Forgive me, I can't go on.'

"It was a terrible thing for Prentiss. Terrible! But he understood by then that his mother would never be what she would have wanted to be again, and I think he was comforted a little by that knowledge.

"Kate died in the early summer. I took three month's leave. Prentiss and I went to Colorado and spent the summer in the mountains in an isolated cabin. We had no telephone, a black-and-white television set which rarely worked, and we slept on lumpy bunk beds. We fished and hiked and swam. We photographed wild animals—even rigged up a dark room to develop our film. We listened to the radio in the evenings and read everything we could get our hands on. We went into town only to get supplies and pick up more books at the library. We cooked wonderful meals over a campfire and sat in the dark afterward, talking for hours.

"We talked about Katherine and her illness. We talked about the tragic little baby who had been a part of our lives for such a short time. We talked about how he felt about everything that happened, and we talked about how I felt about it, at least as much of it as I could say to a fifteen-year-old boy without causing him further anguish. We began to recover a little.

"We talked a lot about what he wanted from his life. He wanted to go to West Point. He took high school ROTC when we got back to Boston to see if he liked the military way of doing things. He thrived on it.

"I worried about him at first, that he might be substituting the structure of the military for something he had lost during his childhood, but he was fine. He graduated from West Point, and he's doing his third tour in Germany. I try to see him as often as possible.

"After the baby died, I was furious that my profession couldn't save people from what we went through. I went back to school to study birth defects. It comforted me to try and prevent another family from experiencing the tragedy of our loss. It was a long time before I had any peace of mind, but my work helped.

"I haven't cared for anyone since Katherine died, other than very casually, and I honestly didn't expect to again. Until now. You've become increasingly important in my life. I've fallen in love with you, Maggs, and I didn't mean to. What's worse, I think I've allowed you to fall in love with me too. If I'm wrong, just say so, but I don't think I am."

They walked close to the water's edge, and he put his arm around Maggs. Her head was on his shoulder, and she could feel his breath on her hair. She didn't know how to stop him, didn't know if she wanted to.

"I want you, Maggs, all of you, all the time. I don't want to go home at night without you. I don't want you to go back to Mobile and Stephen and your life there.

"I've been considering how I could ask you to come with me when I return to Maine. I didn't think it was fair to ask you to give up your life and follow me to a remote place where harsh winters are a way of life. Many people can't handle the isolation. Katherine detested it. She couldn't bear the quiet.

"The house was my mother's. I kept it after she died, and Prentiss and I went up there as often as I could get away. Prentiss loves it as much as I do. After he left for West Point, I sold my home in Boston and went to live there full time.

"The house has a magnificent view of the ocean from the cliff where it sits. There's a wildness there, a natural beauty everywhere you look. Spring can take your breath away, summers are filled with wildflowers and wild berries, and regattas chart their course past the house. Fall brings the whales, which are magnificent to watch, and in winter, northeasters blow the snow-covered dunes into frosted whirlwinds. There are fishing villages up and down the coast, and great restaurants where you can have a lobster that's just been taken out of the trap cooked for your lunch. I know you'd appreciate all these things, Maggs, I just don't know if you could live with them. Or if you'd even want to."

He fell silent. She lifted her head from his shoulder in order to see his face. He was watching her intently. His body was tense, and his face reflected the depth of his feelings. He appeared strangely haunted, but relieved at the same time. And somehow hopeful. As if everything that mattered depended on what she said. She looked at him in a kind of dazed silence until she could no longer bear the intensity of his gaze. He was holding both her hands and suddenly the diamond in her engagement ring caught a moonbeam and flashed it back to her, reminding her with a stab that she should never have allowed herself to be in a position to even have such a conversation.

She had known there would be a reckoning for what she had allowed to happen between them, but somehow she hadn't envisioned it's being this serious. When she had thought of it at all, she thought the most that could happen would be a short, intense affair. She never imagined that it might lead to anything life-changing. Yet even as she stood here trying to collect her thoughts, she knew she found the idea of spending great chunks of time isolated with Christopher Allendale unbearably appealing. She might even want to spend the rest of her life with him. But she wasn't prepared for the monumental upheaval which would be necessary in order for them to be together. It would be, after all, her life that would be turned upside down, not his.

As the thought went through her mind, she knew he wouldn't expect her to do something so momentous without considering the consequences. She turned her face up to him, the tears on her lashes glistening in the moonlight. He was waiting for some kind of response.

"Christopher, I don't know how to answer you. I do care about you, deeply I think. But this has come too soon and I don't know if I have the strength to make such a decision right now, especially one that will change my whole life."

He kissed the tears from her eyelashes, and, holding her face in his hands, he said, "But don't you understand what happened tonight? This offer to join the staff of the university would make it possible for us to stay here. You can keep Myrtlewood and I can keep the house in Maine, and we can share both. I've always loved Charleston, even when I was a boy. We could have the best of both worlds. I don't think many people have a chance like that. It's almost as though it was meant to happen, Maggs."

He kissed her again, her face and her eyes and then finally, her mouth until all her resistance was gone and she was tense with the same desire she could read in his eyes.

"Please, Christopher," she said shakily. "This isn't fair. I can't think when you do this. Let's go home and we'll talk about it some more after I've had time to think."

She started to walk away, but he pulled her back and said, "Maggs, let's go away this weekend. Somewhere that we can be alone. I know of a house with an isolated beach on a small island south of here. It belongs to a friend of mine, and I have a standing invitation to use it. Let's go and see how we like each other when there's no one else around."

Before she could answer, he kissed her again, and his kiss was more insistent, more demanding. He looked into her eyes.

"Maggs, I want you to marry me, not just sleep with me. I don't think you can make a sound decision until we have a chance to really know each other. I never expected to feel this way, but I do, and I can't lose you now. Please come with me."

"What would I tell Molly? And what if Stephen or the children needed me? I don't think this is a good idea, Christopher. And Uncle George—I couldn't bear his thinking I would do something like this."

He outlined her mouth with his fingertip and said, "I'm sure Molly suspects what's happening between us. I think she may even be doing what she can to foster it. As for Uncle George, he asks no questions about my coming and going. He won't even know you're not at Myrtlewood. And you can check in with Molly. Will you come?"

His pleading expression and the anticipation in his eyes caused her to smile involuntarily at his unapologetic vulnerability, and then her smiled turned into a giggle.

Sensing he had won, he laughed too, and kissed her again. "Do you find me amusing? I'll be willing to bet you'll find other adjectives to describe me before I bring you home. We can leave first thing in the morning. I don't have classes Monday, so I'll have three days to see how many ways I can please you. Listen to your heart, Mary Margaret, and give me a chance."

His words struck an eerie echo in her mind. "Okay, you win. But don't blame me if this turns out to be a disaster. I warn you,

Christopher, I'm a long way from being somebody's weekend diversion, and we'll both have my conscience to deal with, so you'd better be sure this is what you want. I don't know why I'm doing this, but yes, I'll come with you."

He reached for her again, but she put her hand on his chest and said, "I think you'd better take me home unless you want me to be sleepy all day tomorrow and have awful circles under my eyes."

"Fat chance," he said. "You'll have to come up with something much more unattractive than dark circles to disenchant me. And you can sleep in the car on the way. Because you won't be getting much sleep once we arrive. Come on, then, let's go. I don't want to leave you, even for a few hours, but I guess I must. Tomorrow night will be very different. I'll ply you with wine and candlelight and poetry and music, and we won't sleep until the sun is up again. I'll be irresistible. You'll see."

One more lingering kiss, and then they walked back to the car with his arm around her shoulders. Her head was spinning. She was astonished that she had agreed to go, and she certainly questioned what she was doing. But she knew she wouldn't change her mind; she had known it when he challenged her to follow her heart. She had taken the first chance when she came to Myrtlewood despite Stephen's objections; she would take another and see what happened.

She would unquestionably have to deal with the morality of her choice at some point, but she would think about that tomorrow too. *No wonder Scarlett used that tactic so often*, she thought. It works!

Chapter 13

The beach house rose from the dunes and faced the ocean confidently, the soft gray patina of its walls shimmering softly in the sunlight. Years of battering from Atlantic storms had given it a muted, weathered appearance that spoke of strength and endurance and permanence. A breeze ruffled the sea oats that grew from the dunes on either side.

Christopher stopped the car in the driveway and came around to open the door. As she stepped out, he caught her to him and kissed her.

"I'll get all this stuff out later," he said as he unlocked the back door. "Come and see the view from the porch. It's wonderful."

The house was spacious and well equipped. The furniture was traditional, with a few good antique pieces scattered here and there and good prints on the walls. Comfortable and lived-in, this was a home on a beach, rather than a "beach house," and it was perfect. A basket of seashells and a piece of shiny driftwood were the only evidence of its purpose.

Glass doors, floor-to-ceiling windows and a full-length porch opened the back of the house to the ocean view and filled the rooms with air and light. The porch was furnished with high-backed wicker chairs, an assortment of tables, and a wrought iron dining table. Ceiling fans relieved the humidity when island breezes were reluctant, and a stand for a double hammock stood at one end of the porch.

Maggs stood at the railing with the breeze blowing her hair and watched the dazzling shimmer of the green-blue water while Christopher brought out the cushions for the furniture. He connected the last hook on the hammock and deposited his long body into it. Maggs heard his sigh of contentment and turned to find him beckoning to her. She laughed happily as she walked over to him, realizing she hadn't felt so carefree in a long time.

"This is so beautiful, Christopher. I can't believe I'm here. It seemed almost too easy."

Christopher caught her hand and pulled her down to him, catching her as she fell. She landed on top of him, and they laughed uncontrollably as they tried to position themselves side by side while the hammock swung crazily. Maggs's laughter and the violent swaying were both stilled as Christopher kissed her.

She responded instantly to the tenderness with which he held her. She answered his kiss with all the yearning she had fought to control since she had first realized she was attracted to him. She was overwhelmed by the intensity of her desire. Sex with Stephen was familiar and comfortable, pleasantly routine. It had been so for some time now. This would be quite different.

As their kisses grew more urgent, Christopher began to undress her, slowly caressing her with his mouth and murmuring her name. She put her arms under his shirt and pulled it up. He released her momentarily, pulled the shirt over his head, and threw it aside, and reached for her again. As the sea breeze fanned them, she moaned and pressed closer to him. Her movement caused the hammock to sway wildly again, almost tossing them to the floor. The situation was too funny to ignore, and they couldn't stifle their laughter.

"Damn this thing for an instrument of hell," he swore, "Come with me, my darling. I don't think I'm going to impress you much under these circumstances. Let's see if we can find something a little more conducive to what I have in mind."

She stood up and faced him in the glittering light of day, exposed and willing, feeling abandoned and utterly desirable.

He looked at her with wonder in his eyes and breathed, "My god, you're beautiful, Maggs. I've never been so moved by anything in my life as the way you look right this minute. I have to be the luckiest man alive."

Tears filled her eyes, making them brighter than the water gently washing up on the sands beyond them. She looked directly into his eyes.

"I'm yours, Christopher. For this time, for right now, I know this is right, and I'm certain this is what I want. Can we accept it for just that for the time being? And deal with everything else later?"

She wrapped her arms around his neck, leaning her head against his chest. He trembled involuntarily, holding her so tightly that she was almost unable to breathe.

"Whatever you wish, my darling. But I think it's only fair to warn you, I'll never willingly let you go. You were meant to share my life. And somehow, I know you will."

He picked her up effortlessly and carried her to the bedroom. He placed her on the bed and leaned over and kissed her lingeringly.

"Wait right here. And hold the thought. I'll be back in a heartbeat. I want to get some champagne."

He left the room, and she heard the back door open and then close again. She lay still, watching the slow-turning blades of the ceiling fan and enjoying the cool air on her bare skin. The draperies were open, and she could see the vast expanse of the ocean covered by a blue-white sky. Seagulls circled lazily over the water. She felt relaxed and totally uninhibited. She adjusted the pillows under her head and closed her eyes. She didn't hear Christopher any longer and wondered idly what he was doing. She was eager for him to return.

When she opened her eyes again, it was to the dimness of early evening. The draperies were still open and she could still see the water but it was a much darker shade of green now.

In the distance she could hear music playing, and she caught the delicious scent of something being grilled. She was covered by a soft cotton throw, and at first she didn't know where she was. When she removed the cover, everything came back in a rush.

She must have fallen asleep. She couldn't believe it. She could hear Christopher whistling somewhere. As she stretched her body languorously, she had an idea that would not only surprise him but also finish what they had left unfinished earlier.

She tiptoed into the bathroom, brushed her hair up, and pinned it on top of her head. Christopher had brought their luggage in while she slept, and she rummaged through her suitcase for a scarf. She worked it into her hair so that it covered the lower part of her face like a veil. She added a pair of large, dangling earrings, and tiptoed silently out to the back porch, clad only in the veil and earrings. Christopher stood in front of the grill, barefooted and bare-chested, a long fork in one hand. He was still whistling softly. His back was to her, and she noticed that he was already well tanned. White shorts emphasized his broad shoulders, and his muscles moved smoothly as he bent over the grill to turn the steaks.

Maggs tiptoed silently up behind him and ran her arms around his chest, pressing her body against his back. He gasped as she caressed his chest, and then turned to face her. He held her at arm's length and devoured her with his eyes.

"Oh my god, Maggs," he said hoarsely. "I thought you'd sleep until I had dinner ready. You were so tired I didn't want to wake you. Although I must admit, a nap wasn't what I had in mind when I left you. But this! Tell me you're not a figment of my imagination."

She wound herself against him and into every bend of his body before pulling herself free, dropped her head demurely and curtsied.

"No figment of imagination can fulfill your desires as I soon will. Come with me, my lord, I have treasures to share that you have only dreamed of."

She danced away as he reached for her. He started after her and then swore as he remembered the steaks on the grill.

"Damn! Don't go away. I've got to take our dinner off the grill or it'll be ruined."

She taunted, "Don't take too long. Your harem girl might fall asleep again and be someone else entirely when she awakens the next time."

He stumped his toe as he carried the platter into the kitchen and swore again. Maggs laughed and danced into the bedroom.

Christopher followed and took her in his arms. They fell onto the bed, locked into each other with such total abandon that when their passion was finally spent, they could only look at each other.

Christopher recovered first. He kissed her tenderly, honoring her with the softness of his mouth. She returned his kisses hungrily, reaching for him when he seemed inclined to stop. She sighed deeply and stretched, the silky feel of the sheets against her bare skin soothing her exhausted body. She closed her eyes and snuggled into his neck. He caressed her shoulders and her back with the softest touch she had ever known. They slept in each other's arms, and when she awoke this time, evening had fallen and she could see the stars in the night sky reflected in the water.

She stirred, and in his sleep he pulled her closer. She kissed him awake and felt his immediate response. This time they made love slowly and voluptuously, taking time to explore and savor, awakening a depth of sensuality in Maggs that she had been unaware of, feelings that were fierce and erotic and tender and caring all at the same time.

Afterward they watched the stars through the open window. They didn't talk about what had happened, but Maggs knew the intensity of her pleasure was the result of Christopher's desire to please her. She felt complete. Not just satisfied—not just content—but truly happy.

Christopher nuzzled her ear and said, "Are you hungry, my little heathen?"

"Famished, my lord," she replied, pretending a timidity denied by her recent actions.

"Well, let's see if the steaks are ruined beyond saving. You'll find the makings for a salad in the kitchen. The potatoes are ready for the oven and the wine is cooling. Can you control yourself long enough for me to feed you?"

"I can if you can. I'll just have a quick shower and I'll be right with you."

After her shower, she put on a bright printed sundress and tied her hair back in a ponytail. She slipped her feet into pink sandals and went to the kitchen. Christopher was back on the deck, trying to salvage the steaks, she supposed; and after she finished washing and chopping the vegetables and making a dressing for the salad, she went to join him.

The night sky was very clear and stars were scattered like daisies in a spring meadow. A full moon spilled a liquid shower on the calm sea below. The wet sand at low tide was alive with all kinds of night-scurrying creatures scavenging for their supper. The air was cool and clean, and the breeze from the ocean was as soft as a gossamer web on her bare shoulders.

Christopher turned and held out his hand to her as she came outside. He whistled his approval softly.

"I thought we'd eat on the porch, it's such a beautiful evening. The steaks are almost ready. I hope they're not ruined, but if they are, it was well worth it."

She leaned against him with his arm around her until the steaks were ready. He carried them to the table while she went to get the rest of their supper. In the center of the table, a candle protected by a hurricane globe flickered slightly when the breeze kicked up. Christopher seated her and poured the wine. The stereo inside played something soft and dreamy by Henry Mancini.

They ate with relish, talking and laughing all the while, and then refilled their wine glasses, kicked off their shoes, and walked down the deserted beach with their arms around each other.

It was late when they returned. Christopher helped clear the dishes and clean up the kitchen. "Are you tired, darling?" he asked as he put away the last dish.

"Yes. But too happy to go to sleep. Let's not call it a day yet. Could we lie in the hammock and watch the stars?"

"Of course. If we can stay in it, that is," he said.

They went back to the porch and settled into the hammock. Maggs noted how perfectly their bodies seemed to fit together. She felt a warm rush as she remembered their earlier lovemaking and anticipated the night ahead. But for now, she really was tired, and in no time she was asleep again—in Christopher's arms.

Some time during the night, Christopher awoke and carried her inside to bed. She curled up against him and slept on. Early the next morning, she was awakened by his insistent kisses and his questing hands. They made love, slowly and drowsily at first, letting their passion build gradually and then explode in a storm that left them both drained and satisfied. They slept again.

When the sound of seagulls woke her, Christopher was already up. She found him on the porch drinking coffee and reading the newspaper.

"Good morning, my love," he called as she came out, wincing a little from the brightness of this morning's sunshine and last night's wine. He poured her a cup of coffee and leaned over to kiss her. He smelled of soap and sunshine and salt air. Delicious.

"What would you like to do today? We can go around to the other side of the island and play some tennis and have a late lunch. Or we can play a few rounds of golf if you like. Or rent a boat and go sailing. What's your pleasure?"

She stretched her arms over her head and then realized how skimpily she was clad. She blushed slightly. "I want to go for a swim in those gorgeous waves and then I want to soak up some of that glorious sunshine, and I would be perfectly content not to leave the beach all day. You don't know it, but I'm a compulsive sun worshipper. Would you mind if we just stayed here today? I don't need to be entertained, Christopher. All I want is to be with you."

He smiled his wonderful smile and said, "That's what I hoped you'd say. I'll go for a swim with you after breakfast, and maybe do a little surf casting while you soak up some sun. I might even catch a few rays, myself."

He got up and started inside. "I stopped by the bakery for sweet rolls when I went for the newspaper. Do you want one or are you up for a heartier breakfast?"

"Sweet rolls sound perfect. Let me help you."

She went inside with him and poured orange juice while he put the sweet rolls on a plate. They took the tray back to the porch and discussed the headlines while they ate.

Maggs cleared the table while Christopher read the sports page. She rinsed out the dishes they had used, and when the kitchen was tidy again, she changed into her swimsuit. She looked at herself in the full-length mirror behind the bathroom door, viewing herself critically from all sides. She had lost a few pounds since she had been at Myrtlewood. She was fairly satisfied with the way she looked in her bathing suit.

She got her hat and sunglasses and beach towel and put them in her beach bag. She applied suntan oil generously. Christopher was already at the water's edge. She put the beach bag on the sand, spread her towel beside it, and walked down to where he stood with his ankles in the water. He cast the rod and then worked it into the sand.

"The water feels pretty good, maybe a little cool," he said. "Come on, I'll race you to the sandbar." He plunged in with swift, sure strokes, and she jumped in right behind him. They swam hard for a few minutes. Christopher reached the sandbar first. He stopped and waited for her to catch up.

He held his arms out to her and when she was close, he pulled her the rest of the way to him and kissed her hard. She kissed him back and the passionate spark in them leaped to flame again. He reached for the straps of her bathing suit, kissing her hungrily while he removed her bathing suit. She clung to him while the waves rocked them to and fro and their desire for each other was once again sated.

Afterward she looked around for her bathing suit and discovered it floating several feet away. "Christopher, you lost my bathing suit! You'll have to get it. I can't come out of the water without it."

He swam after it and brought it to her, holding it just out of arm's reach. "You don't have to worry. There's no one within miles of this beach. You can sunbathe without it if you want to. You certainly have the body for it."

"You, sir, are quite depraved. I may seem to you as if I have lost all sense of decorum, and I may even feel slightly that way myself, but I don't think I'll be parading around outside in the altogether, whether there's anyone to see or not."

"You're not outside. You're in the water." He laughed.

She grinned at him wickedly and added, "Of course, you'll have to help me get back into this suit you so obligingly helped me out of. I hope you don't mind." He did as she asked, getting distracted more than once as he tried to steady her in the jostling waves while she put the bathing suit back on and adjusted the straps.

They swam back to the shore. He pulled her from the surf, and they stumbled to their towels. She lay down on her back on the warm sand and waited for the sun to warm her. He lay face down beside her, his forehead resting on his arms.

They lay quietly, eyes closed, relaxed. After a while, she turned her head to look at him. She thought he had fallen asleep, but he seemed to sense her watching him and turned on his side to face her, propping his head on one arm.

"Maggs, I know I promised not to pressure you about a decision this weekend, and I intend to keep my word. But I do think we need to talk about what's happening between us and what we want to happen next. I'm deeply in love with you. You know it and I know it. If there was ever any doubt about it, there isn't now. I want to know if we have a chance. Can you at least give me an idea of what you're thinking? I promise I won't bring it up again until you're ready. Whenever that happens to be."

She turned on her side to face him. Their bodies were very close. She placed her hand on the side of his face and reached over to kiss him. His hopeful expression triggered something long forgotten. How long had it had been since what she had to say affected anyone more than superficially?

"Christopher," she said, tentatively, "I believe I'm in love with you too. I believe I could spend the rest of my life happily in your arms, in Maine or at Myrtlewood or in a tropical rain forest. But there is much more than my own happiness at stake here, you have to understand, and I can only tell you that I'm considering every aspect of this unexpected turn of events. You've renewed my spirit and brought me great joy. But this happiness can only be mine at such a high cost to others. It would be unbearably hard to hurt those I care so deeply about. My children would be disappointed and bewildered beyond explanation. My friends would be shocked. My entire life as I know it would cease to exist.

"And then there's Stephen. Our marriage hasn't been what it should be for a long time. I realize that in a much more objective way than I ever would have if I had never left Mobile. But he has been good to me in all the important ways, and despite whatever oversight of my emotional needs there may have been, he doesn't deserve my departure from his life without even a chance to bridge the distance that separates us now. We had a wonderful life in the beginning, and I loved him completely for many years. Part of me always will. I don't know if I can just walk away without giving him a chance."

She lay back, closing her eyes and turning her face up to the sun. She continued, "But I don't know if I can walk away from you, either. I want you. I want to stay with you, but I don't know if I have it in me to hurt my family this deeply. It seems too cruel to think about. So you see, I don't have any answer to give you, except that I'm trying desperately to unravel all these tangled feelings. All I can tell you right now is that I don't feel any more certain about going back than I do about staying.

"Can you accept my indecision for right now and give me some time to work this out? If I don't decide on my own, I might blame you or Stephen if it turns out that I can't live with my choice. What I decide can't be influenced by either of you. Do you understand?"

He leaned down and kissed her lightly.

"Of course, Maggs. I wouldn't have it any other way. It just seems as if my very life is at stake. I never expected to need someone else to make my life complete, especially at this stage of my life, and I guess I'm trying to force the situation. I do understand your need to be sure. If you choose me, it has to be because you know it's right for you. That's essential to any chance we might have. I'll wait as long as it takes you to be sure. I'm sorry I added to the pressure you're under. And I promise you this: the next time we discuss this, you'll bring it up. Is that fair enough?"

She reached up and pulled him down to her, her mouth eager for the kisses that could make her forget this was all such a dreadful muddle. She got the desired response, and then, in one swift action, pushed him from her, jumped up and ran toward the water and plunged into the waves. She looked back and laughed at his astonished expression when he realized what she had done.

She swam rapidly toward the sandbar, with Christopher overtaking her easily and swimming in long, powerful strokes alongside her, their bodies gliding through the crystalline water, their problems temporarily neutralized.

She turned onto her back, still swimming with smooth, even strokes, watching his powerful body beside her. This deserted beach, the sparkling clear water, the sun overhead to witness our pleasure, and this wonderful man who loves me just as I am are surely my consolation for the agony of the choice I'll soon have to make, she thought. If this is all I'm to have, I'll make the most of it while I have the chance.

Because in spite of what she had said, and in spite of what she wanted, she realized at this moment, somewhere deep inside, that she probably couldn't knowingly cause the kind of pain a decision to stay with Christopher would mean for those she loved. Stephen would be the only winner in this unexpected turn of events, and he would never even know she had faced such a terrible choice—or what it had cost her.

She understood with sudden clarity that she was in love with Christopher Allendale and that he was offering her a fascinating world she could explore as a cherished partner and equal. She understood that she wanted not just Christopher, but that rare state of preeminence in someone's life. But she also understood, sadly, that she had probably already made her choice, and that it would certainly cost her all that. She was filled with despair that she was like Aunt Eleanor—too afraid to choose her happiness at someone else's expense. She could only hope that, unlike Aunt Eleanor, she wouldn't always regret it.

She would have to deal with her heartache and Christopher's pain eventually. But for now, they had this glorious weekend—the only time they would ever have. She would do her best to make it memorable for them both—something she could savor on long winter evenings in years to come if memories were all she had.

She reached the sandbar and felt the firm sand underneath her feet. She stood waist-deep in the gentle swell of the ocean, the water streaming from her shoulders, and held out her arms to Christopher. Their kisses were salty and sweet and their passion slow and tender, almost poignant.

It was a long time before they swam back to shore and went inside. The phone was ringing when they came in the door.

Chapter 14

Christopher crossed the room to the telephone in long strides. Something stirred in the pit of Maggs's stomach as he turned to her.

"It's for you. It's Molly."

He handed her the receiver and went into the bedroom.

"Hello, Molly," she said. "How are things at Myrtlewood?"

"Fine here, Ms. Maggs," Molly said. "I just thought you would want to know that Mr. Stephen called yesterday afternoon and again this morning. I told him you had gone to the coast with friends for the weekend and that I was sure you'd be calling soon. He asked me to have you call when I heard from you. Says it's nothing urgent, just something you need to discuss. I told him you had tried to contact him before you left and couldn't reach him at work or at home. He said he'll be at home all day." She paused. "Are you having a good time, dear?"

"It's wonderful here, Molly. I can't begin to describe how relaxing it is. I'm not sure I want to come back at all. But I guess it's true that all good things must come to an end. I'll be home tomorrow night, but it may be late. Don't worry about dinner and tell Tom he needn't wait up for me. He needs his rest. I'll see you Tuesday morning."

"Fine, dear. And Ms. Maggs?"

"Yes, Molly?"

"I'm sure there's nothing to worry about. Enjoy the rest of your weekend."

Maggs hung up the receiver thoughtfully, wondering what Stephen wanted and what Molly was thinking—and recognized the sick feeling in her stomach as guilt. The reality of the outside world had intruded upon this brief, happy interlude as if to remind her of what awaited her.

She considered whether to call now or wait. She decided to wait. She went to the refrigerator and poured herself a glass of wine. She could hear the shower running and decided to surprise Christopher by joining him. She poured a second glass of wine and started for the bedroom.

She was halfway there when she realized it wouldn't work. She couldn't be spontaneous knowing Stephen was waiting for her call and not knowing what he wanted. She sat the glasses down and took the telephone out to the porch.

Stephen answered on the first ring.

"Hello, Stephen. Molly said you wanted me to call. Is anything wrong?" She heard the anxiety in her voice even as she said the words and chided herself for reacting so predictably.

"No, everything is fine. I just wanted to talk to you, and we don't seem to connect very often lately. How are you doing?"

"I'm fine. Very busy with my novel. And I've been entertained a lot—I had forgotten how social this little community is. The neighbors have been wonderful, and I've been showered with invitations. They all ask about you and send their regards. How about you? Are you doing okay?"

He replied, peevishly she thought, "Yes. I'm busy too, though not nearly as entertained as you seem to be. Mostly business here. I'm dealing with lawyers and architects and contractors in an attempt to get construction under way. Sometimes the meetings go into the night. And the next day, we start all over again. I hope it won't be too long before we can break ground, but right now I'm swamped with decisions and complications."

She heard him take a deep breath before he said, "Maggs, this is not a good time for you to be gone. I miss you, and I need you to be here for me. I don't suppose you'd consider coming home early, would you?"

The tone of his voice was one he employed to charm her into doing something against her wishes. She recognized it immediately. And resented highly the pleading, little-boy-lost tactic which had been so grossly overused. Her anger fired so quickly that she realized it still sizzled barely below the surface.

"Actually, Stephen, your supposition is correct. You know this is a commitment I feel I have to honor. And, as usual, you're not thinking of me at all. It happens that I'm making a great deal of progress with my novel. I think it's quite good. I've discovered that I have some talent, and I'm enjoying the work enormously. I want to finish what I've started.

"I don't quite understand why you want me to come back anyway. You're never home, so what's the point? Do you want to know what I think? I think you just want things the way they've always been—arranged for your convenience. Well, I'm sorry, but I'm not going to come home any earlier than I had planned. In fact, I may even stay a little longer."

Realizing she was on the verge of shouting, she took a deep breath and said, "I'm sorry. I didn't mean to go off on a tangent. I seem to have a lot of unresolved anger, and I didn't mean to let it get out of control. Let's just leave it that I plan to stay at Myrtlewood for the time being, and we'll talk about it later."

Stephen said, "I don't seem to be able to communicate with you any longer, Maggs. I don't know what's happened to you. You're not the same person you used to be. I'm sorry if our family is no longer a priority with you, but I think it's your problem and not ours. You'll come to your senses in time, I hope.

"In the meantime, the reason for the call is Mike. Graduation has been set for June 17. There is a reception for the graduates and their parents the afternoon before. The invitation requires a response. I assume you'll want to go? If so, we'll have to make reservations right away. Meredith's parents have already made theirs. Shall I make arrangements for us, or do you have other plans for that time too?"

She decided to ignore the sarcasm and said, instead, "Yes, I think you should. You should also check with Leah and Sassie and find out what their plans are."

Stephen said, "I've already talked to them. Leah and Matt will drive up. Sassie is still in New York with her friends, but she'll be home next week. She plans to ride with Leah and Matt. That just leaves us. Shall I reserve separate rooms or will one suffice?"

"Don't be ridiculous, Stephen. Make the reservations for Friday and Saturday nights. I'll let you know when I'll be back as soon as I've decided. At any rate, I'll be back by the sixteenth. Now I really have to go—this is not exactly the best time to be having this discussion. I'll call you when I get back to Myrtlewood."

"Would it be out of line to ask just who the friends are with whom you're spending the weekend? Or would I be better off not knowing?"

The sarcasm was overt now, and she responded before she could stop herself. "You don't know them, Stephen, so their names wouldn't mean anything if I told you. Leading questions often provoke leading questions in response, Stephen, and you haven't been exactly easy to locate yourself. Shouldn't we perhaps just leave it at that for the time being?"

"You're right, of course," he answered coldly. "We don't seem to have much to talk about lately, do we? I'll make the reservations as you suggest, and we'll talk later."

The line went dead in her hand, and as she hung up the receiver, something inside her seemed suddenly disconnected too. She sat watching the repetitive wash of the waves and thought about all the things that had led to this state of affairs. Her anger at Stephen over the deterioration of their life filtered into anxiety about how to resolve the situation. Or whether to even try. Everything seemed to be breaking apart, and it saddened her. At the same time, it didn't prevent her feeling a guilty happiness when she thought of Christopher.

The telephone conversation had certainly not encouraged her intention to try to work things out with Stephen. It had only made the choice more questionable, and she was furious with him for making it harder.

As she sat staring at the horizon, Christopher came out to the porch, a towel wrapped around his waist, drying his hair with another. The faint tinge on his shoulders left by the morning's exposure to the sun was already darkening into a deeper brown. He walked over and kissed the top of her head.

"Anything wrong, darling?" he asked, sitting down beside her.

She started to dismiss it but thought better and decided to tell him what happened. He watched her thoughtfully as she explained. He remained silent for a few moments when she had finished.

"Maggs, I'm sorry to be the cause of your pain. Because I am obviously responsible—not Stephen. If you hadn't been here with me, you would have felt much differently about what he said.

"But I'm not sorry you're here, and I'm damned if I'll say I am. I don't think you are either, really. I think it's just your strong sense of fair play working on you. The situation is no better or no worse now than before you talked to him. The choice is the same, and you're still free to make it without pressure from me. If your decision is what I hope it will be, I'll go to Stephen and explain everything, taking full responsibility for what has happened between us."

The compassion and understanding in his eyes almost pacified her nagging doubt. Almost. But she resolved to put it aside and not let this weekend that had begun so magically be ruined. She had chosen to take advantage of this chance to be with Christopher, and she wouldn't let one untimely telephone call spoil it.

She put her arms around Christopher, and he pulled her into his lap. "I know what you need," he said. "Let's go around to the other side of the island and rent a sailboat. I'm a fair hand with a canvas sail, if I do say so myself. We can get a picnic supper. We'll find a little island to eat on and then sail home in the moonlight. How about it?"

She murmured against his chest, "I'm sorry for putting a cloud on our horizon, Christopher, but it's gone now, and I think a sail is a marvelous idea." She got up to go inside.

"I'll call the marina and arrange for a boat while you're showering, and we'll leave when you're ready," he said, following her inside."

They took their time getting dressed and then drove to the marina on the narrow ribbon of asphalt that was the only road on the island. Sea oats rippled in the breeze, softening the effect of the scrub vegetation that threatened to reclaim any cleared areas, and the glittering, swelling ocean was never out of sight.

The marina and the small shops that surrounded it were the only businesses on Tarpon Island. No resorts or condominiums or spas here. There was a fair golf course and several adequate tennis courts. Two or three good restaurants, all locally owned, offered excellent seafood. Nothing was fancy. The facilities here existed for the convenience of the locals, mainland owners and the few renters who knew about the island only by word of mouth.

The islanders had consistently ignored the big money offered by developers who turned barrier islands like this into gaudy tourist traps. Most of the houses on the island were privately owned and had been in the same families since they were built, scattered far apart, weathered and independent, like the handful of year-round inhabitants who were determined to keep their island the way it had always been.

Maggs had been enchanted with the snug little harbor when they arrived on the island. Glad for a chance to explore the shops, she exclaimed her approval enthusiastically. They browsed in the delicatessen for picnic fixings. Christopher bought everything she pointed to, paid the bill, and they made their way to the slip where the rented sailboat was moored. It was white with freshly painted red trim, and the name Mon Coeur was lettered across its stern.

Maggs knew nothing about sailboats, with the exception of the small Hobie Cat she and Stephen had always kept at the beach house in Heron Bay for the children. This sailboat was much larger, but Christopher assured her it wasn't too much for them to handle. He was an experienced sailor, he promised, and she had no reason to worry. Not totally convinced, but willing to try, Maggs helped load their provisions.

She watched his sure handling of the sails and the wheel as they left the marina and was immediately reassured that Christopher knew what he was doing. He gave explicit instructions, and in short order they were working effectively as a team. As the wind blew her hair and the trim little craft skimmed smartly across the water, Maggs was totally exhilarated.

They sailed for a while and then scouted the numerous small islands for a picnic site. They selected one where they could anchor the sailboat close to shore and waded ashore in their bathing suits. When they found a suitable spot and were satisfied that there were no undesirable inhabitants, human or otherwise, they went back to the boat and Maggs handed the bags over the side to Christopher and then followed him back to shore.

They spread the blanket under a cluster of palm trees that provided shade from the late afternoon sun and unpacked their provisions. After they finished eating, they lay back on the blanket and interspersed sips of wine with soft kisses while they watched the enormous red sun slowly sink into the glassy blue bowl of the sea. It appeared so close that Maggs almost caught herself straining to hear the sizzle when it touched the water.

When the last lingering ray had followed the sun into the sea, they swam in the shallow water, finished the wine, and ate the last bite of pastry, before packing up all evidence of human trespassers, leaving the tiny island deserted and pristine once more. When everything was back in the boat, Christopher sailed them home as the moon began its lethargic journey across a midnight sky. They sailed close in front of their house and then sailed more slowly on to the marina, delaying their return as long as possible.

Most of the boats in the slips were dark, the occupants either gone ashore or turned in for the night. Christopher and Maggs furled the sails and secured the boat, removed their belongings, and climbed onto the dock. They logged out with the sleepy night clerk in the marina office.

The drive home in the moonlight was slow and romantic, with Christopher slowing the car often to kiss her drowsy face. When they arrived home they left everything in the car, too tired to bother unloading. They undressed mechanically, leaving their clothes where they dropped, and fell into bed.

Chapter 15

When Maggs awoke with Christopher's arms around her, it was midday, and her first thought was that this the last day of their weekend. Her second thought was how perfectly she fit into the shape of Christopher's body. She withdrew slightly from his embrace without disturbing him and lay quietly watching his sleeping face, a lump in her throat. He had endured a lot of pain in his life, but it hadn't kept him from being the most gentle, caring person she'd ever known, and the thought of hurting him was unbearable.

As her dismay registered in her eyes, he seemed to sense her absence from his arms, opened his eyes and smiled sleepily.

"Hello, gorgeous. How can you look so beautiful before you even touch the floor? And why are you so far away?"

She smiled indulgently and said, "You're not too bad yourself. As to why I'm so far away, I honestly don't know." She snuggled back into his embrace and as his arms tightened to enfold her, she knew she would probably never feel this cherished again.

Impulsively she murmured, "Oh, Christopher, I don't want to go home today. I don't want to ever go home. Why can't we just run away and keep going, and not have to make choices and decisions that affect everyone but us?"

"We can—if we're brave enough, Maggs," he said softly. "All it takes is the right choice."

She shook her head emphatically against his chest. "I don't want to talk about it. I'm sorry I brought it up. I was just thinking out loud. Surely we can find something better to fill this last glorious morning with?"

His response was immediate, and her passion matched his though hers was tempered by a sweet melancholy that this was probably the last time she would be this much a part of him.

When she was next aware of time, the sun was blazing white-hot outside the windows. She gathered her things for the shower while Christopher lay quietly in bed and watched her. There was a look of vulnerability about him that caused her heart to contract painfully. It was almost as if he, too, now realized that it was over and was trying to memorize her somehow.

When she finished her bath, she could smell bacon frying, and she went into the kitchen to help. He grinned at her, his somber feelings evidently replaced by a resolve to keep everything light, for today at least.

"Want me to finish up while you get your bath?" she asked as she put her arms around his waist. "I know you probably don't believe it from what you've seen this weekend, but I really am a very good cook."

"That wouldn't be your greatest attraction, my love, but I'll take you up on your offer." He handed her the spatula. "After breakfast we'll decide how to spend the rest of the day. I thought we'd make the most of it." He turned back to face her. "Unless you need to get back early?"

"No, not at all. I told Molly I'd be late getting in. We'll have the rest of the day and the evening."

She drained the bacon and fried his eggs the way he liked them, buttered the toast and found some jam. She took the coffee to the porch, poured herself a cup, and sat down to wait for him. He joined her, dressed in white shorts and a white knit shirt that emphasized his dark good looks. He was barefoot, and his hair curled damply; and as he poured himself a cup of coffee and refilled hers, she felt a stab of impending loss so sharp that the pain seemed physical.

She got up quickly and said, "The plates are warming in the oven. I'll just get them. Will you pour the juice?"

Her voice betrayed her distress, and as she passed him, he caught her hand and pulled her to him. He held her tightly, wordlessly, for just a moment. She understood that he knew what she was thinking and was trying to lessen her pain. She was reminded again of how he always seemed to know the right thing to do for her.

When she returned with the tray, they ate their breakfast in a mood of forced joviality. Christopher put his napkin down and said, "Okay, Lady. You've convinced me of your culinary skill. I'm of the opinion that you'd be worth keeping around just for that. To discover that you're multi-talented is almost too much."

She couldn't hide the pain his words caused quickly enough, and he saw her reaction in her expression. He hastened to apologize. "I'm sorry, Maggs. That was terribly insensitive of me."

He pushed his chair back and came around to her. He took her hand and said, "Let's leave this for now. I think we need to take a walk and clear the air. We seem to be on a course to self-destruct at the last minute, and I don't like it. We've been too comfortable with each other to let our last day be awkward."

His expression was grim as he led her down the steps, and his determined pace was too quick for her to keep up with easily. They walked in silence—Maggs struggling to keep up with him.

Finally he slowed his pace and said, "Maggs, I know what you're doing. You're projecting the possibility that this will be the last time we're together and it's making you unhappy. I told you I wouldn't bring the subject up again, and I won't. If you have some idea of where we go from here, or more to the point, where we don't go, and don't want to share it with me yet, so be it.

"I can handle your decision, whatever it is. What I can't handle is the idea that we've had such a wonderful time together and might let the remaining time we have turn into something quite different. We have the rest of this day and as much of the night as it takes us to get home. I want to spend every minute of it doing something that makes us happy and ends this weekend as memorably as it began.

"This doesn't have to be an ending at all unless you decide to make it one. That's your decision. But if that's what you've decided and it's making you this unhappy, you might want to reconsider."

He stopped and faced her, his face so close to hers that she could feel his quickened breath.

"All I want, for your sake as well as mine, is that you don't let it make us uncomfortable and tense with each other for whatever time we have left. Can you do that? For us both? Can we go back to where we were when we woke up this morning in each other's arms and end our trip the same way? Then we'll face whatever comes next as best we can."

His expression was so troubled, his pain so evident, that she put her arms around him and held on to him fiercely, as if she could prevent some unseen entity from tearing him from her embrace.

"Of course, my darling. Of course we can. You're exactly right. I know I'm letting my fear of what's ahead spoil what we have right now. I just don't seem able to stop. Please forgive me. Let's do just as you say. We'll spend the rest of the day doing something wonderful."

He looked into her eyes and saw her brave attempt to smile. He kissed her lightly, took her hand again, and they walked back to the house leisurely, stopping to pick up a seashell or look for dolphins playing beyond the sandbar.

"Would you like to go for a swim? Or maybe play a set of tennis? We're not far from Hilton Head. I have friends there who would love to give us a drink. What would make you happy today, Maggs?"

She considered his question while they walked, and finally said, "I think I had enough sun yesterday and I'm not in the mood for tennis, either. I just want to spend the day with you. I want to feel your arms around me and see your face smiling at me. What if we buy some lobsters for dinner and spend the afternoon here? Afterward, we could go for a walk on the beach and drive back to Myrtlewood late tonight."

"Sounds great to me. Let's go get the lobsters."

They crossed the warm sand and went back to the house. When they drove into the parking lot at the marina, Maggs could see the "Mon Coeur" dancing brightly in the sunlight. She will certainly be part of *my* heart, she thought. Forever.

Maggs said, "Do you know how to select a good lobster?"

He nodded his head. "I come from the ultimate lobster country, if you remember, and I know pretty much everything there is to know about them—how to catch 'em, cook 'em, serve 'em, and eat 'em. Trust me, I'll soon present you with the two best lobsters to be had in these parts."

She smiled at him as they went into the fish market, where after careful deliberation, he finally made his choice. They bought the remaining items on their list, and by the time they had everything they needed, Maggs was almost happy again.

Back at the house, they put the groceries away and went out to the porch. The sun was already starting to descend, and the porch was shaded and cool. A brisk breeze blew and sunbeams danced erratically on the incandescent water. When they set about positioning themselves in the hammock to read, it began to swing out of control again, but with some effort, they managed to arrange themselves side by side. They read until the sun was much lower in the sky and the tide was going out.

Maggs stretched and said, "I don't know about you, but I'm about to fall asleep, and we have dinner to prepare. What about a quick swim before dinner?"

"I'm right behind you, my love," said Christopher.

They changed into their swimsuits and swam to the sandbar with long, even strokes. They stood with their arms around each other for a long time watching the horizon and then swam slowly back to shore, the exercise erasing the last vestige of tension.

When they had dried off, they went inside and Christopher made a pitcher of something tropical while Maggs handed him the ingredients and sampled the drinks until they were just right. They pulled their chairs up to the porch railing and sat, shoulders touching, not talking, as the setting sun spilled an orange glare across the water.

When the last glimmer faded and the evening breeze was picking up, Maggs reluctantly rose from her chair, refilled their glasses from what remained in the blender and said, "I'm going in to change. We should start dinner soon."

Christopher's gaze was fixed on the horizon and he seemed unaware of her presence. She wondered what he was thinking. She ran her fingers through his soft curls and turned to go inside. He nodded absentmindedly when she handed him his drink. In the bedroom, she leaned over to turn on the shower when she heard him behind her, and turned to see an almost strangled expression on his face. He pulled her to him, kissing her roughly. He picked her up and carried her to the bed. She was frightened by the intensity of his expression and the ferocity of his behavior until she realized he was overcome with emotion. Trapped somewhere between anger and pain, his lovemaking was alternately fierce and tender, as if he wasn't sure whether he wanted to take something from her or wanted to give her something of himself.

His desperation touched an answering chord in her, and their coming together was a whirl of mumbled endearments and impassioned pleas, an outburst of energy both would have thought beyond their capability, and an uncontrolled expression of raw emotion which held nothing in reserve. When emotion could no longer sustain them and they found the release possible only in surrender to the need that drove them, they lay side by side, still, silent. Wanting neither to speak nor move, Maggs felt locked in time, joined to him for infinity, fearful that any sound or motion might sever the tenuous connection forever.

Lying beside him, listening to the throb of his heartbeat as it gradually returned to normal, Maggs wondered, not for the first time or for the last, how she was going to accept that they were sharing this kind of closeness for what was probably the last time. There was, of course, no answer.

When the slow whirling of the fan blades eventually began to chill them, they went into the bathroom and showered together. Words were superfluous. Something angry within each of them had been dispelled; tenderness and solicitude were left in its wake.

When they were dressed, they sat on the side of the bed. Christopher said, "Maggs, I hope I didn't frighten you. I don't know what came over me. I felt as though I'd already lost you and I think this was one last, all-out attempt to hold on. I hope you know this isn't typical behavior for me. Believe me, it was much more significant than that."

She could see the concern in his eyes. "Oh, god, Christopher. Don't you know I feel the same way? Except I happen to be the one responsible for the pain we're feeling. But it's for you that I regret it most. I probably deserve what I'll suffer, but you don't, my darling, and I must hurt you regardless. I hadn't intended to tell you until we got home and we had these memories safe, to keep forever. But I can't be less than honest with you after what we just shared.

"When you take me home tonight, I don't want to see you again. I'll use the time before I go back to Mobile to consider everything we've meant to each other. I'll try every way I know to justify staying with you. But I have to tell you that I feel compelled to at least try to salvage what's left of my marriage and keep my family together. I don't want to leave you with any false hopes.

"I'll give you my decision before I leave, I promise. I won't go without seeing you. That you will allow me the time and the distance to make the most important choice of my life is something I don't doubt.

"If I go back to Stephen, I have to do it with a full commitment to making my marriage work. I don't know how I'll do that, loving you the way I do. But I'll have to try. I don't know how I'll be able to live without the love you offer. I know that love would always be there. And I have such a need for it. I honestly don't know which is worse: finding a love such as ours and losing it—or never having known it at all."

She bent her head as tears began to trickle slowly down her cheek. Christopher lifted her face gently and wiped her tears away. She looked at him helplessly and saw that he had tears on his face too.

"Maggs, I never expected to love like this. But I do love you, more than I can tell you, and it sounds like I'll have to learn to live without you. But I'll never stop loving you. It will be harder to give you up knowing you love me too and knowing you're making a mistake. But I'll pray for your happiness. You know I wish only the best for you."

He was silent for a minute, as if trying to assimilate what had happened. Eventually he smiled at her and said, "Come on, let's see about getting these lobsters steamed. It's getting late."

"Christopher, I really don't think I can eat anything. Would you mind terribly if we just packed and started for home? I don't think I can bear to stretch this out through dinner."

He smiled crookedly and said, "Of course not, darling. I seem to have lost my appetite too. We'll give the lobsters to the night clerk at the marina when we leave the island. We can go as soon as we're packed."

Unable to bear the pain in his eyes, she turned away and began to remove her clothes from the dresser. When they were packed, Christopher made them a drink and they walked out onto the porch. Under a starless evening sky, the sea appeared dark and brooding. The breeze had stiffened, creating whitecaps on the choppy waves out beyond where the tide was holding. The moon was hidden by clouds.

Maggs turned to Christopher. "I'll never be as happy again as I have been here with you. I know I won't, and I'll never forget this time as long as I live. I love you, Christopher, with all my heart."

She lifted the glass to her lips and finished the drink in one long swallow. Christopher did the same and then abruptly turned and went inside without speaking. He loaded their luggage into the car. They checked the house, rinsed the glasses and left them side by side in the drain; and without further conversation, turned out the lights and locked the door behind them.

The drive home was silent and strained, and when the car pulled up in front of Myrtlewood, Maggs's resolve was weakening. Quickly, before he could open his door, she said, "Don't come to the door, darling. Let's make this as painless as possible. I'll call you as soon as I've made a decision."

He didn't protest. She leaned over and kissed him hard, opened her door, and ran into the house without looking back. As she ran upstairs, blinded by the tears in her eyes, she heard Christopher open the front door and put her luggage in the foyer, but she didn't look back. From her bedroom, she heard his car leaving and felt every bit of the desolation she had seen in his eyes with her last glimpse of his ravaged face.

She lay face down on her bed and sobbed. "Oh, Aunt Eleanor," she said out loud, "how did you ever manage to send him away?"

She heard Molly's knock on her door some time later but didn't respond. She cried long into the night. When she finally slept from sheer exhaustion, her dreams were troubled by confused images of Stephen and Christopher and Aunt Eleanor and her tiny grandmother; and none of it made any sense. She awoke, drenched in perspiration, and crept silently through the open French doors out onto the cool balcony.

She sat on the chaise, her feet drawn up under her, huddled under the afghan, cold from the night air on her damp skin. She was visited by her demons, one by one. Remorse, guilt, anger, disappointment and fear paid their relentless calls. She confronted each in turn; and as the sun forecast its imminence with a faint lightening in the east, she had acknowledged her shortcomings, determined the cost, and formulated a plan for restitution.

She was left with only heartsickness. She wasn't afraid of any consequence that might befall her as a result of her actions. She would do what was required and accept whatever came her way because of it. She was strong enough for that.

She wasn't afraid that Stephen would leave her. Punish her—probably. Never let her forget—almost certainly. But leave her—she didn't think so. And if he did, she could bear that too. She could certainly understand it.

She fervently hoped that the aftermath of clearing the air with Stephen wouldn't include her children's learning of her lapse from all she believed in and had tried to teach them to believe in. But it wasn't necessary that they understand *or* forgive, either. She could handle their disapproval or even their rejection, if that was also to be part of the cost.

Her complete and utter desolation originated from surrendering to a life that would leave her devoid of joy and spontaneity. Freedom to be herself and be totally accepted would not be possible without Christopher. She was shattered by the knowledge, but concluded that the enormity of her guilt more than justified the enormity of her atonement.

Something inside stirred faintly at her rigid determination to sacrifice herself so completely, but she acknowledged it only momentarily before rejecting it and confirming her commitment to pay for her sins.

"What sins?" said a still, small voice, but she wasn't listening.

She cried for Christopher, her dear and true love, and the life she might have shared with him. She cried because of the pain she knew he would experience once he accepted her decision. She cried because of the pain Stephen would experience when he understood what she had done. She cried because her heart nearly burst inside her with her own unrelenting pain.

But with the gradual brightening of the new day, she had made her decision and she knew she wouldn't look back. She would cry no more futile tears. She would return and make the best possible life she could for Stephen and her children, and maybe in time, the leaden feeling inside her would diminish and finally disappear altogether.

The still, small voice said, "Want to bet?"

Chapter 16

*H*er solitary debate was interrupted by Molly's insistent and determined knock on her bedroom door. Knowing Molly would have to be faced sooner or later, she wrapped the afghan around her more closely and called out, "Come in, Molly."

Molly brought the coffee tray out to the balcony. In the early light, she took one look at Maggs's face and the dark circles under her eyes, and her own broad Irish countenance instantly reflected the misery she saw.

"Whatever has happened, darlin'? Has Mr. Chris upset you? Oh, I'm sure it was unintentional, whatever he did. He thinks the world of you, unlike some as I could name." She put her arms around Maggs. "Never you mind, dear, I'm sure you'll feel better after you've had a bit of coffee."

She set the tray down and poured Maggs a cup of coffee. Ignoring the intractable expression on Maggs's face when she handed her the steaming coffee, Molly went on, "I don't mean to pry, dear. You don't have to tell me what's troubling you, if you don't want to. You've ever been one to keep it all inside. Much like your Aunt Eleanor, come to think of it. But it's no good bearing it all alone."

Maggs sipped the strong coffee. It burned her raw throat as it went down. She made no response to Molly's comment, staring down into the cup as if there were some answer to be found in its depths.

Molly waited patiently a few minutes and when it was obvious Maggs wasn't talking, she finally said, "I'll just be in the kitchen, if you want me. I'll prepare your breakfast when you decide what you'd like."

When Molly opened the bedroom door to leave, Maggs cried out, "Oh, Molly, please don't go. I don't think I can bear this. I don't think I've ever been so torn in all my life. Please, may I talk to you?"

Molly closed the door and was at her side in an instant. "Of course you can, darlin'. What's troubling my little love? You know you can tell me anything—and you know it will never leave this room."

Maggs struggled to regain her composure. She didn't want to talk, but she felt she would explode if she didn't talk to someone. She didn't need advice or absolution from Molly. She had already made her choice. She just needed to share her heartache with someone who would understand, and the only other person who would was no longer available to her, by her own stipulation.

Slowly, painfully, she confided the whole story to Molly. She told her not only the facts, but she shared all the feelings that had led her to fall in love with Christopher. She shared the futility she had felt for so long, and the joy and enthusiasm that returned to her life when she discovered her love for Christopher.

She didn't portray Stephen as the villain; rather she went out of her way to make him the injured party in the whole sad business. She told Molly what she had decided to do and what it was costing her to go through with it. She didn't cry again. Molly kept silent while Maggs talked, holding her comfortingly in her arms, occasionally brushing the hair back from her face.

When at length Maggs was quiet, Molly held her at arm's length, looked directly into her swollen face and said, "Ms. Maggs, I'm going to overstep my bounds here and say something to you I should have said to your Aunt Eleanor many years ago. I held my peace then, and I've regretted it ever since. More than I can tell you.

"You know there was a time in Ms. Eleanor's life when she faced just such a moral dilemma as you are now facing. I watched her struggle with the choice she had to make and I watched her suffer once she had made it. I'll never know if I could have made a difference if I had spoken my mind to her then, but I'll not make the mistake again of holding my tongue while someone I love goes blindly head-on down the wrong path.

"I've observed you for many years now with your Stephen. I know that he must be a fine man and that he's provided you a stable, comfortable life. I know he's the father of four wonderful children who have made up for any other lack you might have felt in your life. But I've watched you together, and I've never seen anything close to what I see in Mr. Chris's eyes every time he looks at you."

As Maggs began to protest, Molly continued emphatically, "I'm not blind, you know, darlin', and I wasn't born yesterday, neither. I have known for quite a time now that things were developing between you and Mr. Chris. I could see you were troubled when you first arrived here, and I could see some joy return to your eyes as time went on. I was happy to see you happy, and I've always been partial to Mr. Chris, as you well know. I didn't expect it to become this serious, but maybe it was inevitable. Who's to say?

"It occurs to me that the circumstances that allowed your affections to be engaged by someone else are the real issue here. Same as with Ms. Eleanor. And I'm afraid that you're going to make the same pointless sacrifice of your happiness that she did. You read her diary. You know it was the sorrow of her life that she hadn't fought for her chance to be happy. She even implied as much to you in the letter she left you."

Maggs's face immediately evidenced her amazement. She started to speak, but was cut off, as Molly continued.

"I know. You had no idea I knew about the letter, but Ms. Eleanor showed it to me when she wrote it. She wanted my opinion as to whether it was too much to ask of you. She asked me to keep it to myself so that if you found yourself unable to oblige her request you would feel no sense of letting anyone down. But I knew her well enough to know there was more messages in that piece of paper than a mere request to spend a month at Myrtlewood.

"I would never have betrayed her confidence if this unfortunate set of circumstances hadn't come about. But having gone this far with it, I'm going to have my say now.

"You are making a most grievous mistake, Ms. Maggs. If you don't take your fate in your own hands and fight for the love you deserve, I'm terribly afraid you will spend many years regretting that you didn't have more courage. I say that fully appreciating the morality of the question you're deciding, dear. Sometimes things happen that aren't just a question of simple morality."

She kissed Maggs lightly on the forehead and stood up to leave. "I know it's a terrible quandary you find yourself in, and I know there's no way out without hurting somebody you care about, but I really and truly believe you must do what's best for you. Ms. Eleanor would give you the same advice if she were still with us, I don't doubt for an instant. Loyalty and devotion are powerful forces—and never to be taken lightly. But love is what keeps us alive. Sure, I'm not talking about our bodies now. I'm talking about our souls. Believe me, there's more than one way to die. I watched it happen to Ms. Eleanor, and I have no desire to see it happen to you. It was a most terrible thing to behold!"

Molly sighed deeply, as if she understood that her words were having little or no impact and accepted her powerlessness.

"I know you will come to your decision in your own way, dear, and that's as it should be. I'll support you, whatever you decide to do. I just thank the Lord for the chance to have my say this time. Now wash your face and come downstairs. You'll feel better after you eat something. You still have lots of time to think about what to do."

Maggs was too tired to argue. She went into her bathroom, took one look at her haggard face in the mirror and her first impulse was to climb back into her deep, warm bed and never come out again. But she washed her face and combed her hair and found something bright to put on, hoping it would make her feel a little better. It didn't, of course, but she went downstairs anyway.

When she finished eating, she went back upstairs. Molly had already straightened her room and unpacked the suitcases Christopher had left in the entrance hall last night. There remained no visible evidence of the weekend.

Except burned into my heart, she thought.

Knowing she had to stop this kind of thinking, she sat down in front of her computer. The blank screen stared at her expectantly, and she realized writing was not going to be an escape this morning. She put everything away, turned off the computer, and went back downstairs.

She looked at the clock; it was still very early, but she decided to go for a walk. She told Molly where she was going and started off disconsolately in the direction of the woods. She walked at a brisk pace for a while, managing to put aside her misery until she approached the sandbar.

Memories came flooding back, and she turned away from the pain they brought and retraced her steps. Back at the edge of the grounds, she glimpsed a canoe on the river and her heart leaped. She looked closer but it was no one she recognized. It wasn't even the right kind of canoe. She didn't know whether she was relieved or disappointed.

She went inside and wandered listlessly through the house. Molly was busy with her household routine. Maggs decided to pass the time with Tom, but she couldn't find him. She went into the library and browsed among the old books for a while. She checked her watch; it wasn't yet noon. She considered driving into town to shop but rejected the idea.

Maybe she could write now. Back upstairs, she managed to put a few thoughts on paper, but when she reread what she had written, she crumpled the pages and threw them in the trash. The hours seemed to creep by as she realized how much of her time had been spent with Christopher. Would there now be nothing to fill the days? She had a sinking suspicion that the nights would be even worse.

She thought of going home right away, but there remained several days of her promised to stay at Myrtlewood, and the commitment was important to her. Painful or not, she would stay and see it through.

She picked at her lunch and then tried to take a nap, but her mind was too jumbled for sleep. She got up and washed her face and went out to the balcony. She sat in the swing and thought about what Molly had said to her this morning, what Aunt Eleanor had said in her letter, what Christopher had said about its being meant for them to be together. She thought about what she wanted to do and what her family would want her to do. It all went round and round in her head until she wanted to scream her frustration into the wind.

Finally, it was time to change for dinner. It was the first evening in many that she had dined alone, and she wasn't looking forward to it. The experience was as grim as she had expected, and as soon as she was done, she went back upstairs.

She took a hot bath, climbed into bed, and turned on the television. It failed to hold her interest; she turned it off and picked up a book. Unable to concentrate, she laid it aside and turned out the lights. She lay in the darkness for hours, thinking. Exhausted by it all, she fell asleep, only to awaken before dawn with still another long day ahead.

This day, however, found her able to concentrate a little better, and she spent the morning at the computer. She was less than satisfied with the results of her effort but thankful that she had accomplished anything at all.

After lunch she thought of calling Stephen, but she didn't want to talk to him yet. She thought of calling Christopher, but she didn't know what to say to him yet, either. She was disappointed that he hadn't called and chided herself for it. She had asked him not to call, and he had agreed not to. She had known he wouldn't break his promise, so why was she disappointed? Another solitary dinner preceded another night of tossing and turning and sitting for hours on the balcony, sleepless and alone, her thoughts as black as the night that surrounded her.

Long, agonizing nights followed by days made up of endless hours to fill set the pattern for the remainder of her stay at Myrtlewood.

She declined all invitations for fear she would run into Christopher, or at the very least be questioned as to his whereabouts. She assumed people were wondering at her sudden withdrawal, but their speculation was preferable to their outright questions. And they *would ask.*

She made some progress with her novel, but it was tedious and uninspired. She was surprised to discover how important it had become to discuss her ideas. Something was missing that had once lent a vitality to her work. The something was Christopher. She knew that he was neither the inspiration nor the motivation for her to keep writing, but his sudden absence created a dull ache within her that left no room for enthusiasm about anything. She prayed that when the pain dissipated, her muse would still be around.

She decided to go through Aunt Eleanor's belongings and box up what she would give away. She hadn't gone into her aunt's bedroom since she returned, and it had to be done. There were some fine pieces of jewelry among Eleanor's collection, including a ring with three large emeralds in a platinum filigree setting that had been promised to Maggs when she was a little girl. Most of the jewelry was far too valuable to keep around the house and should have been in the safe deposit box, but Maggs had simply not had the heart to go through it.

She told Molly to reserve the next day to box up Aunt Eleanor's clothes and go through her belongings. She cataloged the jewelry so that Tom could take it to the bank. At the last minute, she slipped the emerald ring on her finger, hoping it would make her feel closer to Eleanor and maybe in some way give her the strength she needed for what lay ahead. Instead, the stones gleamed in the light and winked at her insistently as if trying to share some elusive secret.

Going though Aunt Eleanor's personal effects had a peculiar effect on Maggs. She finally decided to box up the clothes for charity and leave everything else in the room as it was. Several ball gowns would be prepared for storage along with the historic collection in the attic, and Maggs told Molly to keep any of the clothes she would like to have.

When they finished taping the last box, Maggs picked up Aunt Eleanor's silver and pearl rosary. "I want you to have this, Molly. I know Aunt Eleanor would have wanted it too. No one will value it more than you will."

Molly's eyes brimmed with tears as she took the rosary. "I don't know what to say, Ms. Maggs. I've never known it to be very far from the dear lady herself. But you should surely keep it. It's much too fine to give away."

Molly offered it back, but Maggs closed her fingers over Molly's and pushed it back to her. "Molly, I'll be very happy knowing you have something she treasured so much. Please take it." Molly bowed her head, wiped her eyes, and put the rosary in her apron pocket.

Maggs turned back to the task at hand. She would take the China vanity set and the monogrammed silver brushes and hand mirror back with her. But when she removed them, she couldn't bear the sight of the dressing table without them. She put them back in their place.

When she and Molly had finished and closed the door behind them, Maggs had taken only the Victorian sewing stand which contained Eleanor's silver embroidery scissors, her tiny gold thimble, and some unfinished lace she had been working on at the time of her death. She would keep the sewing stand next to the chaise beside her bedroom window in Mobile, where she often did her own needlework.

She spent the remainder of her time at Myrtlewood in a somber, contemplative mood. She repeatedly challenged her decision to go back. At times she decided to let the chips fall where they may; she and Christopher and their love for each other would be enough even if that love cost her everything and everyone else she cared about. But in the end, she couldn't reconcile the loss of her children with the chance for happiness in a future secured at such a cost, and she returned invariably to her original decision.

The month approached its end. The first of June fell on a Sunday, and after much agonizing, she booked her flight on that day. Once she had done so, she phoned Stephen. She was surprised to find him at home.

"Stephen, I've made arrangements to come home Sunday morning. My flight will arrive at 9:45 a.m. I would appreciate it if you could pick me up. Or arrange for someone else to, if you can't."

His voice was remote and cool as he said, "Of course, no problem."

He offered nothing further. Maggs found his sulky attitude and his expectations of being coaxed into a good humor too trivial to be worth the effort. Without intention, she compared Stephen's habit of getting what he wanted by manipulation and passive aggression to Christopher's straightforward manner of dealing with others. Stephen suffered much by comparison.

Right now, she was just plain exhausted and not at all in a conciliatory mood. She said, curtly, "All right then. I'll see you Sunday." She thought she heard him say "wait, Maggs" as she removed the receiver from her ear, but she wasn't interested in prolonging any further unproductive exchange and returned the receiver to its cradle.

It didn't bode well for her homecoming that it had begun on such an unpromising note, but it couldn't be helped. She had left with Stephen angry, and she was returning with him angry. When he heard all she had to tell him, he would be even more so. It didn't distress her unduly to consider the resulting recrimination she was sure to suffer. By now, she almost welcomed it.

This negative frame of mind resulted from the numbing sense of resignation and capitulation she felt about her unequivocal surrender. She shouldn't go back and attempt to pick up the pieces of her life with these feelings uppermost in her mind, but she didn't know how to neutralize their power.

Now that she had committed herself to returning, she felt only a giant void, a seemingly bottomless despair. A great deal of that despair derived from the necessity to face Christopher and confirm what he must already have concluded. Perhaps when she had completed that onerous task, she would feel a little relief.

She lifted the telephone to make the call and experienced such an acute premonition of all the years ahead without Christopher that she was overcome with despair and literally unable to move. She was shaking all over, drenched in perspiration, and couldn't think. Molly found her thus, replaced the receiver, and led her out to the back porch. She set Maggs down on the glider while she went to get her a brandy.

"Here, darlin', drink this."

Maggs took the glass in stiff hands and raised it to her mouth. Molly wisely didn't question or comfort her; she left the brandy and went back into the house. Maggs sat, dazed and ill, for a long time before she felt in control again. She had finished the brandy and felt its dizzying effect as she stood up. She hadn't eaten all day, she recalled, and the brandy must have gone straight to her head.

She thought she was going to be violently ill and made her way quickly to the downstairs bathroom. She splashed water on her feverish face until the feeling lessened and then dried her face and went into the kitchen in search of something to counter the empty, sick feeling. She had no idea what time it was. She didn't really care.

Molly had set out a cold lunch. She wasn't in sight, so Maggs sat down at the kitchen table and after forcing a few bites down, the trembling subsided and she managed to eat a little more. When she finished, she carried the dishes to the sink and washed them. She was putting them away when Molly returned.

When she put the last plate in the cabinet, she said, "Molly, I'm going upstairs to lie down for a while. Please don't call me unless it's important."

"Very well, dear, I'll see you're not disturbed." Molly put her arm around Maggs's shoulders and walked her to the staircase. She had the look on her face she always did when she had something to say and was doing her best to keep from blurting it out.

Maggs recognized the expression and said, "What is it, Molly? You don't have to hold your tongue with me. We've been through far too much for that."

"Well, it occurs to me that your body is trying to tell you something your mind won't consider, Ms. Maggs. I hope you'll not be holding it against me for saying so, but it may be that you literally can't stomach what you're doing.

"I know you think you're doing the right thing, and I know you'll not likely reconsider, but I'm seeing you suffer over something that's not necessary at all. That's all I wanted to say. Except for one tiny bit of advice, if you'll forgive my presuming to tell you what to do."

Maggs nodded, wishing Molly would just get on with it.

"If you're determined to go through with this, you'll be better served to go ahead and tell Mr. Christopher and make a clean break of it. You'll feel better for it even though you may hurt the most while you're getting it done. That's all I wanted to say. Now go on upstairs with you. I'll call you when dinner is ready." She squared her shoulders as if satisfied that she had done her duty and went back toward the kitchen.

Maggs went slowly up to her room, mulling over Molly's advice as she climbed the stairs with feet that seemed to be weighted with lead. She lay down on her bed and dozed fitfully.

The sun was low in the afternoon sky when she awoke. Her head was pounding insistently but her queasiness appeared to have vanished. She went out to the balcony and sat gazing at the river. She couldn't avoid the memories of the hours she and Christopher had spent in the tiny canoe, drifting idly down the river looking for an inviting place to go ashore. The Ashley was a beautiful river, as he had promised it was, and she would miss its steady flow. It was well suited to the pace of life at Myrtlewood, and she felt a sharp pang of regret as she realized how much she would miss everything about this place. Especially the river.

Thoughts of the river and Christopher inevitably led her back to the dreaded telephone call. There was wisdom in what Molly had said. She wouldn't feel better until she had told Christopher what she intended to do. And there was nothing to be gained by procrastinating.

She picked up the telephone and dialed his number. As it rang on the other end, she discovered she was holding her breath.

At length he answered. He sounded irritated and out of breath. "Hello, Christopher Allendale speaking."

She found herself momentarily at a loss for words. When she found her voice, she said, "Hello, Christopher. It's Maggs. I'd like to talk. Do you have plans for tonight? Could you possibly come over after dinner?"

There was a long pause on the other end of the line. She was beginning to think he would refuse, when at last he said, "Of course, Maggs. Shall I come around eight o'clock?"

"Yes, that will be good. I'll see you then." She hung up the phone, hating how much she would hurt him before this night ended.

Chapter 17

She had Molly serve dinner early and rushed through the meal. While she showered and dressed, she searched for the right words to say to Christopher. She carefully selected what she would wear, choosing a simple moss green silhouette with a copper belt and matching flats. She brushed her hair and let it swing free around her face, unaware of how vulnerable she looked.

She rehearsed what she would say to Christopher. She assumed he knew, but she wanted desperately to soften the effect of her decision, to make him understand it had nothing to do with him. She hoped he would be able to put their time together in perspective and get on with his life, and that he would ultimately be happy again. Her own feelings didn't matter.

When she heard the doorbell, the sick feeling returned to the pit of her stomach. She glanced quickly in the mirror, smoothed her hair nervously, and went downstairs to the library.

He stood in front of the fireplace poking at the fire with one of the fire tools that had been there forever. *He looks so right here*, she thought as her heart gave a lurch, *and oh, how badly I have wanted him here*.

When she entered the room he turned to face her, a spontaneous smile of delight spreading from his sensitive mouth to his beautiful dark blue eyes. A lamp on a table beside the door provided the only light in the room, other than the glow of the fire.

He said only one word: "Darling!"

Every part of her responded to him, and she fought to maintain control. She wanted to run to him and feel his arms around her while he assured her everything would be fine. She wanted to feel his mouth on hers in an embrace so fierce she couldn't breathe. She wanted to stay wrapped up just like that, ignoring everything else.

Instead, she walked across the room to greet him, stiff and aching with longing, holding out both hands to him. "Hello, Christopher. It's good to see you. Thank you for coming on such short notice." She let go of his hands quickly. "Would you like a drink?"

A look of surprise replaced the glad expression he had worn when she entered the room. She knew she sounded stiff and formal and hated it, but it was necessary if she was going to get through this. "Brandy. Please," he said simply.

"That sounds good. I think I'll have one too." She poured the drinks and brought the glasses to the fireplace where he stood motionless, watching her intently. Her heart was jerking hard, and she was sure he knew it.

"Shall we sit down?" She led the way to the old leather sofa. He sat down beside her.

"Christopher, this is the hardest thing I've ever had to do. I don't think it will surprise you that I'm going back to Mobile, but I feel I owe you an explanation. I don't mean explanation, exactly. You know all the reasons why I feel I have no other choice. I just wanted to face you when I told you and to hear whatever you want to say.

"I accept full responsibility for what happened between us. I was frustrated and lonely, and I felt very unappreciated when I came here. I was flattered by your attention and enjoyed your company. I should have never allowed it to go any further than that. I'm not free to have a relationship that goes beyond friendship. You are, but I'm not. I should have stopped it when I realized I was attracted to you, and not having done that, I should certainly have stopped it when I became aware that you felt the same way.

"I can't tell you that I don't love you. I do, honestly and deeply, and for always. You've made me happier than I've been in a long, long time. But it has to be over.

"For the rest of my life, I'll cherish the memories we made. They are all I will have. But I want you to go on with your life. I want you to find someone to share all the wonderful things you can offer a woman. I wish that woman could be me, and I know right now that you do too, but it can't. I want you to find someone who is free to love you.

"I know you're angry with me, and I know you hurt, but I have to ask you for one more thing. Please don't regret what we shared. I ask a lot, I know, but this is very painful for me too, and if I thought you were sorry that we fell in love, I couldn't bear it.

She looked directly at him and said, "I'm going home Sunday, Christopher, and I won't see you again. I hope you'll understand that I made the only choice that will allow me to live with myself. I hope your life will be as wonderful as you deserve, my darling, and that in time you will forgive me.

She lowered her head. Her eyes filled with tears. Some of them escaped down her pale cheeks. As she talked she had watched his expression change from hope to despair and then to resignation. There had been no hint of anger. Now that she was finished, she couldn't bear to see his pain, and she couldn't look at him.

She fought not to break down. She had promised herself she wouldn't put either of them through that. But it was so hard.

He didn't speak. He held the brandy snifter between his hands, not moving. She could hear him breathing. At length he put the glass down and very gently lifted her chin until their eyes met. In his face she saw the one thing that might make this impossible.

He looked at her with eyes totally filled with love. And pain, great pain. But no anger. And yes, she couldn't believe it, but there was also acceptance. His own tears glinted in the firelight, but he was utterly calm.

"My dearest, dearest love," he said softly, "how could you think I wouldn't understand? The qualities that make this decision necessary for you, this choice that hurts me so deeply, are the same qualities that make me love you so completely.

"I love your honesty, your character, your ability to see the heart of a matter. I love your need to be at peace with yourself, to do the right thing. These aren't the only things I love about you, but they are the essence of you. Only someone who is truly good puts the needs of others ahead of his own. I anticipated that you would do that and have come to terms with it. I don't want to accept that our relationship is over, but I can. And I promise you, I will.

"As far as regret is concerned, I can honestly tell you I regret only two things. I think you're making a mistake, Maggs, and I regret that. For both of us. I know I have to let you go, and I won't add to your unhappiness by arguing about it. And I also regret that our time together was so short. I wish there could have been more time for making memories.

"But I could never regret the love we shared, love I had never expected because I didn't know such love existed. I'll cherish the memories as much as you do.

"The other thing I want to say to you is this: If there is to be accountability for anyone's pain or disappointment, I won't have it as being yours. I saw what was happening as clearly as you did. I not only allowed you to fall in love with me, knowing you weren't free, I actually did all I could to make sure you did. The fact that I was already in love with you is no excuse. I don't want you ever to think that what happened is your fault.

"If you can go back to your world and make your peace with it, I can make my peace with the fact that you have to go. I hope it works out. If you change your mind, you know where to find me. Because nothing will change my feelings for you. Maybe time will bring some solace to us both."

He kissed her, picked up his brandy and walked over to stare into the fire. She wiped the tears from her cheeks and joined him. He put his arm around her shoulders and they stood in silence, abjectly gazing into the flames.

"What will you do about the appointment you've been offered?" she asked, at last.

"I don't know yet. I'll have to think about it. I love the South, particularly Charleston, and Riverside will be mine one day, the same way Myrtlewood came to you, though I hope not for a long time. But it'll be hard to stay here without you. I'll just have to see how I feel when the summer is over."

He turned to face her. "What have you decided to do about Myrtlewood?"

"I can't think objectively just now. I called Grover Houston and told him to leave things as they are for now. He has the information about putting Myrtlewood on the historic register. I'll think about that after I get back to Mobile."

She gave a small sigh and said, "For now, it's nice to know Myrtlewood will be here. I don't think I could part with it, too, and still go on. I may need a place to be one day. Anyway, I'll have plenty of time to decide."

They fell silent again—knowing their parting was at hand, not wanting it to happen, but not able to postpone it.

Finally Maggs said, "I guess we've said all there is to say, Christopher. Except that I have loved you totally, and I will treasure your love as long as I have breath in my body. I think we should say good-bye now. I think that would be best," she repeated in a voice that was almost a whisper.

She looked into his eyes—for the last time, she couldn't help thinking, and her voice expressed the emotion she felt. "Good-bye, my very dear love. You have given me so much more than I can tell you."

He pulled her close and said, "No more than you returned, my darling. I won't forget you, either, and I'll be only a whisper away if you ever need anything. Remember that I will love you always."

His voice broke too, and they embraced, both fighting for control. He raised her face to his and bent to kiss her trembling lips. She kissed him one last time, with all the longing and all the passion and all the hunger she was no longer able to deny. They held nothing back. It was the expression of all the emotion they were feeling and the knowledge of all they were giving up. It accelerated in intensity, demanding any alternative to their love other than parting; and they were swept into a turbulence that precluded an awareness of their surroundings or their circumstances, aware only of each other and their insistent need.

Maggs came to her senses as he lifted her in his arms and carried her to the couch. "No, Christopher, we can't do this. It will prove nothing. It will only make it harder. Please, darling," she said, as she tried to make him hear her. "Please let's end this with dignity and not do something that will diminish what we've shared." She was crying as she took his face in her hands and forced him to look at her. "Please?"

He finally realized where he was and what he was doing, and his remorse was instant. He placed her gently on the sofa and looked at her anguished face.

"God, I'm sorry, Maggs. I don't know what happened. I thought I was okay with this. I guess I'm a little further from it than I thought. Please forgive me. I don't want our last moments together flavored with regret."

She took his hand and raised it to her lips. She held it against her cheek and said, "It wasn't your fault any more than mine. We both went a little over the edge. There's nothing to forgive. But I do think it's time to say good-bye. You need to go home, and I need to finish packing."

He said, "Will you walk me to the door?"

The walked into the foyer, arm in arm. At the door he kissed her softly, just once, saying nothing. Then he walked down the steps to his car without looking back.

She watched him as he drove down the driveway and out of her life. "But not out of your heart," the still little inner voice said. "What will you do now?"

"Pick up the pieces and try to go on," she said out loud, "that's all there is left to do." She turned and went upstairs to her room.

Chapter 18

After another sleepless night, Maggs rose early and attacked the chore of getting ready to leave with a vengeance. Molly found her already hard at work when she brought the coffee. The sun was shining through the open French doors and the birds were singing, but the look on Maggs's face was stormy. Molly took one look and wisely didn't question the outcome of the meeting with Christopher.

"What would you like for breakfast this morning, dear?" was all she said.

"I'm not hungry. And don't argue. I'll just have coffee and get as much packed today as I can. There seems to be so much more to take back than I brought." She sighed and kept on with her work. "It feels so unnatural to be removing all the evidence of my life here for the past month. It must be because I don't really want to leave."

She sat down and looked at Molly beseechingly.

"Well, darlin', you know you don't have to take everything this trip. You'll be coming back to close up the house later in the summer. You can leave what you won't need right away. What will you do about the computer?"

Maggs thought a moment and said, "I guess I'll box it up and get Tom to take it to Riverside after I'm gone. Christopher wants me to keep it, but I wouldn't feel right about it. I probably won't be here long enough to write any more, and he may have gone back to Maine before I return." She shuddered involuntarily as she thought of his absence from her life.

Molly watched her quietly, and still said nothing. Maggs looked at her worried face and said, "Molly, it's all right. Christopher and I parted on good terms. He understands what I have to do and why. He'll get over this in time, and I pray that I will too. I've just got to make the best of it until I get grounded again.

"This has been a wonderful time, close to Aunt Eleanor's memory and coming to feel a true part of Myrtlewood. I've learned a lot about my aunt and a lot about Myrtlewood. I've felt such total acceptance while I've been here.

"I've also learned a lot about myself, I think. For one thing, I've rediscovered some qualities I hope will help me reorganize my life. I've made a commitment to allow time for myself, to be true to my own needs. I'm not going to be so accessible to those who ask for my help before they try to help themselves."

She continued, looking into Molly's face, both of them sad that Maggs was leaving. "I want you to know how happy you and Tom have made my life here. If things were different, I could easily imagine my life continuing here with you forever. I owe you both so much for your loving care, your constant concern, your support and your loyalty. Particularly you, Molly, as I've made such a muddle of things with Christopher. I've never felt any sense of being judged, and I appreciate that. I'll miss you both, and I'll call often to check on you."

Maggs looked around the familiar room and sighed again. "I think I'll take your advice and leave everything I don't need right now. But there's still a lot to pack, and I'd better get to it. I know, I know, I can see it in your face," she laughed, "I'll be down for lunch, I promise. I'm just not hungry right now. Please?"

Molly left the room, muttering under her breath, and Maggs resumed her task. When she had her suitcase packed, she went to her desk and copied her book onto floppy disks, wondering if she would ever finish it now. The enthusiasm that had kept her going for the last four weeks was gone. She hoped the spirit of her characters would call to her strongly enough that she would come back to them.

When Molly called her to lunch, Maggs still had no appetite and ate only to appease Molly. She went back upstairs to pack her great-grandmother's wedding dress. Her anticipation of sharing its history with Sassie and Leah helped take her mind off the sharp throb that used to be her heartbeat. Molly had confirmed that the dress had indeed been worn by Gramma Patrice when she married but it had belonged originally to Gramma Patrice's mother, as Maggs had suspected. It was a small part of Myrtlewood that Maggs could take with her.

When everything was packed, she went out to the balcony to rest. The river breeze fanned her hair and caressed her cheek, lulling her and providing a short respite from the pain that never seemed to subside.

She took a leisurely bath and dressed in a caftan of watered silk. She added small gold earrings and put on gold slippers. She applied just enough makeup to brighten the pale face that looked back at her from her mirror. She wanted this dinner to be a fitting end to what had been an unforgettable time in her life. Tonight she would concentrate on the wonderful part. She would deal with the other part later, when she was far enough away that she couldn't turn back from her decision. Not tonight.

In the dining room, the candle flames were reflected on the polished tabletop. Quiet music played and champagne was chilling in the Georgian silver wine cooler. The setting exemplified the grace and charm of life at Myrtlewood and implied a continuity that was non-existent, of course; but Maggs embraced, if only briefly, the illusion that this was merely one more in a string of undisturbed evenings that had no beginning and no end.

Molly had gone to a great deal of trouble with dinner, and Maggs took her time, savoring the meal and the experience. She had coffee and dessert in the library in front of the fire. The illusion continued as Maggs lingered over her coffee. It was late when she finally poured a brandy to take upstairs and went to find Molly and Tom.

They were at the kitchen table drinking coffee, faces grim. After Maggs thanked them for dinner, she kissed Molly and hugged a stiffly uncomfortable Tom. Nothing was said of good-byes or partings, as if by unspoken mutual consent.

In her room, she sipped the brandy while she prepared for bed. Her departure seemed a little easier now that it was definite, just the tiniest bit less upsetting. She put on her robe and took her brandy out to the balcony to sit in the silvery glow of the moonlight one last time.

She was comforted by the soft moonlight, the rich scent of flowers carried by the night breeze, and the loveliness of the view. She sat peacefully in the dark, her mind, momentarily at least, free of emotion. She was rising to go inside when her eye was distracted by an almost imperceptible movement on the river.

Holding her breath, praying it wasn't Christopher, praying it was Christopher, not knowing *what* she was praying for, she realized as her eyes focused in the dark that it was indeed his canoe gliding silently on the water. If she had turned her head a split second sooner, she would have missed him altogether. She stood transfixed, watching as he rowed out of sight, her heart pounding wildly inside her chest. She had seen him on his solitary night-journeying when she had first returned to Myrtlewood, and now, again, on the eve of her departure. The two instances were separated by much more than a matter of weeks; they were separated by matters of the heart which would leave neither of them completely whole again for a long time, if ever. Icy shards of pain seemed to slice her heart into slivers as she rushed inside. She cried with huge, uncontrolled, gasping sobs until she fell asleep at last, shattered and exhausted.

With her devastation came the first glimmer of a grim suspicion that this experience might not be something she could successfully put behind her, try as she might. If she managed at all, it was going to be a monumental achievement.

Morning's first light found her pale and tired, her face showing the ravages of last night's grief. She was bathed, dressed and ready to go long before she went downstairs, silent and tense. She ate mechanically and then went for a brief walk around the grounds while Tom loaded the car.

Molly watched her anxiously, but made no small talk this morning, her own face dismal and unhappy. When Maggs came back inside she had filled her mind with images of the beauty she was leaving, images enough, she hoped, to last until she returned to close the house.

She stiffened her shoulders, raised her chin, embraced Molly tightly, stifling the impulse to cling to her, and said, "I'll call you soon, and let you know how I am. You and Tom just carry on as usual, and I'll let you know when I'll return. You know how to reach me if anything comes up. Thank you for all you have done." Her voice trembled, cracked, and she could say no more.

She looked into Molly's dear face and knew she had to get into the car immediately or she wouldn't be able maintain her hard-won self-control. Tom held the car door open but wouldn't look at her as she climbed inside. She rode down the long, oak-lined driveway without looking back, her heart a small, cold stone.

Afterward she only vaguely remembered the trip home. When she walked into the terminal of the Mobile airport a few hours later to find Stephen and Sassie waiting, the coldness in her chest twisted into an anxious little knot of dread and shifted to the pit of her stomach. Sassie held flowers and smiled an excited welcome as she ran to greet Maggs.

Stephen, reserved and unreadable, waited until Sassie released Maggs and gave her a perfunctory embrace. "Hello, Maggs. You look tired. Did you have a rough flight?"

"No, it was fine, but I am tired, I guess. I'm glad it's over." She understood the expression in Stephen's eyes, but he took her claim check without further comment and went to collect her luggage. Sassie was full of news about her trip to New York and chattered all the way home. Maggs was grateful for the non-stop narrative that made conversation unnecessary.

When they got home, Sassie jumped out of the car and said, "I'm going to meet Mary Elizabeth, Mom. We've found an apartment that suits us and we need to make some decisions about it. I want you to look at it before we sign the lease—Dad's already given his approval—but there's plenty of time next week to do that. We just need to check a few things. You two need to be alone, anyway. I probably won't see you tonight," she said, kissing Maggs first and then Stephen. "Jeff is meeting me there and we're going to a movie later, but I'll make breakfast in the morning to celebrate your homecoming, okay?"

She got into the little convertible sports car which Stephen had given her against Maggs's wishes and which she always drove too fast and sped down the driveway.

Maggs gave Stephen an awkward smile, realizing with dismay that she had counted on Sassie's presence to keep things impersonal as she and Stephen made the transition into this awkward reunion. Sassie had understood the tension and the need for them to be alone to work through it. So much for breathing room.

Stephen's smile was equally uncomfortable as he carried her luggage into the kitchen. He set her bags down and looked at her questioningly. Neither seemed to know how to break the ice.

"I'll just put these in some water," she said finally, looking at the flowers in her hands. While she filled a vase with water and arranged the flowers, Stephen still stood as if glued to the floor. Finally he said, "I'll take your bags upstairs. You'll probably want to change and rest a while. I'll make some martinis, and you can join me in the study when you're rested."

He seemed to expect no reply. Maggs followed him upstairs, miserable, uncomfortable, her unhappiness evident on her face, saddened that there was no pleasure for either of them in this homecoming. She suspected that Stephen felt bad too and that that was only a small part of what he was experiencing. But she also knew he wouldn't share what he was feeling.

"I'll just freshen up and be right down, Stephen," she said as he set the suitcases down and turned to leave. "I don't really want to rest right now." She walked over to her dressing table and removed her jewelry, waiting for him to leave the room. Strange that she felt he had to leave before she undressed. He felt it too, she sensed. He smiled again awkwardly and closed the door behind him.

She washed her face and put on bright green linen slacks and a white silk shell. She added a lightweight navy blazer and navy flats, applied enough makeup to disguise her paleness, and went downstairs.

He sat in his favorite chair, legs crossed, a martini glass in his hand. He looked tired too and as unhappy as she did. What has happened to us, she wondered, and how are we going to be able to find our way back to where we were?

He went to the bar and poured her a drink, added an olive and handed her the glass. She took the glass and walked to the open French doors and looked out. The garden appeared to be well tended, but it didn't feel as though it belonged to her. Nor was it the view she was accustomed to. She felt as if she were a visitor, that she had no real connection here anymore.

"Maggs," Stephen walked up behind her and placed his hand on her shoulder, "I know we have a lot to work through. I'm not sure what happened to us or why, and I don't know where to start to work it out. The only thing I know for sure is that I do want to work it out. I hope you do too. I assume you do, since you're here.

"But I don't think this is the time to get into that. I'm aware you feel uncomfortable with me, and to tell you the truth, I feel pretty uncomfortable myself. Let's put all this on the back burner for right now and just go have dinner. We'll take things slow until we get used to each other again."

She turned to face him and her eyes probed his. She was surprised by his words and moved by his obvious distress. She regretted instantly that she was responsible, even as she understood he had played at least an equal part in it. His part in their dilemma didn't prevent an army of protective instincts, finely developed in her over many years, from marching smartly to the forefront of her thoughts, as if there had been no break in the continuity of their marriage. She found herself responding as predictably and sympathetically as she always had when she believed him to be threatened. Except that now she recognized the trap as one she must avoid. She couldn't get caught up in his misery at the expense of her own well-being.

She had expected him to be sullen, accusatory, or at the very least, cool and indifferent. His apparent insight was the one thing she hadn't expected. Time would tell if it was an improvement over what she had been prepared for, or if it was even real.

She continued to gaze at him thoughtfully. She had known this wouldn't be easy. For the moment, what mattered was that he was right. She decided to accept his offer at face value.

She smiled her gratitude, sipped her drink, and said, "I think that's a great idea. Where do you want to go?"

"It's a nice night, let's eat on the water somewhere. We can drive to Point Clear if you like. We can talk on the way. I'll fill you in on Mike's graduation and you can catch me up on news from Myrtlewood. I also have a lot to tell you about the business, if you're up to a little shoptalk."

He took her hand. "Maggs, I know it's a long way back to where we started, but I want to get back very badly. I won't rush you, I promise. I've moved my things into the guestroom, and I'll give you all the time you need. Just know that I want more than anything to make it work again and I'll do everything I can to help."

She squeezed his hand and said, "I appreciate your candor, Stephen. I hope we can work things out too. That's why I'm here. But there is a lot that needs talking about, and I agree that we need to go slowly. We could start by establishing some straightforward communication. It's been a long time since either of us said what we really meant."

"I think that's as good a place to start as we're going to find," he replied, "and I'm all for it. All in good time, of course. Why don't you write Sassie a note, and I'll go change my coat."

Maggs wrote the note and propped it on her desk. She rinsed their glasses and put them in the dishwasher. Funny how some actions are so ingrained that they seem almost to get done of their own volition.

They drove leisurely to the beautiful old hotel on Mobile Bay. Nestled among aging moss-covered oaks, the Grand Hotel at Point Clear was a landmark in coastal Alabama, as well as a sentimental part of their own history. During a moonlight stroll there, Stephen had proposed to Maggs, and it had been a favorite place for special occasions ever since. The significance of his choice wasn't lost on

Maggs, and she accepted the offering in the spirit in which it was intended.

While he drove, Stephen filled her in on the status of the merger. He was enthusiastic about what had been accomplished in just a month. Groundbreaking had finally been scheduled, and the grand opening was planned for late fall. The complicated snarl of plans, schedules, negotiations, and contracts that required all of his time and energy was almost finished.

"I believe this merger has come at a very fortuitous time, Maggs. There will be time for us now, and I hope that when everything is settled, I'll be able to take you on a trip. If you want to go, of course," he added quickly. "I've even picked up some travel brochures on the Greek Islands. You've always wanted to go. Or we could go to Mexico. We haven't had a real vacation in years. I think it's high time we did, and I think we should do it right."

He paused expectantly, glanced at her sideways, and when she didn't speak, he said, hesitantly, "It's just something for you to think about, Maggs. I've thought a lot about the fact that we don't spend time together anymore, and I hope this can be a chance to get back into the habit."

They drove for a while in silence. At length, Stephen said, "I talked to Mike last night. He got accepted to law school, and he's really walking on air. I don't think he'll come down for a month."

Maggs noticed the expression on his face with considerable surprise. He was actually talking about Mike and *smiling*.

When he caught her watching him, he shrugged self-consciously. "I know what you're thinking, Maggs. The distance between you and me hasn't been the only one. Mike and I have some fence mending of our own to do. I've been thinking about that too—a lot. In fact, I went up and spent the day with him recently. We played a little golf and had dinner.

"We talked about what we had done to each other and what we meant to each other and a little bit about what we'd like our relationship to be. I think it was a good start. We enjoyed the time together. At least, I know I did, and I think he did too. He said so, anyway. He wanted me to stay overnight, but I had an early meeting the next morning and I couldn't. I think he was actually disappointed. So was I. Gave me quite a jolt.

"Meredith is her usual amazing self. Thank God, Mike found someone like her. Jennifer is fine too, growing so fast you can almost see it. I managed to spend a little time with her before I left. Took her to the toy store. That child has a way with her grandpa's heart, let me tell you."

Maggs couldn't help thinking that "that child" had a way that was exactly like her father's, if Stephen had ever looked closely enough to find that out, but she didn't say it. Mike had effortlessly won everyone's approval all his life—except his father's. Maybe things were going to improve between them before it was too late to rebuild any sort of connection; maybe they were finally realizing what she had tried so many times to make them understand.

After dinner, Stephen paid the bill, and they walked in the garden. When it got cool, Stephen placed Maggs's jacket around her shoulders, his hand remaining lightly on her shoulder. They sat on a wrought iron bench and looked out over the water.

Maggs felt very receptive toward Stephen right now. He had found just the right touch for this homecoming she had so dreaded. She felt a faint pulse of the cold little stone in her chest, almost as if it were trying desperately to resuscitate itself.

On the drive home they discussed local gossip and the trip to Tuscaloosa for Mike's graduation. Stephen pulled the car into the garage and they walked into the kitchen as they had hundreds of times before. Then, unexpectedly, the awkwardness was back, and neither of them seemed to know what to do next.

"Nightcap, Maggs?" he asked.

"No, I don't think I have room for anything else. I'll sit with you while you have one, if you like," she offered.

"No, I don't really want one, either. It was just something to say. Look, Maggs, I think this has gone exceptionally well and I also think this is a good place to end our first day. Why don't you go on to bed—you must be exhausted. I'll lock up and then go to bed too. I'll see you in the morning."

He kissed her forehead, turned her in the direction of the stairs and gently pushed her toward them. Gratefully, she did as he said. It really had been a long, stressful day. That it had turned out as well as it had was no small credit to Stephen. She knew he was capable of this kind of sensitivity—it was just that he hadn't shown it in such a long time.

She closed the bedroom door, put on her gown, and then sat down at the vanity to brush her hair. She looked around at this room that had been her sanctuary for so many years and which now felt so alien to her. Her face in the mirror reflected her weariness. The physical manifestation of her fatigue would dissipate with a good night's sleep; the emotional aftermath would just have to be dealt with.

She turned back the spread on the bed, running her fingers over the familiar carved posts. It was the first piece of good furniture she and Stephen had bought and she had never considered replacing it. More history, she sighed. She turned out the bedside lamp and slid between the sheets. She lay very still in the unfamiliar darkness, hoping sleep would find her quickly; but it didn't, and she found herself wondering what the moon looked like tonight from the balcony outside her bedroom at Myrtlewood, and whether there was a ghost canoe making its silent way along the swirling, misty river. She heard Stephen's footsteps on the stairs and then a pause outside her door before proceeding down the hall to the guestroom. She heard the door close. Her mind raced erratically for a long time before exhaustion finally won out and she slept deep and dreamlessly.

Chapter 19

Stephen had already gone to work, and the house was quiet when Maggs woke up. The sunlight was brilliant, but it flooded the bedroom in an unfamiliar way. She looked toward the balcony doors, didn't find them, and realized she wasn't at Myrtlewood. Then she heard Sassie downstairs making breakfast noises. She was home.

Home? How strange that sounded. This didn't feel like home. Myrtlewood felt like home; she could feel its strong pull in spite of the short time she had been its mistress. She would have to put an end to such feelings and get on with her life here. This *was* home, whether it felt like it or not.

She slipped on her robe and slippers, brushed her hair, and went downstairs. Stephen had taped a note to the outside of the bedroom door saying he had a meeting this morning but would be home in time to spend the afternoon with her.

Sassie's delighted smile helped a lot. At least it felt natural to be with her. Maggs hugged her tightly, reluctant to let her go, until Sassie laughed and said, "Mom, I've got to turn the bacon before it burns."

Maggs poured a cup of coffee and sat down. Sassie had put fresh flowers on the table and the kitchen looked warm and familiar.

"Breakfast will be ready in a minute, Mom, and then we can talk."

Sassie removed a bowl of fresh fruit from the refrigerator and took the croissants out of the oven. She drained the bacon and placed it on a platter, poured the juice, and then sat down across from Maggs.

"It's so good to have you home, Mom. We've missed you terribly. Especially Dad. More than he expected to, I think. He seemed kind of angry and distracted when you first left. I'm not sure exactly what was going on with him. He was awfully busy with the merger, but it was more than that. But lately he seems to have worked his way through something, and he's been totally different. It must have had something to do with the way you parted."

She helped herself to some bacon, offered the platter to Maggs and continued. "I hope things are going to be okay between you and Dad now, Mom, but I also want you to be happy. I know something happened while you were in Charleston, and I don't think it has necessarily made you happier. I don't know what it was, and I'm not asking you. I just want you to know I'm old enough to understand that things happen sometimes without planning, and things change sometimes too. I know there are things you and Dad have to get worked out. I love you both. And I will, whatever happens now."

Her smile was frank and open, and as Maggs opened her mouth to reassure her, she said, "Mom, you don't have to explain anything. I just wanted to get that said in case I'm a concern in whatever happens next. I don't need to be. Now let's change the subject. On the way in from the airport yesterday you said you had something fascinating to show me. What is it?"

Maggs looked at her earnest open face and knew how blessed she was to have such a daughter. Understanding that the rift between Maggs and Stephen was more complicated than either let on, her first priority was to reassure Maggs. She possessed Maggs's talent for getting to the heart of a problem and starting there to find a solution.

Maggs smiled at her now and said, "Darling, thank you for your sensitivity. But you needn't worry. We'll work this out. It's not too serious. You'll see."

She took a deep breath. "Now that we have that out of the way, let's get on to the fun part. In the attic at Myrtlewood, I found the wedding gown that belonged to my great-grandmother, and it's in almost perfect condition. It was also worn by Gramma Patrice when she married my grandfather. I couldn't resist bringing it home. It's very close to your size, and I thought it might be fun to see how it looks on you. Shall we invite Leah and Matt over for dinner, and afterward you can try it on? Melody will love it too. It will be like playing dress up."

Sassie's response was predictably enthusiastic. "Sounds like a winner to me. I have one class this afternoon, and I'll come straight home and help make dinner. Would you like me to pick up anything at the market?"

"No, your dad is taking the afternoon off. We'll eat on the terrace. It should be a lovely evening for it. I have steaks in the freezer, and it looks like someone stocked the refrigerator before I got home. Was that someone, by chance, you?"

"You bet. We've lived on take-out food and dinner at the club too long. I'm ready for some home-cooked meals for a change. I bought all my favorites, and I'll even help with the cooking. You can't ask for a better deal than that."

Maggs laughed. "Definitely not. Now, tell me about the apartment you and Mary Elizabeth have found."

Sassie was off and running, her words tripping over each other. It sounded as if they had made a wise choice. The price was reasonable; the apartment was located close to the college and in a safe neighborhood. Mary Elizabeth's parents had already given their approval and so had Stephen. Sassie was excited at the prospect of being on her own and couldn't wait to show Maggs the apartment. They arranged to see it the next morning. Maggs caught Sassie's excitement and was soon thinking of things in the attic that could be donated.

When the kitchen clock chimed, Sassie said, "Goodness, I've got a class at eleven, Mom. Got to grab a shower and rush. Sorry I can't help you clear away the dishes."

"Run along, dear, it won't take me but a few minutes."

Maggs loaded the dishwasher and tidied up before going upstairs. She stopped on the way to her bedroom and made up Stephen's bed. A small stack of crumpled telephone messages lay on the dresser, and as Maggs started to leave, the name on the top message caught her eye: Terry Matthews. She picked it up, not really meaning to but not feeling there was any reason that she shouldn't. The time was noted as 9:15 a.m. yesterday, and the message read: "Ms. Matthews wants to know if you can meet her for an early lunch before you go to the airport. Please call her."

She placed it back on top of the stack, finished tidying the dresser before going thoughtfully on to her bedroom. As she unpacked her luggage and put things back in the spaces they had always occupied, she considered the message. It surely wasn't an unusual occurrence if Stephen's secretary could deliver the message. It was probably just a business matter, but why was it necessary to have lunch with him before he met her plane? Had he gone?

What difference did it make anyway? Terry was his partner. And if there was more to the relationship than business, as she suspected, Maggs was in no position to be prying. She certainly hadn't doubted Stephen's sincerity when he expressed his hopes of working things out. It was curious, however, that while filling her in on all the news, he hadn't mentioned Terry's name once. Was Terry the meeting he had this morning?

Maggs put the question out of her mind and went on with the process of settling back into her home. Leah called to welcome her back. Her words were cordial, but Maggs detected the faint note of disapproval behind them as she was meant to. Not surprised by Leah's censure, Maggs ignored it. *Leah on her high horse* was how the family described it when Leah took it upon herself to judge what she considered someone else's shortcomings. Maggs invited her to dinner and got off the phone. She finished unpacking, did a few chores, and was sitting on the terrace with a glass of iced tea when Stephen came home at noon.

"Hi, Toots!" he said merrily, loosening his tie. He had called her Toots in the early days of their marriage, but it had been many years since she had heard him say it. "How was your morning?"

"Pretty good. Sassie and I had a lovely breakfast. Leah called a little later, and I've gotten settled in. How was your meeting?" she asked.

"Oh, just another tedious detail that needed working out. Bet you wouldn't pour me a glass of that iced tea while I go change, would you?" He was taking his coat off as he went inside. "Don't go away—I'll be right back."

She walked over to the tray and poured him a glass of iced tea and then sat down to wait for him. It was very shady here, and the quiet was lovely. The generous backyard was surrounded by a high brick wall. Huge trees and overflowing flowerbeds effectively disguised the existence of the busy neighborhood street just the other side of the wall. In the garden all sounds were muted. A cast-iron fountain tinkled delicately into a small reflecting pool, adding to the serenity of the setting.

She thought of the peaceful hours she had spent here swinging her children to sleep on mild spring evenings. Now she occasionally did the same with her grandchildren. She and Stephen had hosted countless pool parties and cookouts. The children had played in the swimming pool with their friends on hot summer afternoons all through their school years. This had always been a happy place, and she had never taken it for granted. When something troubled her, she put on old clothes, got her garden tools, and worked in the dark, rich soil until she got some sort of perspective on the problem.

There's a lot to be said for having a history with someone, she thought. Maybe it's enough in the end. "I fervently hope so," she breathed, in the softest of voices.

For there was unquestionably a long history. When Maggs first met Stephen, he was just the pest who sat behind her in third grade. A year older than Maggs, he had been held back a year because of a serious bout with rheumatic fever. He had a smile that would melt her heart in later years, but at this early stage it was merely open and friendly—if a tiny bit superior. He eventually skipped a grade and ended up a year ahead of her.

When Stephen was in the tenth grade, his parents were killed in a plane crash. They had been generally unaware of almost everything that affected Stephen as he grew up. Neither his mother nor father had expected this late-in-life child who would intrude upon the placid, intellectual life they lived. They provided for his needs, gave him an absentminded affection and left him pretty much in the care of people paid to look after him while they continued to travel. They were stingy only with their time and attention, which was, of course, the only thing he wanted.

After their death, an elderly uncle cared for him until it was time for him to go away to college. His parents had provided for his education. If he had felt any sense of personal loss at their death, he never showed it. That he had fared as well as he did through an emotionally barren childhood was a tribute to his sunny disposition and his ready sense of humor. Only in later years did Maggs come to understand how adversely his childhood had affected him. In the formative years of their love, he was just a shining, handsome boy who loved her as devotedly as she loved him.

He alternately aggravated and protected her until the summer before Maggs's senior year of high school when they found themselves at loose ends one humid night and went to the local hangout for a coke and a hamburger. They ended the evening sitting outside Maggs's house, talking for hours, discovering that they felt the same way about most of the things in their world. When the evening ended, without putting it into words, they were forever a couple.

Parked one night in Stephen's convertible, watching a star-scattered sky make twinkling reflections in the calm waves of the Gulf of Mexico, his kisses suddenly became more insistent; and Maggs responded with all the ardor her sexual innocence permitted. Stephen was leaving for the University of Alabama in the fall; she had another year in high school before she could join him, and she didn't think she could bear the separation. During that intense summer their relationship deepened, and by the time Stephen left for Tuscaloosa, they were engaged.

Her parents were pleased. Stephen had been accepted around her house long before he and Maggs fell in love, and although Maggs may have been surprised when she realized it was Stephen who sent her blood singing through her veins, her parents had thought that would happen all along.

Maggs pined for him her entire senior year of high school and then finally joined him in Tuscaloosa the following fall. Their college years were good ones, filled with football games, fraternity parties, homecoming parades, studying together late into the night. And as time passed, coming to know and trust each other in all ways—sexually, of course, with all the breathless passion of the uninitiated, but also morally and intellectually.

They married the summer Stephen graduated, and Leah was on the way almost immediately. Maggs graduated too, but her plans for graduate school were first postponed and eventually canceled.

Those times, and the years that followed, had been significant in shaping their life; and from the vantage point of thirty years down the road, their importance had not diminished.

"Why the solemn face?" said Stephen, coming out the door. He was dressed in shorts and sneakers. Always handsome, it was evident even when he was a child that he would one day grow splendidly into his tall, lanky body. Over the years he worked hard to remain fit, eating moderately and exercising conscientiously. The payoff for his efforts was that he always looked good, and Maggs admired him silently as he took his glass from the table and walked toward her. He leaned over and kissed her cheek before taking a long drink and sitting down in the swing beside her.

Maggs said, "I was just thinking about all the hours we've spent in this garden. It doesn't seem possible that so much time has gone by and we're still here in the same spot. Most of the time it's a positive feeling, but sometimes it's a little deadening. Do you know what I mean? Do you ever have that feeling?"

"Of course. Probably not as intensely as you do, but I know what you're talking about, Maggs. Life goes on. It goes on through the good times and the bad times and the just plain ordinary times. The trick is to hang in there and take it as it comes. There's an art to making the most of life, and if you ever master it, the result is a parade of events that began long ago and culminates in the present. It's all somehow connected, and it turns out to be your life. I believe it happens the same with everyone. The difference is, in some people's lives the events are more fortuitous than in others. I think we've been part of the fortunate few. Don't you?"

"Yes, I guess I'd have to say I agree, all things considered," she said. They sat quietly, the need for words temporarily allayed, as comfortable with each other as only two people who have remained together for a long time can be.

After a while, Stephen cleared his throat nervously. Maggs could almost feel him physically bracing himself.

"Maggs, I don't know how you'll feel about what I'm going to say, but this is probably as good a time as any to bring it up. I'm not naïve, and I'm not insensitive either, contrary to how I may act sometimes. I know what we're confronting is more than just differences about how we want to be treated and what we want from each other. I don't know who has claimed your interest or how deep that attachment goes, but I know someone else has become important to you.

"I must assume that whatever it meant to you, you've chosen to put it aside and resume our life together. If I'm wrong, set me straight, and I'll shut up. But I think I'm reading you right on this score. I hope to God I am.

"I've done something I'm not proud of and justified it because of injured pride or anger or spite, so believe me, I'm not casting stones or placing blame. I'm simply trying to say that I regret it. That's not an excuse. There is none. I'm not being vague to keep from owning complete responsibility for what I did. I'll be happy to give you any details you feel you need. But I don't believe it would serve either of us to give names or dates or detailed explanations of how and why it happened and what it meant. In my case, it meant nothing, which probably shows a greater lapse of character than to say that it did, but nevertheless that's the truth. It's over, and it will never happen again.

"I have this terrible dread that in your case, you probably won't be able to say it meant nothing. And that terrifies me. But I promise I'll ask you no questions. You can share part of it or all of it or none of it, as you prefer. The point is, I feel very strongly that the life we've shared can be an incentive to work this out and regain our mutual respect and our trust in each other. I want to do that.

"The real issues have to do with our relationship, and that's what I propose we focus on. I'll abide by what I said last night. I won't rush you. I'll keep my distance until you want it otherwise. But I really think we have to deal with what needs correcting between *us* rather than what happened with someone else. If you agree, we'll go forward in that direction, and anything else will be put to rest forever. If you don't, we can handle it however you choose. It's up to you."

He took a deep breath and exhaled. He had spoken for the most part with his head down. Now he looked directly into her eyes, expectant, vulnerable.

"I don't know if this was the right time to say this, Maggs, but I don't know when would be a good time. It had to be said. I intend to take as much time as we need make this work, so there's no rush. I think that's been a major factor in where we are right now—there just hasn't been enough time. I can see now that time isn't given to us like a magical gift. We have to make it. And take it. And give it to others. I plan to do that from now on. If I have the chance."

He fell silent as if suddenly the well of thoughts was exhausted. He didn't seem to expect a response. It appeared to be enough that he had said what was on his mind. Maggs knew how hard it was for him put all his feelings into words.

For a few minutes Maggs didn't reply. She didn't know what to say. She had been prepared to have this conversation when she got home yesterday, but events had taken a course that lulled her into thinking it wasn't imminent. Now the issue was before her again, and she couldn't remember how she had planned to explain about Christopher.

She left the swing, refilled her glass, and walked to the edge of the terrace. She leaned over out of habit to pull the dead blooms from the flowers in the brick planter. After a moment, she turned to face him.

"Stephen, I appreciate what you've told me. I appreciate the way you're handling this whole thing. I agree with most of what you say. I agree with all of it, in fact.

"The problem is, my affections, as you tactfully put it, were very deep. Deep enough, in fact, that I considered not coming back at all. Deep enough that I considered making a new life with someone who came to mean everything to me that you no longer did. A very wonderful man, Stephen, whom you would be proud to have as a friend under different circumstances. It was no peevish fling."

She paused, thinking about how to express what she wanted to say next, and then just plunged ahead. "He wants me to marry him."

She looked directly into Stephen's face, saw the shock register, followed by a look of dismay that pierced her heart.

"In the end, I turned him down. I'm not entirely sure of all the reasons why I did, but I did. The reason I considered not turning him down is that he accepted me in a way—appreciated me in a way—that no one ever has before. Not even you, in our best times together. And when I left him, I also left a part of myself.

"I don't regret my choice, and I don't intend to change my mind. It's as over as what was between you and, I assume, Terry Matthews. But *I'm* not over what happened. I'm not over *him* completely though I will be eventually, and I'm not over the depth of what I felt and what it cost me to give that up.

"I came home because I thought it was the right thing to do. Also because I have no desire to hurt *you*, Stephen. I care for you a great deal. We've made a good life together. Another part of why I came home is that I'm a little bit of a coward too. I came home for our children and our grandchildren. I came home because I doubted the wisdom of what I was considering. I came home because I didn't know what else to do. There are lots of reasons, Stephen, some I'm not sure are even valid.

"Believe me, for my sake as well as yours, I wish I could tell you that it didn't mean anything, but it did. It meant everything. It meant I was alive again. It meant there was joy when I woke up every morning and happiness when I went to sleep at night. It meant there was someone to talk to who really cared what I think. I want those feelings in my life again, Stephen.

"I came home to see if I can find them with you. If you can accept what happened and get beyond it, and if you really want to try, I'll try too. But it won't be easy, and it won't happen quickly. If you want me back on those terms, we'll see what happens. But if you can't put it out of your mind, this won't work, Stephen. I know it won't. So I guess that means it's not totally up to me—a lot depends on you.

"I'm truly sorry for the pain this is causing you. I wish it could be different, but I have to be honest with you if we're to have a chance."

She walked back to the swing and sat down beside him. The anguish in his eyes was terrible to see. She sat quietly, saying nothing further; she knew this needed time to sink in. And it was always his habit to carefully consider his options.

After a while, she said, "Leah and Matt and the children are coming to dinner tonight. I thawed some steaks to cook on the grill. Sassie will be home in a little while to help. Do you feel up to it, or shall I postpone it?"

He rose slowly, as if he ached all over, tucked in his shirt tail and said, "You've given me a lot to think about, Maggs. Fair enough, I asked for it. I don't think we need to do any more talking tonight. Let the kids come on as planned. It'll be good to have the family together again and to spend some time with Jason and Melody. I know you must be eager to see them."

He took her hand and pulled her to her feet. "I want to say one more thing, Maggs, since we're being completely honest. I didn't expect you to tell me you lost your heart. It hurts more that you made an emotional commitment to him than that you shared your body with him. I realize I shouldn't be surprised—I know a meaningless affair would never tempt you. That you were vulnerable at all is because I haven't been what you needed. I'm responsible for that. But I still want us to be together again, and I still think it's possible. In time. In time, I hope."

They went into the house together, her hand still clasped firmly but lightly in his, both more than a little overpowered by what they had learned about the other in the space of an hour's conversation. Honesty wasn't going to be simple or painless, it was apparent, but it would be infinitely preferable to the way they had been before. She hoped it would be a lot easier to live with, once they were accustomed to it. For both of them.

Chapter 20

The next two weeks proved difficult in many ways, but in others it seemed to Maggs as if she had never been away at all. The routine of her days was quickly reestablished as friends found out about her return, and invitations and appointments filled her calendar again. She was busy with her house and her grandchildren and plans for Mike's graduation.

She helped Sassie and Mary Elizabeth get moved in, shopped with them for household necessities and knickknacks to personalize the small apartment. She shared Sassie's joy reservedly, realizing, even if Sassie didn't, that she would likely go from this first heady taste of independence to marriage and a home of her own. For all practical purposes, Sassie was now fully fledged, and although she was in and out of the house frequently, it didn't feel the same.

Stephen understood Maggs's silent grieving and went out of his way to provide distractions. Maggs was astonished when she realized that he was grieving too. They comforted each other, and it brought them closer.

For the next few weeks, true to his word, Stephen came home on time almost every night. They often had dinner out and sometimes went to a movie or for a drink in a local pub they had enjoyed years before. Many nights found them in the terrace swing as the hour grew late, talking about what had gone wrong and how it could be avoided. Maggs felt Stephen was really listening to her for the first time in years. He was responsive and understanding, taking measures to remedy the slights and neglects that had become habit without intention over the years.

Maggs visited the construction site and made plans to decorate the new showroom. They discussed the budget and reviewed the prospectus and solved the problems that occasionally arose. Maggs made suggestions unobtrusively, sensitive to the prerogatives of Terry Matthews as Stephen's partner, but there was never a problem as far as she knew; and although she half expected to run into Terry some time, Maggs was relieved that it never happened.

They opened the beach house the weekend before Mike's graduation. They informed everyone that they didn't want company. Their wishes were respected, and they had three days free from the demands of work and family and social obligations.

If being at the beach revived memories she was trying hard to eradicate, Maggs ferociously berated the still little voice which nagged her in quiet moments and went on as though she didn't remember Christopher's hard, strong arms or his warm, soft mouth.

Nights were the hardest. As he had promised, Stephen made no attempt to return to her bed, and Maggs's nights were filled with long hours of actively suppressing thoughts of Christopher while she lay sleepless in the dark before inevitably succumbing to her need for him when she was caught, exhausted and defenseless, in the no-man's-land of dreams, unable and unwilling to resist any longer.

Though she fought really hard to forget Christopher, she was unsuccessful for the most part. She finally realized that as long as she wasn't making an effort to replace the memories that haunted her with new ones, she would remain unsuccessful. She talked frankly to Stephen about her feelings, and he remained patient. His sensitivity encouraged her to suggest that it was time to resume the physical part of their marriage.

Stephen was quietly delighted and suggested that they follow Mike's graduation with a second honeymoon. She agreed at once, and he came home the next afternoon with reservations for the Tutwiler Hotel in Birmingham. He had even made dinner reservations at a new restaurant she had mentioned once. He was excited and hopeful. She knew him so well, she realized, as she listened to him outline their weekend.

She was less optimistic, but she understood she would have to make this transition if they were to make any further progress. She shopped for a new negligee and a new dress, packed with Stephen's preferences in mind and tried to match his enthusiasm.

In Tuscaloosa they attended the tea on Friday afternoon and took everyone to dinner afterward. The graduation ceremony the next morning was long and hot, but her discomfort counted for nothing when she saw Mike accept his diploma and search the crowd for Stephen when he finally had it in his hand. The pride in Stephen's eyes brought tears to her own. Was it really possible that Stephen and Mike had realized how much they needed each other?

By mid-afternoon, Maggs and Stephen were on their way to Birmingham, both preoccupied with putting their relationship back on solid ground. Inevitably, instead of romantic and natural, their reunion proved to be awkward and strained. But Maggs felt enormous relief that it was a fait accompli and suspected Stephen felt the same way. It hadn't left her breathless or drained, but it was done, and it was fine. There had been too much of a purpose to allow for spontaneity. Maggs reassured herself that the sexual part of their marriage would improve when everything else was back to normal.

The following weekend Maggs kept Jennifer so that Mike and Meredith could spend two days at the beach. Maggs invited the rest of the family for dinner Saturday night, straightened up after everyone, and kept everything running smoothly all weekend. It was wonderful to have the house full again, if exhausting; but when the house was quiet again Sunday night, Maggs was glad she and Stephen were alone.

In the ensuing weeks it seemed life was back to normal. Normal in the sense that it used to be, she would think occasionally in the midst of one of the meaningless engagements that filled her days, but she stifled the thought as quickly as it occurred. Stephen was preoccupied with his business again, and the number of hours he worked gradually increased to ten or twelve hours, and sometimes more. Sassie was working, happy with her independence and her apartment. Leah was busy with Matt and her children. Greg wrote that he was planning a trip home for Christmas.

Maggs phoned Molly every week and was invariably informed that she and Tom were well, they missed her, there were no problems at Myrtlewood. She gossiped about local doings but never mentioned Christopher, and Maggs never asked. Molly didn't ask how things were working out with Stephen.

As the weeks turned into months, Maggs began to find it harder to keep the old resentments at bay. She tried denying her feelings, rationalizing what was happening, keeping an even more hectic schedule. As their relationship approached its previous stalemate, she and Stephen stopped talking about what was bothering them and went back to guessing what the other was thinking. Maggs realized this failure to communicate could derail everything, but she perversely did nothing to change it, justifying her inaction with the excuse that if Stephen was too busy to make the effort, she was too.

She tried to work on her novel, but the telephone invariably rang, or someone needed something, or she had too much scheduled for that day, or she just wasn't inspired. She tried to talk to Stephen about it, hoping for some encouragement; but she caught him on a day when a contractor had defaulted on a major phase of the project, and he had little time and no encouragement. In spite of the efforts he had initially made to respond to her needs, he remained oblivious to how important this novel was to her.

Dissatisfaction with her superficial routine increased. As time progressed, she realized the problem wasn't dissatisfaction—it was depression. But it wasn't an overwhelming depression, and not having any experience with it, she didn't realize at first that it was depression at all.

It didn't immobilize her. It came insidiously when she looked at the dinner table after she had made a special dinner for Stephen and he hadn't come home. Or when she called Sassie and caught her on the way out with no time to chat. Or when she accepted the chairmanship of a new committee she wasn't the least bit committed to because it met on Tuesday nights, and she didn't have anything else to fill Tuesday nights with. Or when she watched old black-and-white movies on television late at night because she couldn't sleep and found that the happy endings left her in tears which she thought were about the movie until she understood finally that they were really for herself—and the happy ending that didn't seem to be materializing for her.

Still she resisted; strong people simply didn't succumb to depression. Nevertheless, the sense of futility continued to intensify. She denied it as long as she could while her days grew emptier and her nights grew lonelier. Her despair became so consuming that she finally had no choice except to acknowledge its reality.

The admission of depression forced her to explore the cause. She stubbornly rejected what was at first a suspicion and then a certainty: She had indeed made the mistake Molly had tried to talk her out of, only to discover that her old life was simply not enough anymore. That realization was harder for her to accept than the idea that she could be seriously affected by depression. She was horrified when she finally admitted what was troubling her. Because now her choice was simple: stay and stagnate or leave and accept everyone's censure. She didn't know what to do, but it was no longer possible to deny what was going on.

More and more frequently she would cancel appointments and stay in bed most of the day, only getting up in time to dress and prepare dinner before Stephen came home. Her hopelessness manifested itself in angry eruptions at Stephen over insignificant matters. He responded with concern at first, but he soon tired of humoring her unreasonable moods and reacted angrily as well. After a while they talked only when necessary.

Sassie realized something had changed and tried to talk to her, but Maggs denied that anything was wrong. In the face of such absolute rebuttal, Sassie had to withdraw. She dropped in less often. Maggs knew it was her doing, but at the same time she was irrationally hurt by Sassie's imagined indifference. Unable to bridge the gap, Maggs grew more depressed.

After several weeks of erratic behavior, Maggs realized she had to do something. There was only one person she could discuss her feelings with because there was only one person who knew the whole story. That person was Molly. She longed for Molly's strong arms and gentle acceptance and her practical no-nonsense approach to life. Molly always saw things as they were, and Maggs badly needed an objective opinion right now.

Early one afternoon when she was no longer able to bear the lethargy that gripped her, she dialed the number at Myrtlewood. When she heard Molly's voice, Maggs completely lost her composure. "Oh, Molly, you were right," she wailed. "I've made a terrible mistake. I've committed myself to this choice, and it's all wrong. It was all along. And now it's worse for the whole family than if I had never returned. I'm confused, and I can't think what to do.

"The only thing I know for sure is that I don't love Stephen the way I need to in order to stay here. I'm not sure he even loves me. But I do love Christopher, and pretending I don't isn't going to work. Molly, I need to talk to him. What do you think he'll say if I call him?"

She had blurted it all out, her pain palpable, undisguised and unmistakable in its urgency. Having finally admitted her distress to someone else, she was strangely calm inside as she waited for Molly's answer.

There was a long pause on the other end of the phone before Molly said, "Oh, my poor darlin,' my poor, misguided, darlin.' I'm so sorry to hear what you're saying. I had so hoped that I was wrong and that you could make it work. You were so convinced you could."

She paused again and finally said, "Ms. Maggs, I'm sorry to be the one to tell you this, but Mr. Christopher has returned to Maine. He finished the term and then packed up and left. He turned down the offer the university made him. Said he felt he had to go back where his roots were. He's been gone about two weeks. Nell tells me Mr. Huntingdon is desolate over his departure, but he couldn't talk him out of it. Something happened to Mr. Christopher, Nell says, but no one knows what it was.

"I wasn't going to tell you this, dear, but he came around one afternoon just before he left and asked if I thought you were happy. I had to tell him that as far as I knew, you were making the best of your choice and it seemed to be working. He said, 'I really loved her, Molly, and I can't stay here without her. If she's happy with her decision, please don't tell her I talked to you. I know you'll understand why I have to leave, but you'll probably be the only one who does. I wanted to say good-bye to you and Tom. If Maggs ever needs me, Molly, she can reach me through Uncle George, but I can't stay here and wait when there's nothing to hope for.'

"I felt real sorry for him, he was that dejected. Oh, Ms. Maggs, why couldn't you have listened to what I was trying to tell you and what your Aunt Eleanor was trying to tell you? Now what are you going to do?"

Maggs said, brokenly, "I honestly don't know, Molly. I think I'm coming home. To Myrtlewood, I mean. This isn't working with Stephen, and I've finally figured out that it's not going to. I've hurt him so badly, Molly. I've got to make a decision before I hurt him anymore. Oh, why didn't I realize I would only hurt him more in the long run by trying to hold on to something that no longer exists?

"I've got to talk to him and explain how I feel. He's going to be devastated, but I truly don't think he's any happier than I am—he just won't admit it yet. And if he can't forgive me, I'll just have to live with that burden. I'll also have to talk to the kids. They're going to be shocked and hurt and probably mad as hell too, but they have to be told. As soon as I figure out what I need to do and get it all settled, I'll let you know."

She was quiet a moment. Then she said, "You know, Molly, ever since I've been back, this hasn't felt like home. And every time I've used that word, I've realized it was Myrtlewood I was thinking of. I've made such a mess of the last few months that I may not be able to straighten it out. I'm such a mess myself. It's not going to be easy, but if I can straighten myself out anywhere, I can do it at Myrtlewood.

"If you should hear from Christopher, please don't tell him any of this. Right now my only concern has to be Stephen and how I'm going to tell him I can't stay. If I can figure that out, I can manage the rest of it."

"How long do you think all that will take, dear?" Molly asked.

"I don't know. I'll probably tell Stephen this weekend, if I can find the courage, and I'll tell the kids after I talk to him. Then I'll have to make some arrangements. It shouldn't be complicated. I'll sign the house over to Stephen, and the rest should be fairly straightforward. I won't need his financial help. It's possible I could leave in two or three weeks. I'll keep in touch, Molly. Pray for me, please? That I'm not making another mistake? I don't think I could bear it."

She was crying softly, and Molly said, "Now hush, dear, and get on with what you have to do. Deciding is always the hardest part, and grieving is the next hardest. You've made the decision already. You've proved what you had to prove to yourself. Come on home now and do your grieving. You're strong enough to get through this, you know. And don't you be worrying, there's never a night that doesn't find you in my prayers. I'll just add a little extra to them. It will be all right, you'll see."

Maggs replaced the receiver and gave way to the utter desolation she felt. She put her face down on her arms and cried in great wracking sobs. She could remember crying this hard only one other time in her life and that was the night she had sent Christopher away. As she fought for control, she heard a faint sound and raised her head to find Stephen watching her from the bedroom doorway, his face white with shock and anger.

"I think we need to talk," he said, without a trace of emotion, "and I see nothing to be gained by putting it off. I didn't mean to eavesdrop on your conversation, but having heard what you had to say, I think we need to come to an understanding. Suppose you wash your face and join me in the study?"

He turned and closed the door soundlessly behind him. Maggs was stunned. She was totally unprepared to do this right now. She needed time to gather her thoughts. She had wanted to break this to him gently, and now that wouldn't be possible. She dreaded facing him, but she pulled herself up from the bed and went into the bathroom to bathe her face and her swollen eyes with a cold cloth.

She brushed her hair, put on some lipstick, squared her shoulders, and faced herself in the mirror. "Okay, if this is what you want, you have to have enough character to face the consequences of your choice," she said to her reflection. "You're no coward, Mary Margaret Masters. You never have been. And you're no quitter. So just get on with it."

She turned off the bathroom light and went downstairs to face Stephen, her heart in her throat, not having the slightest idea what to say to him.

Chapter 21

Stephen handed her a martini when she came into the study. He was very pale, his expression grim. Maggs knew how hard it was for him to maintain the rigid control he was exhibiting, and her heart ached for him. She accepted the drink, her own face white with shock, and seated herself on the sofa. She took a sip, then another, and finally, taking a deep breath, she said, "Do you want to go first, or would you prefer that I do?"

He looked levelly at her and said, "Maggs, I really believed we would be able to work this out, but I guess some things can't be repaired. Sometimes the damage is just too severe. I've been aware that our relationship has pretty much reverted to the old pattern. I've also realized you weren't happy. I haven't wanted to look too closely at the reasons, so I directed my frustration into working harder, knowing it wouldn't solve anything. But I honestly didn't understand how miserable you are until I overheard what you told Molly. Maybe I should have, but I didn't.

"I'm not convinced this has nothing to do with someone else in spite of what you said to Molly. I suspect it has more to do with him than you realize. But the bottom line is, I can't make you happy. And I don't want you to stay here because you feel responsible or obligated—or for any other damned reason except that this is where you want to be. From what you said, that isn't the case."

He paced the floor as he talked, and she knew he was in a great deal of pain. He would hate her knowing it, but it was true. He stopped pacing and looked questioningly at her.

Her eyes were blue crystal pools as her tears overflowed and ran slowly down her face. "Stephen, I really thought I did the right thing when I came home. I really thought we could work it out too, and I really thought I should try. I know now I came home for all the wrong reasons, and they simply weren't strong enough to support a bad choice. I never wanted to hurt you. Part of the reason I came back was because I didn't want to do that, but it turns out that's all I've done. I hurt you when I left, I hurt you when I returned and told you what had happened, and now I'm hurting you again.

"You may never believe this, but I do love you, and part of me always will. We've spent most of lives together, raised four great kids, and we have wonderful memories. When I came home, I thought our past would be enough to hold us together. I see now that it isn't, but that fact doesn't invalidate the memories. I'll always care what happens to you, and I'll always want you to be happy. But I can't assure that happiness at the expense of my own any longer. I'm suffocating here, trying to do what makes everyone in this family happy, to be what everyone in this family expects of me, and I've finally understood that everyone in this family *except* me is basically already happy. They don't need my sacrifice to keep them going. They've all found their own way. You have too though it may take you a while to realize it.

"I have to find a way to live for myself now, to find out who I am, apart from an extension of someone else. I want that chance. It's very painful to know I'm the cause of your unhappiness. And the kids will also be hurt. But I will pray that in time you can all forgive me."

She walked to the bar and refilled her glass. She added an olive and turned to him. "Would you like another?"

He shook his head, his eyes fixed on hers. She left the drink on the bar, walked over to him, and laid her hand on the side of his face. She could feel the tightly clenched muscles of his jaw. His eyes were not their normal shade of blue. He removed her hand from his face.

"I don't know how much you overheard," she continued, returning to the bar to pick up her drink, "but I don't want you to give up the house. I'll go back to Myrtlewood. I'll be able to take care of myself financially. I don't want this to be complicated or ugly, and I hope you won't either."

"How soon will you leave?" he asked. The monotone of his voice was the only indication of what it was costing him to maintain his self-control.

"I'll tell Sassie and Leah tomorrow. I'll write to Greg, and I'll talk to Mike. I'll explain that this is my fault, and I'll let them have their say. I have some obligations to get out of. I'll do that as quickly as I can and leave as soon as possible. I'll try to handle everything discreetly, Stephen, so that you and the children will have the least amount of gossip or speculation to deal with. Whatever reason you want to give for my departure is fine with me. I know you will be fair.

She looked at him intently and hesitated while trying to decide whether to say what was on her mind. She decided she must.

"I'd like to repeat that this really has nothing to do with Christopher. I haven't heard from him since I returned. He has left Charleston and knows nothing about this. If he knew, he would be sorry it didn't work out. He's a good man, Stephen. I can't promise nothing will ever come of our relationship, but I can assure you that it won't happen until I come to terms with everything that has happened in the last few months and until I know exactly what I want. Then I'll have to see if he fits into any of it.

"I'd like you to believe this is not about Christopher and me, but about you and me. Mostly, about me. If you blame anyone, Stephen, blame me. I've hurt you, and I truly didn't mean to. I hope one day we can be friends, but if that's asking too much, I understand."

For a split second, the anger surfaced in his eyes but it was only a moment before he regained his control.

He said, "How long do you think that should take, Maggs? Do you really believe it's even possible? It certainly won't be any time soon. I'm trying my damnedest to understand what happened. How can two people who meant so much to each other for so many years let it all get lost? I'd do anything to make you change your mind, but I can't think of anything that would. I don't see that I have any choice but to accept what you're doing and try to salvage what's left of my life while you go in search of God knows what to make your life complete.

"I'll try to make the best of it, but I damn well don't have to like it, and I'm on record as letting you know right here and now that I damn well don't. I hope you'll be happy, Maggs, but I don't think I'll ever feel anything but anger over what you've done."

He turned to leave the room, hesitated, and then turned back to her.

"I'll pack a suitcase and take a room in town until you leave. I don't think I can stand being around you. You can have Grover Houston get in touch with Pat Delaney when you're ready. I'm sure he'll represent me. I can't think of anything we can't agree on, so perhaps it will be as easy to dissolve thirty years of marriage as you seem to think it will. Good luck, Maggs."

He glared at her as if the anger he was trying so hard to suppress was preventing him from saying something more. He held her gaze a long time, frustration visible in every line of his face. Unable to find the words, he shrugged his shoulders in defeat and stormed out of the study, slamming the door behind him. She heard his footsteps going upstairs followed by the sound of dresser drawers and closet doors slamming. She remained where she was, transfixed. She wasn't surprised that he was so angry. Only that he had controlled it so well.

After a while he came downstairs and slammed the kitchen door as he went into the garage. She heard the sound of the car engine as he drove too fast down the driveway.

The house was suddenly very silent. She sat perfectly still for a long time before rising wearily and going into the kitchen. Dusk was closing in and the emptiness of the house was suddenly unbearably oppressive. She turned on some lamps in the living room. It was time to prepare dinner, but she had no appetite and there was no one else to prepare for. She switched on the small television set in the kitchen and caught the end of the local newscast. The news was as grim as she felt. She switched it off, put the kettle on for tea, and went out on the terrace to wait for the water to boil.

At the table where she had sat so many times planning her week over a cup of coffee, she viewed her garden in the fading twilight and was aware of how much its beauty and serenity had always comforted her. She thought of her children playing with their friends and realized that her expectations of seeing her grandchildren play here as they grew up had vanished with the same conversation that had just concluded her marriage to Stephen. She would no longer be part of the activities that took place here. She was stricken by the reality of that.

Her agitation was such that she found herself wondering if anything was worth all this pain. Pain she was suffering, pain she was causing others. It all hurt so badly—maybe the easiest thing would be to not feel anything. There were ways to accomplish that. She had never understood how anyone could consider such a solution, but maybe those people desperate enough to make such a choice knew something she didn't. Or maybe they were just braver.

The kettle began to whistle, and the shrill sound jolted her back to reality, horrified by what she had been thinking. She was doing the only thing that made any sense. It was also the only thing that made sense for Stephen; she was just sorry for the pain he would experience until he realized it.

The next ordeal would be to face Sassie and Leah. She debated whether to tell them separately or together and decided on the latter. She would do it, as she had told Stephen, as soon as possible. Tomorrow, if she could arrange it.

She went inside and made herself a cup of tea and found some crackers. She turned out the lights and went upstairs. It was completely dark outside now. The house was quiet, and she felt completely alone for the first time in her life. There had never been a time when she was strictly on her own. She considered herself a strong person, but she wondered if she could get through the coming days if she didn't have Molly and Myrtlewood to turn to. She thanked her aunt silently for the sanctuary, wondering what Aunt Eleanor would think about the course her life was taking.

There was no way to know, but Maggs was pretty sure she would have understood.

Sassie was out. She called Leah next and asked her to come over tomorrow before work. Sassie returned her call right away and agreed to do the same. To their questions she replied only that she didn't want to discuss it over the telephone.

She got ready for bed and turned on the television, just for the noise, but the senseless gibberish bothered her nerves. She brushed her hair and then tried to read, but after she reread the same page for the third time, she closed the book and turned out the light. She lay sleepless and inconsolable for hours before exhaustion finally overcame her.

The next morning she was up before the sun, and she started packing immediately. She would get everything ready to ship—she didn't want Stephen to find her things everywhere he turned when he came back. It would be hard enough for him as it was. She was interrupted by the sound of Sassie's car and went downstairs to greet her. Leah arrived before they got inside.

Maggs put the coffee carafe and cups on a tray. "It's such a beautiful morning, let's have coffee outside."

They followed her outside, exchanging quizzical glances before turning apprehensively to her.

"What's up, Mom?" asked Sassie, pouring fresh cream into her coffee. "Why so mysterious?"

Maggs handed Leah a cup and said, "I've got something important to tell you. It's going to be hard for you to accept, but I hope you will try. I don't know any way to tell you except to come right out with it. Your father and I are separating. We're going to get a divorce."

She watched Leah's mouth open as though to refute what she heard and then quickly close. Sassie was watching Maggs intently, and her face remained expressionless.

"I'm going to be frank with you," Maggs continued, "because I want you to understand. I am not leaving your father for someone else although there is someone else I've come to care for. He is not a part of what is happening. Your father and I have been growing apart for a long time. The situation kind of jelled when Aunt Eleanor died and I decided to comply with her request to spend a month at Myrtlewood, against your father's wishes. That's when I met someone else.

"Sassie, you'll know I'm talking about Christopher Allendale. He has since gone back to his home in Maine, and I haven't heard from him since I left Myrtlewood. He doesn't know I'm leaving your father.

"I don't know whether we have a future or not, but that isn't a consideration right now. I'm telling you all of this because I think you deserve to know the facts. I have to get through this on my own and for the right reasons. I plan to live at Myrtlewood, and I plan to leave as soon as I can make the necessary arrangements. Stephen will continue to live in this house. He has gone to a hotel for the time being, but he'll be back as soon as I'm gone. Before I leave, I'm going to Tuscaloosa and talk to Mike."

Leah was looking at Maggs incredulously, as if Maggs were talking about a stranger. Sassie's expression still had not changed.

Maggs continued, "I want to be as much a part of your lives as I am now. The only difference will be that I'll be a little farther away. We can talk on the phone often. It's not a bad drive to Charleston, and I hope you and the children will visit me as often as you can. You must know you will always be welcome at Myrtlewood.

"I know this comes as a shock, but if you think about it, things won't be so very different. You children are grown. You're all busy with your own lives. I'm more a background for you now, and rightly so. My role should be to provide love and support—and help, if you really need it—and I can do that from Charleston.

"That's what I wanted to tell you. I'll answer your questions as openly as I can. What do you think?"

She refilled their cups, sat back in her chair, and looked at her daughters. Leah, as usual, was the first to do battle.

"I can't understand this, Mom, and I don't understand what you can be thinking. How could you leave Dad? After all these years? And how can you leave us? I need you in my life, and I want you to be a part of the kids' lives. Here. Not off in Charleston with some strange man we don't know anything about. This is absurd, and I can't believe you would even consider it."

As she talked, her voice got louder and shriller until she was fairly shouting.

"Leah, I'm willing to discuss this objectively, but I won't engage in a shouting match. Christopher is not a strange man, and this is not about him anyway. This is about differences between your father and me that can't be reconciled. You'll be just fine. You'll probably manage better on your own than you do with me so readily at hand. As far as Melody and Jason are concerned, I've already told you I intend to be very much involved in their lives. Unless you prefer otherwise.

"Your father will be hurt for a while and then he will begin to get over it, just as you will. I don't intend to change my plans. I have lived the last thirty years of my life for my husband and children. You children are grown now, and Stephen's business is so consuming that there's little time for me. I need a purpose in my life, something that fulfills me. I hoped you would understand. I expected your anger, and I find it understandable. I hope we can get past it."

"But, Mother," Leah wailed, "people your age just don't do something this drastic without giving it a lot of thought. This is so sudden. What will I tell my friends? My Mother is going through a midlife crisis and has fallen hopelessly in love with some handsome vagabond who paid her a little attention and is foolishly giving up everything for him?"

Maggs felt her anger rising and fought to control it. "First of all, Leah, I'm not nearly old enough to have no remaining passion for life. Secondly, I am not having a midlife crisis. I find that comment highly offensive and completely inappropriate. Last of all, Christopher is not a vagabond. He's a highly respected professional with a challenging career. He finds me intelligent, interesting, and capable of great understanding. That kind of recognition is something I've had very little of from my family, Leah, you included. But let me repeat that that's not the reason I'm leaving.

"What I want now . . . no, what I *need* now is a chance to live my life to its fullest potential. I'm trying to arrange things in a way that will prove the least disruptive for all of you. My concern is not with what you tell your friends. You may tell them what you choose. Tell them I've suffered a massive hemorrhage which caused severe brain damage and I've been institutionalized, if you find that less painful than telling the truth. Which is exactly my point, Leah. Please try to understand—this is not about you. This is about me. And for a very long time now, most of the concerns in this family have had little or nothing to do with what I need. Now it's my turn."

Leah's sulky expression was a familiar reflection of a battle which had been lost but stubbornly not conceded. Sassie had listened quietly to all that had been said. Maggs turned to her.

"Sassie, do you feel the same way? Do you think I'm in my dotage and throwing away everything for some pathetic romantic fling? Do neither of you understand me any better than that, after all the years I've spent giving you the best I had to give? Do you really think me capable of something so superficial?"

"Of course not, Mom." Sassie took Maggs's hand and held it tightly. "You know I don't. I knew something was wrong between you and Dad, even before Aunt Eleanor died. I didn't want to know it, but I did. I saw the restlessness and the emptiness in your eyes sometimes when you didn't know I was watching you. It was painful to see, and I didn't want to believe anything could separate you and Dad, so I convinced myself I was imagining it. I understand more than you think I do. I know this didn't happen because of Christopher. I think it happened over time without either you or Dad realizing it. And I guess no matter how badly I wish otherwise, it's something that evidently can't be undone.

"I just find it hard to accept that our family is going to change so drastically. And I can't bear the thought of your not being here. I know that sounds selfish. And childish too. But it will be hard to give up the assurance that you're always here if things get too tough for us to handle alone.

"It will be hard to watch Dad come to terms with this and try to get on with his life too, Mom. But I don't think your staying will fix anything for either of you. If you're as unhappy as you say you are and you've found a chance for happiness, you have to take it. I'll get used to it, and Dad will get used to it, and Leah will too. I'll always want you to be part of my life, and I think Mike and Greg and Leah will too, once we have a little time."

She released Maggs's hand and wiped the tears from Maggs's face with her napkin as if she were the mother and Maggs the child.

"You do what you have to do, Mom. It's not going to change how I feel one bit."

She rose from the table and said, "Now, I have to get to work before they wonder if I've resigned." She looked at Maggs and said, "Mom, do you have to go right away? Couldn't we have just a little longer to get used to the idea?"

Her wistful face and her sad expression pierced Maggs's heart. She stood up and put her arms around Sassie. "Oh, darling, a few more days won't make it any easier. And I think it would be even harder on your father. Of all that's happened, what I regret most is the pain he feels. Please be here for him. He'll be fine eventually, but it will take some time, and he'll need you until he's okay. May I ask that of you?"

Sassie hugged her tightly, her head on Maggs's shoulder. She said, "You know I will, Mom. We both will, won't we, Leah?"

Leah remained silent, glaring at them both.

Sassie detached herself from Maggs's embrace and said, "I've really got to go now. I'll come by after work, okay? We'll talk some more then."

After Sassie left, Maggs turned to Leah, who was taking her keys from her purse and said, "Leah, I'm sorry you don't understand. I hope you will think less harshly of me in time. I love you, and I love your precious children. I pray that your anger with me won't come between us. I'll be here a few more days if you want to talk."

Maggs walked over and put her arms around Leah, but it was like embracing a statue.

Leah said stiffly, "I'll call you before you leave, Mother, and I will try to understand. You just don't know how hard this is for me. And I don't know what to tell Melody and Jason."

With that, she fled through the kitchen door, and Maggs's heart jerked painfully as Leah's car went down the driveway. She regretted Leah's anguish and wondered how long it would take her to recognize that a tantrum couldn't change this. It was predictable that Sassie would try to understand and Leah would react solely on the basis of how it affected her, making no effort to understand anything she didn't agree with.

Maggs took the coffee things into the kitchen and put them away before going upstairs to write Greg. It took a long time to compose the letter and satisfy herself that she had broken the news as well as she could. She sealed and stamped the letter and then called Mike and told him she wanted to see him. They arranged for her to come to Tuscaloosa in a couple of days.

She hung up the telephone, reflecting somberly that in the space of a few short hours she had dramatically changed the course of her life and that of her family. Frightening though it was, it was also oddly exhilarating. Thoughts tumbled through her mind. She was free. She was sad. She was scared. She was glad. She was on her way, for better or worse.

She took Greg's letter to the mailbox, and as she walked back to the front door, she looked around at the familiar surroundings. She would carry her memories of this place with her forever. She had been happy here, and she felt a sharp, unexpected pain at the thought of giving it up. She had made the mental transition, but evidently the physical separation still needed some work. Her home had been the backdrop to most of her life, and it was natural that her leave-taking wouldn't be totally free of regret, she reassured herself.

She went inside and resumed packing. She would take her books and her personal effects and leave everything else except the little rosewood desk and chair which her grandmother had given her. The beautiful rice bed would remain here. She didn't want to start her new life with something that had been so intimate a part of the life she was leaving behind. If Stephen no longer wanted it, he could sell it or give it to one of the children.

She sorted her clothes, packing what she would take and putting what she no longer wanted in boxes to give to charity. At the end of the day, she still wasn't finished. For most of the day she had forgotten to eat, and when hunger could no longer be ignored, she went downstairs and ate something, just to keep from getting faint.

Sassie came after work and stayed for a while. They talked of inconsequential matters; everything important had already been said. When Sassie left, Maggs worked on until midnight and then fell into bed exhausted.

The next morning she made coffee and immediately went back upstairs and worked steadily all day. She didn't answer the telephone. When she happened to catch her reflection in the mirror, she was shocked by the grim-faced, driven woman staring at her. But she was determined to remove all possible traces of her existence from this room and this house before Stephen came back, and she kept going. Two days later, she had succeeded so well that this house that she had made so indelibly her own showed little evidence of her occupancy.

She left very early the following morning and drove to Tuscaloosa. She had no idea how Mike would react. Not understanding at first, Mike listened thoughtfully while she explained. In the end, he was sympathetic and supported her right to search for a happier life. He made no judgment and placed no blame—perhaps, she thought later, as she was driving home, because there had been so much judgment involved in his own relationship with Stephen.

Mike was becoming his own man, a rather fine one, she thought. She recognized many of Stephen's admirable qualities in Mike, and thought his willingness to listen and not judge indicated that perhaps he would be more flexible in his own relationships than Stephen was. She appreciated the evidence of this new maturity at this time when she especially needed his understanding.

She spent the afternoon playing with Jennifer and then they all went for an early dinner at a small restaurant she and Stephen had frequented when they were in college. Memories of those times were vivid. But not disturbing, particularly. Mike and Meredith urged her to stay overnight, but she refused even though it was a six-hour drive to Mobile and it was late when she left.

She wasn't tired. She wasn't afraid either. She was filled with energy, excited over the possibilities open to her. Now that she had made her intentions known to her children and listened to their objections, she was anxious to get on with it.

The two-lane highway out of Tuscaloosa was dark and deserted, but the isolation was strangely comforting. It was well after two o'clock in the morning when she got home. The long drive had given her time to balance anticipation about the future against apprehension about the inevitable consequences of leaving everything familiar behind, and she was still satisfied with her decision.

She lowered the garage door and let herself into the kitchen. She poured herself a glass of water without turning the lights on, knowing from years of habit where everything was and went straight upstairs. As she prepared for bed, her mind was occupied with what the next few days would require of her. Indecision and uncertainty were finally behind her, and for the first time in weeks, she felt she could sleep.

Next, she would resign from all her committee assignments, volunteer organizations, and club memberships. Her friends would be astounded at what she was doing. She was astounded herself. But tomorrow or the next day she would load her car and be on her way.

The drive to Charleston would be long, but she would stay overnight somewhere, instead of driving straight through. As she climbed into bed, she made a mental note to call Molly. And before she left, she would call Stephen to say good-bye.

It was done. No regrets. No looking back. "I told you so," said the still, small voice. "You could have saved yourself a lot of trouble if you had just listened."

"Maybe so," Maggs replied out loud as she turned out the lamp, "but I had to be sure this wouldn't work before I gave up on it."

Chapter 22

In weeks to come, Maggs didn't remember much about her actual departure. She remembered the look on Sassie's face as she stood crying in the driveway when Maggs drove away. Maggs cried too, but she kept driving.

She remembered the hostility in Stephen's voice that effectively disguised his pain so that nobody but her would have detected it, but she didn't remember what they said to each other, except that she tried one more time to say how sorry she was. No use telling him she would always care for him; he wouldn't believe it for a long time. If ever.

She remembered the bitterness of Leah's good-bye though not the conversation. She remembered the pain of leaving Melody and Jason. They had been such a joyous part of her days, and she would miss them terribly.

She was numb when she passed the sign that read, "Thank you for visiting Mobile. Please come again." She wasn't sure her heart was even beating until she reached Pensacola, where she stopped for coffee though she hadn't been on the road an hour. She had started shaking and thought eating something might distract her from the suddenly scary finality of what she had done. It didn't, of course. She sat in the bright vinyl booth until the disinterested waitress asked her the third time if she wanted a refill. She washed her face in the restroom and got back in her car. She would drive until she reached Jacksonville. She should be there by early afternoon and then she would rest, perhaps drive out to the beach for a while, have an early dinner and go to bed. Then she could take her time driving the remaining few hours to Myrtlewood.

Driving along, feeling a little better, she remembered a sorority sister who lived in Jacksonville whom she hadn't seen in years. Alicia Delacroix was her name, and Maggs decided to call her when she got to Jacksonville. Maybe they could meet for dinner. Her spirits rose at the thought of seeing Alicia. She and Maggs had spent holidays and summer vacations visiting each other while they were in college. They had "fixed each other up," double-dated, and gone on football weekends together.

Maggs and Alicia and Delaine Packard, their predatory sorority sister, had spent countless hours discussing which dress to wear to a fraternity dance or whispering into the small hours about whether to finally let go of their burdensome virginity. Delaine impatiently advised them to stop talking about it and get on with it. They knew, of course, that she had "gotten on with it" a long time ago. Delaine was a free spirit and certainly no hypocrite.

Maggs and Alicia instinctively understood that they didn't want such a significant step to be the fodder for gossip sessions in the fraternity houses. Sexual freedom might be glamorous, but they knew it also had a price. In time, Maggs and Alicia had cried and comforted each other when they finally crossed that threshold. Maggs smiled at the thought of how serious they had been about sex back then. How times had changed.

It would be good to see Alicia again. Unquestionably a product of her environment, Alicia had married into a wealthy Jacksonville family after college, presented the prerequisite son and daughter, assumed her place in Jacksonville society, and performed admirably the role she had been groomed for since the day she was born. Maggs wondered if Alicia ever felt the twinges of unrest that had plagued her.

When Maggs checked into the hotel, she was tired, but her spirits were definitely on the mend. She ordered a sandwich from room service and looked up Alicia's number in her address book. The telephone was answered by a stern-sounding man Maggs assumed was the butler.

In a few minutes, Alicia's breathless voice said excitedly, "Maggs, is it really you? Wherever are you, darling?"

Maggs took a sip of her Coke and laughed. "Yes, Alicia, it's really me. I'm here in Jacksonville. I'm staying overnight on my way to Charleston and thought I'd see if you're free for dinner. I apologize for not giving you any advance notice, but I'd really love to see you. And Austin too, of course."

"Oh, that sounds divine. Austin is in Dallas at one of those dreary medical conventions, and I have an Auxiliary meeting at four o'clock, but I'll slip out early and pick you up. I'd ditch it altogether except that I'm president this year, and this is a big planning session for our annual bazaar. We'll go somewhere fabulous for drinks, and I'll take you to the club for dinner. I'm simply can't believe you're here. You'll stay with me, of course, I won't hear otherwise—it'll be just like it was at school. I'll pick you up a little after five. What hotel are you staying at?"

"I have my car, Alicia, so just give me directions and I'll meet you at your house around six. That will give you a little more time. I want to drive out to the beach, anyway."

"Why in the world aren't you flying to Charleston, Maggs? It's such a terribly long drive. All by yourself? Well, anyway, if you're sure you don't want to be picked up, I'll see you at six." She gave directions to her house and rang off.

Maggs finished her lunch and changed into a sundress. She got directions from the parking attendant and threaded her way through downtown traffic and out to Highway A1A, where she turned south and drove along the beaches. She parked on a sandy shoulder and made her way down to the beach. The afternoon sun reflected off the blue Atlantic waves in white-hot beams that made her eyelids feel as if they were shrinking. She inhaled deeply several times, filling her lungs with the salty, faintly fishy smell of the shore.

People in the distance were tiny silhouettes and far out from shore brightly colored sailboats flitted along the horizon like butterflies with jeweled wings. She couldn't help thinking of the Mon Coeur. She removed her sandals, unconcerned that no one knew where she was. After walking a while, she sat down to rest and dug her feet into the sand, which was deliciously cool once her toes were past the heat of the surface. It was peaceful here; the monotonous sound of the waves was soothing.

She wanted to stay and watch the sunset, but she had to start back if she was to dress for dinner and get to Alicia's on time. She brushed the sand off her feet, buckled her sandals, and drove reluctantly back to the hotel.

She followed Alicia's directions to the St. John's River area section of Jacksonville where large homes had been owned by most of the same families since Henry Flagler had made Jacksonville the most elegant summer watering hole on the east coast for wealthy northern industrialists. The shady divided streets were quiet and formal.

Maggs was admitted through a wrought iron gate in a high stucco wall by a uniformed attendant. Mediterranean, sprawling, with arches and courtyards and fountains and a terra-cotta roof covering its three stories, Alicia's home was typical of the neighborhood. Luxurious tropical vegetation surrounded the house, and plants of every color and description filled beautifully landscaped flower beds which were scattered everywhere like schools of tropical fish.

Maggs parked her car and lifted the knocker on the massive front door. A stern-faced butler answered the door and led her across a foyer larger than most living rooms and left her in a huge room under a vaulted ceiling so high the massive beams seemed to disappear into the gloom at its apex. Statuary and relics and heavy Mediterranean furniture gave the room a museum-like atmosphere.

Maggs was inspecting her surroundings with considerable awe when she heard the quick tap of high heels in the foyer, and Alicia burst through the double doors in a cloud of expensive perfume and floating silk loungewear.

"Darling, I'm so glad you're here at last! I'm so sorry Max put you in this dreadful mausoleum to wait. Don't you just hate it? I detest it myself. I don't even think Austin likes it, really, but it mustn't be changed, you know. It has always been like this, so it has to remain like this." She took Maggs by the hand and led her across the foyer to the stairs. "Let's go upstairs. I spend as little time down here as possible. Except when we entertain, of course. Then the whole dreadful place has to be opened up and lit with candles and its ugliness paraded for the world to see. When I'm alone, I don't even come down to eat."

At the top of a beautifully carved staircase, Alicia led Maggs down a wide hall covered with Persian rugs and more antiques to double doors which opened into her suite. These rooms were spacious and light and filled with colorful prints and delicate furniture. She could see Alicia's bedroom through a wide arch.

"I'll have Max bring your bags up. You can have the room next to mine. Let's have a drink while I get ready. What would you like?"

"Martini, please. But Alicia, I'm not staying overnight. I'm leaving early tomorrow, and there's no need to disturb your entire household when I go. It will be simpler if I just go back to the hotel." "Oh, but you must stay here! I've been so looking forward to spending the evening together. Please let me send to the hotel for your things. I can't bear it if you don't."

Maggs looked closely at her for the first time. The loveliness and grace was still there. She was carefully coifed and beautifully made up. Her figure was still shapely, and she was beautifully dressed. Her smile was brilliant, but Maggs sensed desperation behind it.

Alicia turned away and busied herself making their drinks as if she realized she had given away too much. When she handed Maggs the martini, her smile was perfect again though her hand shook slightly. This was not the first drink Alicia had had this evening. Something was wrong.

"Well, if you really want me to stay, I guess there's no harm. I was only trying to save you the inconvenience of my early departure," Maggs said.

"Wonderful! I'll have Max collect your bags. You'll be all settled into the guestroom when we get back from dinner. I'm so happy to have you here, Maggs. Couldn't you stay longer? Austin won't be home until next week, and I'd love to introduce you to all my friends."

Again Maggs detected the faint sound of desperation behind Alicia's words.

"No, darling, as much as I'd like to, I'm expected tomorrow at Myrtlewood and I really can't delay. If Austin is gone a lot, perhaps you can visit me there. I'll have lots of free time, and I'll show you Charleston."

Alicia smiled wistfully and took a long drink. "That sounds like terrific fun. I might just do that. Oh, I forgot to ask why you are going to Myrtlewood alone. Are you going ahead to open up the house? Isn't it kind of late in the summer to be doing that?" The silk garment swirled around her as she seated herself in an overstuffed chair. She looked just like an overdressed porcelain doll.

"Do sit down, Maggs. I'll change in a minute. There's this wonderful new bar in town where everyone goes, and I thought we'd start there with drinks. Now tell me why you're going to Myrtlewood. I did so love visiting you there when we were at school. Has it changed much?"

Maggs sat down on the loveseat opposite her, recalling all too well Alicia's frustrating habit of asking and answering her own questions in rapid-fire order. "Stephen and I are divorcing, Alicia. I'm going to Myrtlewood to live. It belongs to me now."

"Oh, how dreadful! You poor darling! How beastly of Stephen to do this to you! Was it another woman? It usually is. But I can't believe you and Stephen are separating. You must give him another chance. These things always run their course, and it's not worth giving up your way of life just to salvage a little pride. Believe me, Maggs, I know what I'm talking about. Austin has his little escapades, but he always comes back. It would cost him too much to leave me, and he doesn't really want to anyway. It's just something men do."

Alicia chattered on, admonishing Maggs and offering advice about how to bring Stephen back into the fold. Maggs began to suspect that the desperation she sensed behind Alicia's glittering facade must be caused by her marriage.

"It wasn't Stephen who wanted a divorce, Alicia. I did. I've been unhappy for some time. Stephen has never mistreated me. We just grew apart. Sometimes it happens. I can't exactly explain my decision to leave. It's just something I have to do."

Alicia's face portrayed her astonishment. "Maggs, how *can* you be so foolish? You have a wonderful life! These feelings always pass. Think how sorry you'll be that you gave up your security, not to mention a good man into the bargain. And I can tell you, a good man is not something to casually toss aside. I could tell you a lot about that."

Her voice quivered, and she dropped her eyes.

"I shouldn't expect you to understand any better than Stephen and the children did, I guess. You'll just have to take my word that I'm doing what's best for me. Now come on, Alicia, get dressed and let's get started if we're going out. I have to get up early tomorrow."

Alicia seemed relieved to end this serious conversation and poured herself another generous drink, chatting away as she searched her cavernous closet for something to wear and spent another hour getting ready. She gave instructions to have someone sent to the hotel to collect Maggs's luggage and ordered the car brought around.

By now Maggs could see the direction the evening would take, but Alicia's desperation touched her and she couldn't back out. The limousine took them to a bar where Alicia had more drinks before they left for the club. Maggs had been right; Alicia was not drinking with pleasure. She was trying very hard to convince Maggs of her fairy-tale existence, but Maggs realized that somehow her choice to leave Stephen threatened Alicia's acceptance of her own marriage, and she was really trying desperately to convince herself.

At the club, Alicia introduced Maggs to some of her friends and ordered another drink. By the time Maggs insisted that they order and their dinner arrived, Alicia had no idea what she was eating. After dinner, she wanted to go to another club, but Maggs declined, pleading her early departure. Reluctantly, Alicia consented to go home.

In the back seat of the limousine, Alicia tipsily confided that she occasionally thought of starting over. "But I'm too scared, Maggs. I don't think I could give all this up. I wouldn't know what to do. Austin would be merciless if I left him. I'd have to stay here and face all my friends, with nothing to fall back on. You don't know how brave you are, Maggs," she whispered.

Maggs helped Alicia upstairs and got her ready for bed. She closed the door behind her and went to her own room with a heavy heart. Alicia would never be able to do anything about her unhappiness. Maggs knew that she was fortunate to have other options, but she was very glad that the trappings of her life weren't so important that she couldn't let go of them.

Maggs slept fitfully and awoke the next morning to a silent house. She bathed and packed and then sat down to write Alicia a note, repeating her invitation for Alicia to visit, knowing it wasn't likely to happen. She collected her bags and walked quietly to Alicia's room. She knocked softly on the door and then opened it and peered into the gloom. Alicia was breathing evenly and hadn't moved from the position Maggs had left her in the night before. She left the note on Alicia's bedside table and thanked God that she had the courage to look for her own answer.

She drove away with her mind full of Alicia's unhappiness, but she felt vastly relieved to be away from that beautiful house where all the privileges of wealth and social acceptance didn't give meaning to a loveless marriage or fill empty days and nights.

When she reached Savannah, she stopped for breakfast at a restaurant where she and Stephen had eaten many times. They both appreciated Savannah's rich tradition and its fierce determination to maintain its individuality. She remembered those times while she sat on the deck enjoying the rich black coffee and idly watched the gulls whirl and swoop over the water. Her reminiscence was flavored with fondness for those times, but she felt no regret when she thought of herself and Stephen here—two people who were a couple no longer. Perhaps that was an omen.

Refreshed and eager to resume her journey, she paid her bill and was on her way again. She would be home in less than two hours.

It sounded so right when she said it aloud: "Home!" Myrtlewood *was* her home now, not merely a cherished childhood memory or a lovely place for an occasional visit, and she intended to make it hers in every sense of the word. With every mile she drove, her heart lifted a little more, and by the time she reached Charleston, she couldn't wait to get through the congested city and out to the serenity of the Ashley River and the entrance to her own driveway. Into Molly's welcoming arms and Tom's dour but nevertheless sincere concern for her well-being.

Chapter 23

It was mid-August when Maggs returned to Myrtlewood. The days were still long though the sun took a slightly different overhead path each day now, and the air was filled with the promise of cooler days. The leaves were already taking on faint tinges of the brilliant orange and red and gold colors of autumn in coastal South Carolina. The change of seasons had an invigorating effect, and the early indications of fall seemed to promise wonderful things.

As her new life gradually took shape, Maggs was at peace. Molly and Tom, happy to have her back, guarded her solitude when she wanted it but were always close by when she needed company. At first she hibernated, recovering from the enormous upheaval in her life that had left her physically and mentally exhausted. Gradually her children came to understand her decision as time and space slowly provided a more unemotional perspective to each of them.

Sassie, the most comfortable with the change in Maggs's life, was predictably the first to break the ice, coming to visit before the fall quarter began. Her roommate was getting married at Christmas, but Sassie had decided to keep the apartment. She buzzed in and out of Stephen's house, and in and out of Myrtlewood, bringing a breath of fresh air wherever she landed.

Leah brought the children for the Labor Day weekend. They delighted in the wide-open spaces and the woods and the riverbank. Maggs took them to her sandbar for a picnic. They roasted wieners as the sun went down and the evening turned chilly. They pulled on sweaters and sat around the fire roasting marshmallows and telling ghost stories, trudging home weary and grimy, singing all the way. Leah even joined in the spirit of the occasion, much to everyone's astonishment.

Leah saw firsthand why this life exerted such a pull on Maggs. She observed the serenity of the days here and the way Maggs had bloomed under that serenity; and she went home beginning to understand the extent of Maggs's contentment. She almost conceded (grudgingly) that Maggs had made the right choice. She confided that her own life seemed to be improving. Matt had landed a job that suited his freewheeling disposition and was successfully employed, at last. Their money problems had eased considerably and, along with that, much of the stress in their marriage.

The night before Leah left, she and Maggs sat on the back porch while Jason and Melody caught fireflies in the twilight. Leah seemed to have acquired some sorely-needed independence and confidence since Maggs was no longer so accessible, though contentment would probably always be relative with Leah. *The change has been good for Leah*, Maggs thought. And she could see a difference in Melody and Jason. Leah's more relaxed approach to her life was reflected in the behavior of the children. Maggs was overjoyed to have the time with them. In such a few short years Jason would leave babyhood behind, and Melody would become a young lady.

Mike called often. He hadn't been able to visit because he was working as a law clerk, but he promised to bring his family for Christmas. Meredith wrote that Stephen and Mike tried to play golf at least once a month and had been to several football games together. They were seriously trying to strengthen the tenuous bond they had established.

Greg had found the divorce hard to understand at first, but Maggs answered his questions without evasion when he called. His hoped-for visit in the fall hadn't materialized, but he promised to come for Christmas. He asked to bring a girl he had met. Maggs was delighted. Greg must be more than casually interested in the girl; he wouldn't bring someone home for the holidays unless she was special. It should be a wonderful Christmas.

By late fall it appeared that Stephen's anger and bitterness was beginning to dissipate. In the beginning, when he called, always for a specific reason, his manner ranged from cool to hostile. Maggs had learned, at first from the children and eventually from Stephen himself, that his business was doing well. It still consumed most of his time. As time passed, he began to call sometimes just to chat, and when Maggs called to congratulate him on his grand opening, he sounded glad to hear from her. He seemed interested in what she was doing in a friendly, nonproprietary way.

Maggs was mildly unsettled (she admitted grudgingly—and only to herself) that he had seemingly adapted to her absence so quickly and so well, but she was mostly relieved. He still maintained their circle of friends and occasionally told her of their doings; but it was like hearing about someone from another era, and though she made appropriate responses, with a very few exceptions, she wasn't at all interested.

In late October, Sassie told Maggs that Stephen was seeing Angela Montgomery. She had recently gotten a divorce, and in the course of being supportive, Stephen had asked her out. He eventually mentioned to Maggs, in an offhand way, that he was seeing Angela occasionally. It felt strange to think of Stephen with someone else; but Maggs took it in stride, aware that he had to start sometime, and she had always liked Angela. She was glad Stephen had found someone to spend time with.

Terry Matthews was Stephen's partner in a business sense only. She had never really been an issue, merely a willing convenience. Maggs had understood that on some level all along. Someone as predatory as Terry Matthews wouldn't hold Stephen's interest for long. Fortunately, Terry was worldly enough not to allow his lack of romantic interest to interfere with their working relationship.

So on this particularly heady late fall afternoon, Maggs felt herself truly fortunate. She was working on her novel, and it was going well. In much the same way as when she had first begun, the words spilled forth prolifically. There remained at most two or three chapters before her story would be finished.

She had overcome her insecurity and submitted the unfinished manuscript to an editor whose name Christopher had given her. The editor had called to say he was definitely interested in working with her when the novel was finished. She had expected rejection, and when it turned out otherwise, she was shocked and disbelieving. Her success might be limited or even short-lived, but getting published seemed almost a certainty. After all her doubts, the editor's favorable reaction was gratifying. Her joy was only slightly diminished because she couldn't share it with Christopher.

As she worked, she could hear Molly bustling around in the kitchen below. When she occasionally looked out the window of her bedroom, she could see Tom getting the flowerbeds ready for the coming cold weather. The days were cool now, and the open balcony doors let in breezes laden with the fragrances of drying leaves and haystacks and late fall roses. A mother blue jay squawked as she fed the last of her fledglings that would soon be left to survive the impending winter on their own.

Maggs looked around the room and experienced a feeling of real satisfaction. She hadn't changed much, just added a few paintings and some personal belongings. She had made a place in the library for the little rosewood desk, sometimes working there when she didn't want to work in her room.

In fact, she had changed little in the entire house. She decided Myrtlewood should remain the way Aunt Eleanor had left it, but gradually Myrtlewood showed the effects of Maggs's unmistakable style.

She filled her days with long walks around the grounds and the woods. She visited the sandbar often. Sometimes she wrote whole chapters, and sometimes she just lay on the blanket and drowsed and dreamed. Her contentment was so complete that even the arrival of the final divorce decree didn't upset her. She was sad that her marriage was over but thankful that the divorce had gone through rapidly and without complications or disputes—as she had hoped it would. She was grateful for Stephen's cooperation.

Maggs had eased gradually back into the social life of the Ashley River community. Fall carnivals and hay rides and barbecues and dinner parties filled every weekend if she chose to be entertained.

She visited Uncle George often, sometimes staying for dinner. He never mentioned Christopher, and she didn't either though she thought of him often. Uncle George was showing signs of failing health, and Maggs dreaded the time when he would no longer be at Riverside. She was acutely aware that a treasured part of her life and a valued member of the community would be lost when George Huntingdon died.

Meredith wrote and invited Maggs to spend her first solitary Thanksgiving with them in Tuscaloosa, and on the same day Maggs received the letter, Stephen telephoned.

"Maggs, I've got a proposition for you. Sassie and Leah came up with this idea, and I think it's a good one. How would you feel about having Thanksgiving here, with all the family? An old-fashioned Thanksgiving with turkey and dressing and all the trimmings. I'll have the club prepare our dinner, and you won't even have to cook. I know Mike and Meredith have invited you to their house for Thanksgiving, but Mike said if you could be persuaded to come to Mobile instead, it would suit them. Rather than having the family scattered, we'll all be together. No strings attached. I think we can manage a couple of days in the same house. How do you feel about it?"

He ended on a hesitant note, as if he had second thoughts as soon as the words were out of his mouth. Or maybe dreaded the answer he would get.

"I'd love for us all to be together for Thanksgiving. But I would really like to cook dinner. If Leah and Sassie will get the groceries, I'll do the cooking when I get there. It sounds like just what this family needs. I'll be looking forward to it."

When she hung up the telephone, she knew she had responded impulsively and wondered if she'd accepted too quickly. But she felt good about it, so it must be the right thing to do. No second-guessing anymore—she would go, and that was that.

After lunch she got the cart and went to Tom's garden to find the best pumpkins to put outside the front door. Halloween trick-or-treaters would be out tonight. She was going to a costume party at Riverside, but she had bought candy for Molly and Tom to dispense. As she struggled to get the pumpkins back to the house, she realized it was only seven weeks until Christmas. It didn't seem possible, but when she got back from Mobile, the holiday season would be in full swing. Thanksgiving in Mobile proved to be a gratifying experience. She and Stephen treasured every minute they spent with Jennifer and Jason and Melody. Their presence helped ease the initial tension between Maggs and Stephen. Everyone helped cook dinner, and though the kitchen was chaotic at times, the dinner that resulted was remarkably well put together.

When everyone was stuffed and the children were taking naps and the men were watching football games, Maggs declared her intention to walk off some of the calories she had just consumed.

"I'll go with you if you don't mind the company," Stephen said. "If you'd rather go alone, just say so."

"Of course not, don't be silly. Come on."

It wasn't cold yet, but there was a bite to the air that Maggs hadn't noticed in Charleston. She pulled her sweater closer. They walked companionably through the neighborhood that had been theirs for so many years. She enjoyed seeing it again but felt no regret about leaving it. Her neighborhood lay along a beautiful, peaceful river, and she was glad.

After a while, Stephen broke the silence. "Maggs, I'd like to tell you how much I appreciate your coming. I think it's been very healing for our children to see that we've put hard feelings behind us and that we can be friends. I didn't believe that would be possible when you left. But I've wanted to tell you for some time that it's okay, and that I hope things work out for you. I know they will for me. I'm not sure just how yet, but I'm confident that they will. Happy Thanksgiving, Maggs."

She looked into the face that was still so dear and leaned into his embrace naturally and unselfconsciously. They stood with their arms around each other, filled with an abiding love and joy that they had overcome the obstacles and reached a place where there was goodwill and where bitterness had no part.

"Happy Thanksgiving, Stephen."

They finished their walk hand in hand, and when they came inside, everyone had recovered enough for dessert. The women had their dessert around the kitchen table with the children, and the men took theirs back into the den for more football games. It felt right to be part of this again.

Maggs left Mobile with a happy glow. This time it wasn't an unhappy leave-taking. The weekend had proved that they could remain close as long as family unity was important enough to make the effort.

Chapter 24

Maggs returned to Myrtlewood to find Molly in the midst of the baking and cooking and freezing that preceded a traditional Southern Christmas. Maggs shelled pecans and stirred batter, grated coconut, and soaked cheesecloth-wrapped fruitcakes with rum. The atmosphere was festive, and Maggs's mood was too.

The round of parties and dinners had already begun. Hospitality on the Ashley River was lavish this time of year, and there was an invitation for every night. Maggs joined in the spirit of the community and planned a party at Myrtlewood for the night before Christmas Eve. After the success of the Thanksgiving weekend, she had decided to invite Stephen and all the children to Myrtlewood for Christmas, and they would all be there in time for her party. Molly and Maggs cooked for days in feverish preparation for her first big party at Myrtlewood. As the date of the party neared, Maggs hired extra help to do the heavy cleaning and get the grounds ready, over both Molly and Tom's vociferous objections.

Maggs and Tom and Molly went into the woods to cut holly and cedar boughs to drape over the windows and doors and railings. She and Molly spent hours making red velvet bows to adorn the greenery. Aunt Eleanor had always made her own and Maggs wanted to do the same. Tom scoured the woods and found what Maggs considered the most perfect tree in all South Carolina. A rare collection of Christmas decorations was brought down from the attic to decorate the tree. When they were finished, the towering tree stood centered in the foyer, the antique glass ornaments reflecting the glow of hundreds of tiny white lights. The effect was magical. When Tom dimmed the lights and they stood back to observe the final result, Maggs was enchanted. From the earliest Christmas she could remember, the first glimpse of Myrtlewood's Christmas tree was a great thrill. Now it was up to her to carry on the tradition.

Molly clapped her hands and said, "Ms. Eleanor never had a finer tree, for sure, darlin'. I just know she's looking down at this one with pride and love."

It was close to midnight when they made the last adjustment to the tree and declared it finished. Maggs dragged herself wearily up the stairs and forced herself to give her hair it's nightly brushing.

Finally everything was done. She had shopped and wrapped, and baked and decorated, and she was exhausted. She was still sleeping soundly when Molly came bustling into her room and shook her awake. "You've got to get up, Ms. Maggs. Mr. Stephen and Ms. Sassie will be arriving at the airport in two hours, and you wanted to meet their plane. Your coffee is on the table in front of the fire. Come on, now, and get up."

"All right, all right. I'm awake, Molly. Ask Tom to bring the car around in an hour."

She turned back the covers and left the warm refuge of her bed reluctantly. She poured a cup of coffee and buttered a muffin and sat down in front of the fire for just a minute. The fire felt delicious to her bare toes. It was a brilliant, sunshiny morning, cold and clear; and she was filled with anticipation.

Leah and her family would arrive tonight. Maggs would be at Uncle George's Christmas party, but Tom would meet them at the airport, and Molly would get them settled. Maggs would see them first thing in the morning.

Mike and Meredith and Jennifer were due sometime the next morning. Stephen had offered to pay for plane tickets, but Mike had insisted on driving. Maggs was proud of Mike for wanting to manage on his own and glad Stephen hadn't insisted on paying their way. She remembered how independent Stephen had been in the early days of their marriage, and evidently he remembered too. Greg's flight was due at noon tomorrow. Then everyone would be here.

Tonight she would take Sassie and Stephen to Uncle George's Christmas gala. Tomorrow night she would be able to show off her entire family at her own party. The whole community would be there.

At the airport, Stephen and Sassie hugged Maggs happily, and as Tom loaded their luggage into the trunk, the weekend looked to be off to a promising start. Maggs made sure that Stephen and Sassie were settled into their rooms and then forced herself to rest, too keyed up to relax, but knowing she would be exhausted by the next few days, no matter how enjoyable they would be.

When she was ready, she came downstairs to the library. A flash in Stephen's eyes confirmed his approval of the deep green velvet gown that hugged Maggs's tall, slender form. To emphasize the old-fashioned look of the dress, Maggs had put her hair up, leaving a few tendrils framing her face. The cut of the dress needed no adornment, and her only jewelry was an emerald bracelet and earrings that had belonged to Aunt Eleanor.

Maggs felt positively euphoric. Myrtlewood was beautifully decorated, and she was proud of its appearance. She was also well pleased with her own appearance, knowing she looked good in that instinctive way all attractive women do when they are dressed for a special occasion. That assurance lent her an extra sparkle. Her family was reassembled—or almost, anyway. Everything was perfect.

Sassie was standing beside her father in front of the fire. Her red-sequined silhouette emphasized the curves of her voluptuous figure and made a striking contrast to the deep green of Maggs's dress. Stephen, handsome in his dinner jacket, poured a glass of sherry for each of them. Molly brought their wraps, and then they were off to the evening's festivities.

At Riverside, Uncle George's butler opened the door, and as a strong gust of wind ushered them through the door, Maggs turned around and looked directly into the startled eyes of Christopher

Allendale, who stood beside his uncle welcoming the evening's guests.

Totally unprepared for his presence, Maggs felt the color drain from her face. It felt as if someone had knocked the breath out of her, and she was at a complete loss about what to do next. Her face seemed frozen into some semblance of a smile, but she couldn't speak. She seemed unable to move any farther into the foyer.

George Huntingdon sized the situation up instantly, and moved swiftly to alleviate any awkwardness. He took Maggs's arm and said, "Maggs, you remember Christopher, I believe. He decided to surprise me by making an unexpected visit, just in time for my party. Truly a treat to warm an old man's heart. And, I must say, you are another one. You look ravishing, my dear, as always. I'm glad you could come to my party."

He kissed her cheek, pulled her gently but firmly into the room, and extended his hand to Stephen. "Welcome to Riverside, Stephen. It's been quite a while since we've met." Turning to Sassie, he said, "Don't tell me this enchanting young lady is the same person who visited me during the summer in a ponytail and blue jeans. Is this really you, Sassie? Come in, come in, child, the evening has turned quite cold. There's wassail in the dining room, or champagne, if you prefer it, and there's a fire in the library. Please make yourselves at home."

As he spoke, Uncle George kept his arm firmly around Maggs's shoulders, his flawless manners and his tactful control giving Maggs time to regain her equilibrium. As he directed them to the dining room, it remained only to speak to Christopher.

Christopher stood slightly behind his uncle, a glass of champagne in his hand. Only his eyes betrayed the depth of his emotions.

"Hello, Maggs, how nice to see you again. Sassie, you look absolutely smashing."

He extended his hand to Maggs, gave Sassie a quick hug and then turned to Stephen. "This must be your husband. I'm glad to meet you, Stephen. I'm sorry we didn't get a chance to meet during the summer. I had hoped we might. Maggs was a welcome addition to our small community."

He released Stephen's hand and turned to Maggs. "I've only just returned. A quick trip, more or less. I hadn't realized your family would be at Myrtlewood for the holidays, Maggs. How long will you stay?"

Maggs, still overwhelmed by Christopher's unexpected presence, opened her mouth to answer him, managing only to get out, "Well, actually, . . ." when they were interrupted by Uncle George.

"Christopher, may I interrupt you a moment. There's someone here who would like to say hello to you."

Christopher inclined his head, excused himself, and turned to the next guest.

Maggs took Stephen's arm and said, in a voice that sounded unnatural to her ears, "Uncle George's Wassail is one of the most looked-forward-to parts of the holidays around here. Let's go try it out."

Sassie was whisked away to dance, and Maggs and Stephen followed the flow of guests to the dining room. A maid was serving the Wassail in silver cups from a huge silver bowl surrounded by a wreath of holly and ivy. As Maggs took a cup, she was mortified to see that her hand shook. She knew Stephen noticed, but his only comment was something about the beauty of Riverside. She took a deep drink of the Wassail and felt it warm her as it went down. She took another, hoping it would calm her inner shaking; and when she had finished, she returned her cup for another refill. The strong ale was helping, but not nearly enough. Stephen led her firmly into the library before she could extend her cup again.

They were quickly surrounded by friends who greeted her fondly while clamoring to meet Stephen. These descendants of many generations born and bred in this beautiful part of the South were a gracious group of people; and though many may have wondered about Stephen's presence here tonight, they welcomed him sincerely and displayed no obvious curiosity.

For her part, Maggs was still unnerved, trying desperately to regain a semblance of calmness while pretending to concentrate on Mrs. Gilden's recitation of her latest medical crisis. As Mrs. Gilden's voice droned on, Maggs was struck by a sudden lightning-bolt realization. *Christopher was the only person here who didn't know she and Stephen were divorced!* And this wasn't the time or the place to tell him. What incredibly dreadful timing!

Riverside's Christmas celebration was always a seated dinner; and while Mrs. Gilden, who had been a close friend of Aunt Eleanor, was still relating the details of her traumatic recovery, a bell called for their attention. Uncle George stood in the center of the foyer. "As we go in to dinner, I want to take just a moment to welcome each of you. It's wonderful to have you here again. I hope you will enjoy the evening."

Stephen helped her find her place at the table. She was seated at Uncle George's right; and to her dismay, she discovered that Christopher and Stephen had been placed almost directly across from each other, farther down the table. Sassie was seated between two handsome young men at another table.

As one course followed another, Maggs managed to keep up a light exchange with her dinner partners, all the while keeping an uneasy eye on Christopher and Stephen. She could see that they were engaged in conversation and could only speculate nervously about what they were discussing. She couldn't remember being at table so long in her entire life. Finally, Uncle George announced brandy in the library for the gentlemen and cordials in the parlor for the ladies.

Later there was dancing, and although Maggs could see Christopher on the dance floor, he never approached her. Stephen seemed to be having a good time, charming her friends with his flawless manners and the casual flirtation that was a time-honored social accomplishment in their circle. Sassie rarely completed a dance with just one partner.

Maggs was barely aware of whom she danced with or what was said. She danced with Stephen several times, and he offered to take her home whenever she was ready. She knew he was being considerate of her discomfort, but she refused, dreading his questions, and knowing an early departure would be noticed by everyone. She would see the evening through to its conclusion.

At two o'clock, Uncle George toasted the musicians, and announced the last dance. Maggs turned around, expecting to find Stephen behind her, and instead found herself in Christopher's arms. As the waltz began and she felt Christopher's arms tighten around her, it seemed as if she was dancing on clouds which swept her higher and higher into a sky filled with twinkling stars, a sky which would hold her a willing captive forever. She could have sworn her feet were no longer on the floor, that she was no longer earthbound. She closed her eyes, not wanting to spoil the feeling by saying anything and not knowing what to say, anyway.

Christopher held her close. They danced in silence, as though he, too, wanted to suspend reality for as long as possible. She never wanted this dance to end. She wanted to talk to him, but that wasn't possible. Much too soon the music stopped, and Maggs found herself unwillingly returned to the dance floor.

As the music faded Christopher broke the spell, saying so softly that only she could hear, "Maggs, I want you to know I'm happy that your decision to return to Stephen has turned out well. I like him very much. I've made myself stay away all evening, but I had to hold you just once more. I'm returning to Maine tomorrow. I'll feel better knowing you're happy. Merry Christmas, Maggs."

Maggs opened her mouth to say she wanted to talk to him before he left and was interrupted before she could speak by the applause of the dancers and the scramble for wraps as everyone began making their way to the foyer to thank their host. Christopher dropped his arms, bowed slightly, looked intently into her eyes, and then turned and made his way through the crowd.

Maggs stood where he left her, looking after him helplessly. Stephen approached with Sassie in tow, their wraps over his arm. He took Maggs's elbow and steered her wordlessly through the foyer.

"Are you all right?" Uncle George whispered in her ear as she hugged him good night. She nodded woodenly.

She waited numbly while Stephen thanked Uncle George and ushered them outside, where Tom waited patiently. The cold night air hit Maggs with a jolt, but it was no colder than the band of ice that encircled her heart. Sassie and Stephen compared impressions about the evening on the drive home; but Maggs remained silent, huddled desolately inside her fur coat, thankful that Stephen was diverting Sassie's attention.

When they were finally back at Myrtlewood, Sassie looked at Maggs's drawn face, kissed her quickly, and said, "'Night, Mom, Dad. It was a lovely party. I'll be up early tomorrow to help you get ready for yours, Mom."

She ran upstairs, leaving Maggs and Stephen facing each other in the foyer.

"He's the one, isn't he, Maggs? Christopher, I mean. The man you fell in love with while you were here?" His face was serious but not accusing or angry.

She couldn't speak, but she nodded, her eyes filling with tears. She dropped her head, and the tears spilled down her face and onto the marble floor.

Stephen gently tipped her chin up so he could see her face. "He doesn't know, does he? That we're no longer married?"

She shook her head, still not able to say anything, the tears threatening to engulf her if she opened her mouth to speak.

"Call him, Maggs. Call him right now. If you care for him, you have to tell him. You should have already let him know, don't you know that?"

Still she stood, unmoving, silent, stricken. Finally she whispered, "I'll tell him in the morning. I can't talk to him tonight. I can barely talk to you."

Stephen pushed the hair back from her face and said, "You know, Maggs, I'll always love you, and I'm very happy to be sharing this Christmas with you. But I know our life together is over. I've accepted it and started rebuilding mine. And I think you know I wish you nothing but happiness in yours. I appreciate that you kept Christopher separate from the dissolution of our marriage, just as you said you would. But I think it's time for you to let him know we didn't make it."

Calmer now, she stepped back and said, "I'll always love you too, you know, and I'll always care what happens to you. Always. You are a truly good man, Stephen, and I've always known that about you. I'm awfully glad you're here tonight."

She slipped off her shoes, taking his arm to steady herself. "Now, I think this day has lasted just about as long as I can possibly stand, and I think we had better get to bed. I've got a lot to do before tomorrow evening."

She stood on her tiptoes and kissed him softly on the mouth. "Good night, Stephen. And thanks. For everything. You really are a prince, and I hope you find someone who deserves you."

He watched her thoughtfully as she climbed the stairs, her shoes in her hand. "Good night, light of my life," he said softly before climbing the stairs to his own bedroom.

Chapter 25

Maggs spent a restless night. She was up well before the sun issued its first frosty rays. Too early to call Christopher, she went to the kitchen and made a pot of coffee. For once, she beat Molly to it. But not by much. Molly came through the back door and found Maggs sitting at the kitchen table, chin in hand, running her index finger around the rim of the cup.

"What's the matter, Ms. Maggs? You couldn't sleep? I figured you'd sleep late this morning, considering the time you came home."

She took in Maggs's expression with a worried look. "Has something happened about Mr. Greg's flight?"

"No, Molly, it's nothing like that. Everything is fine, really. It's just that I ran into Christopher at Uncle George's party last night, and I didn't know he was in town. Evidently he came in unexpectedly. He doesn't know Stephen and I are divorced, and there was no chance to tell him last night."

Her eyes filled with tears. "He saw Stephen with me and assumed we are together. He wished me luck and said he was happy for me. We got interrupted before I could explain. I'm just waiting until it's late enough to call him."

Molly poured herself a cup of coffee, refilled Maggs's cup, and sat down at the table. She squeezed Maggs's hand encouragingly. Words wouldn't help now, and she wisely kept silent.

"I just took for granted that Uncle George would have told him. I can't understand why he didn't," Maggs said.

"Perhaps he understood how upset Mr. Chris was when he left and thought that if it was over, it was probably for the best. No need to add fuel to the ashes. Besides, you know Mr. George is a gentleman of the old school and not one to engage in gossip."

"I guess you're right, Molly. It just shocked me so badly to walk through the door and see Christopher standing there that I'm afraid I acted a total idiot. You would have thought I was seventeen years old. I couldn't even talk. Besides being so overwhelmed, I was extremely embarrassed. For myself, and for Stephen and Sassie too. If it hadn't been for Uncle George recognizing my distress, my behavior would be the main topic of discussion at breakfast tables up and down the Ashley River this morning. I'm really upset with myself over the way I handled the whole situation. Or rather, didn't handle it."

"Now, now, darlin', you know things always look worse from your point of view than from someone else's. Was Mr. Stephen upset?"

"He was a rock! He stayed beside me the entire evening, except at dinner. He was seated across from Christopher, and they made a favorable impression on each other, I think. Stephen knows that Christopher doesn't know we're divorced."

Maggs rose and started to the sink, turned and started to the kitchen door, stopped again, and stood in the middle of the floor. Finally she just sat back down at the table in defeat.

"I've got so much to do today that I don't know where to start. Mike's family is coming in this morning, and Greg has to be picked up at the airport at noon. I've got some last-minute wrapping to do. My dress has to be picked up. And I haven't seen Leah and the kids yet . . ."

"Did they get here okay, was their plane on time?"

"Yes, dear. They got here in good order, just tired. They'll probably all be down for breakfast by the time you're dressed."

"I can't decide what to do first. I'm in such a quandary about whether to try to get this misunderstanding straightened out with Christopher this morning or wait until after Christmas when everyone has gone back home and I can think clearly again. The problem is, Christopher is leaving today. I don't know what to do, Molly. This couldn't have happened at a worse time. I was looking forward to seeing Christopher again after I got my life reorganized, but I certainly didn't expect it to be under these circumstances."

Molly watched her quietly until she was finished. "You're fairly spinning in the middle of this floor, Ms. Maggs. Why don't you give Mr. Chris a call, tell him about you and Mr. Stephen and that you want to talk to him after the holidays, and then go on with these plans you've spent so much time and effort on? Seems to me that would be the sensible way to go about it. You're too distracted to straighten this out right now anyway. And if you and Mr. Chris are meant to be together, then that will surely happen. This isn't necessarily the end of anything. As with most things in life, darlin', time sorts a lot of it out."

Maggs considered what Molly said. It made more sense than any of the solutions she had come up with since last night. She felt like she was drowning and Molly's advice was a lifeline. She grabbed as hard as she could.

"You're right, of course. First I'm going to get ready for the day. It's going to be a long one. Then I'll call Christopher. You're a gem, Molly. As usual, I don't know what I'd do without you!" Maggs rose and took her cup to the sink.

Molly rose too and smiled fondly at Maggs. "Well, that settles it then. As for me, I've got to get breakfast started. I'm sure this crowd will be starving when they all get downstairs.

Upstairs, Maggs showered and dressed in dark green corduroy slacks and a long-sleeved, green and white striped shirt. She pulled a matching sweater over her head and took the telephone out to the balcony.

The sun was fully up now. The day was going to be another glorious gift of the Carolina low country, and though it was crisp and cold, the shelter of the balcony gave her the benefit of the sunshine without the bluster of the wind.

She dialed the number and listened while the phone rang repeatedly. When she was about to hang up, Uncle George answered, out of breath.

"Uncle George, this is Maggs. Did I catch you at a bad time? Where is Andrew?"

"Hello, my dear. How nice to hear your voice. Andrew has taken Christopher to the airport, and I've given everyone else the day off. And, to answer your question, no, you haven't caught me at a bad time at all. What can I do for you?" he asked.

Maggs couldn't keep the dismay out of her voice. "I wanted to speak to Christopher before he left. I thought I would catch him. I didn't know he was leaving so early. I wanted to explain about last night. Uncle George, Christopher doesn't know Stephen and I are divorced. He misunderstood when he saw us together last night. I wanted to tell him, and I didn't get the chance."

She could hear her words coming faster as she talked. She forced herself to slow down and said, calmly, "Please forgive me, Uncle George. I seem to have botched this all the way around, but I certainly didn't mean to bring you into it."

He didn't reply.

In an attempt to relieve the awkwardness, she changed the subject. Trying for a cheerful note, she said, "The rest of my family will get here today, and my grandchildren will be at the party tonight, for the early part of the evening, at least. I can't wait for you to see them. I really must run now, Uncle George, I have a million things to do. I'm sorry I burdened you with this. I'll make it up to you tonight."

"Maggs. Listen to me. There is no need for apology. I'm terribly sorry about what happened last night. I feel it is I who owe an apology for letting you walk in cold to find Christopher at Riverside, but I didn't know he was planning to surprise me by attending my party. His arrival coincided with the rest of the guests.

"I'm not unaware of the situation that developed between you and Christopher during the summer, and I'm not unaware that you were both deeply hurt when it ended. What I'm not aware of is under what terms you parted and what, if any, plans you had for the future. Christopher is a very private man, and he didn't discuss any of this with me, as you have not. So you see, my dear, I'm not in a very informed position from which to counsel either of you."

He continued, "I believe he intended to stay longer but changed his plans when he discovered you were at Myrtlewood. He excused himself by saying that he had some pressing business. He apparently arranged for Andrew to take him into town early this morning, and when I came down to breakfast this morning, they were already gone. I had no chance to tell Christopher that your circumstances are not what he assumed when he saw you and Stephen together last night.

"I'm very sorry, my dear. But perhaps it's better this way. It might be wise for both of you to take more time to sort your feelings out. Forgive me if I'm presuming on our friendship, but I have long felt about you as the daughter I would have chosen for my own, and I know I can speak frankly. You and Christopher are both honorable people. Perhaps a little more time will guarantee that no one ever questions that."

He paused and then said kindly, "Take an old man's advice and give it some time."

Maggs was touched by his concern, and his obvious affection helped assuage the disappointment she was suffering over Christopher's abrupt departure.

"Thank you, Uncle George. I'll take that advice. You're as wise as you are dear to me, and your good opinion is something I treasure more than I can tell you. I'll concentrate on my family and this party tonight, and the rest will take care of itself. I'll be much more in control tonight, I promise you. Just one more thing. I want to thank you for coming to my rescue last night. I don't believe anyone other than you and Stephen knew how incapacitated I was for a few moments, and your tactful intervention saved me great embarrassment. I'll look forward to seeing you tonight, dear Uncle George."

Replacing the receiver in its cradle, she took the phone back into her room, checked her appearance in the mirror, reapplied her lipstick, and went downstairs to start this day she had put so much into.

Molly had already started cooking, and much of tonight's feast was in the oven along with several of the dishes they would have for Christmas dinner. A fat country ham, glazed with pineapple and cherries, it's skin still sizzling and crackling from the heat of the oven, had been placed on a table to cool; and the Christmas goose was in the oven adding its fragrance to the other wonderful smells.

Sassie was all over the kitchen, poking her fingers into everything Molly was cooking while Molly was trying to get her to sit down and eat breakfast. Melody was at the kitchen table eating fresh-baked cinnamon rolls. Stephen sat beside her, a heaping plate of scrambled eggs, grits, country-sliced bacon, and biscuits in front of him. He was putting pear preserves on a biscuit dripping with butter and looked sheepish when Maggs raised her eyebrows questioningly. He grinned and shrugged his shoulders.

"You can't fight Molly when she's determined to feed you, Maggs. You should know that as well as anyone."

Maggs laughed as she gave Jason a quick kiss on the top of his curly head. He was sitting in a high chair that Leah had sat in at this same table when she was a baby. Stephen was tempting him with everything on the table—unsuccessfully because Jason was fascinated by the nonstop activity in the busy kitchen and wasn't interested in eating. His eyes lit up when he saw Maggs, and he raised his arms for her to take him from the highchair. She lifted him out and hugged him hard, stood him on the floor, and went around the table to kiss Melody's sticky face.

As she pulled up a chair beside Melody, Leah and Matt came through the back door. Their cheeks were red from the cold air, but their eyes were shining and they were holding hands. Matt shrugged out of his jacket and helped Leah with hers. He hung them on the coat rack beside the back door.

"Is anyone going into town this morning?" he asked. "I need to do a last-minute errand."

Leah looked at him inquiringly as she walked around the table to hug Maggs, but he smiled enigmatically and ignored her.

"Tom is going to the airport to pick up Greg," Molly said. "I'm sure you can persuade him to take you into town on the way. He has a couple of stops to make for Ms. Maggs, so I'm sure he won't mind. Come along, you two, these biscuits won't stay hot forever. Eat hearty. I won't be having time to feed you after this. You're on your own until the party.

"You too, Ms. Maggs. Time's a'wasting," she said, a question in her eyes. Maggs shook her head slightly and sat down at the table. She sipped her coffee and kept Stephen company while he ate his breakfast. Even Sassie, who normally ate like a bird, finally sat down at the table, cleaned her plate, and had a second biscuit.

When Stephen had finished his last cup of coffee, he pushed his chair out and said, "I feel like a little exercise. How about a quick walk, Maggs, before the last-minute details swamp you? It'll clear your head."

She knew he wanted to be sure she was okay, but she didn't need consolation just now; she really needed time. But the concern he had showed last night at least deserved her reassurance this morning.

"Okay, but just for a few minutes," she agreed. "Then I've really got to get busy."

"Don't know how you're going to get through all you have to do this day without anything to keep you goin' but a cup of coffee," Molly was mumbling under her breath.

Stephen wisely ignored Molly and got their jackets. Once outside, Maggs realized the sheltered warmth of her balcony had been deceptive. It was very cold, with a strong east wind that was constant and biting. The sunshine was brilliant though, and as they walked the path that Maggs had come to know so well, the rich verdant odor of frost on fallen leaves and the cold winter smell of the river reminded her of what was really important.

"Did you talk to Christopher this morning, Maggs?" Stephen asked immediately when they were far enough into the woods to shelter them from the whistling wind.

"No, I missed him. He took an early flight home. But it's okay, Stephen. I've made plans for the holidays that are important to me. This misunderstanding can get worked out in its own time. I'm fine with the delay, really. In fact, I wouldn't have it any other way.

"I appreciate your encouragement, Stephen. But I realized this morning that I don't have to rush anything. What I've enjoyed most about my new life is the fact that I don't have to rush and I don't have to please anyone but myself. That's what I took such a chance for, and I'd be a fool to go back to the way I was before. For anyone or anything. I just temporarily forgot that last night. I won't lose sight of it again.

"I want this to be the best Christmas this family has ever had. I want it to be a time to enjoy each other—a time to accept each other as we are. That's what I hoped these few days would accomplish, and that's what I'm going to focus on now. Speaking of which, I really need to get started."

"Good for you, Maggs. Everything will work out for the best. You told me that once, and I didn't believe you. You may not believe me right now either, but I know I'm right."

He put his arm around her waist, and they turned toward the house.

"Are you going with Tom to meet Greg's plane?"

"Yes," he said. "I thought I might as well. I'll just be in the way around here, and I can see it's going to be a long day trying to dodge you and Molly both. I think I'll be much safer at a distance. I may stop off in Charleston with Matt. I have a few last minute things to do myself."

When they came into the back hall, they heard Molly's excited voice.

"Welcome home, Mr. Mike, Ms. Meredith. Jennifer, you pretty child, come give me a hug. Ms. Maggs and Mr. Stephen have gone for a walk, but they'll be back shortly. I've kept the biscuits warm. Come have some coffee while I scramble you some eggs. Mr. Mike, I remember how much you liked my breakfasts when you were a little fella. Tom will take your bags upstairs later."

"I'll get the bags, Molly," Mike said. "Just give Meredith and Jennifer something warm to drink. The heater went out on our car halfway here, and they're chilled to the bone." He turned to go back outside as Maggs and Stephen came into the kitchen.

"What's this about a broken heater?" Stephen asked, giving Mike a bear hug.

"Just a broken hose, I think, Dad. I thought we could take a look at it after awhile. I don't think it's anything complicated."

"Sure thing, son. Tom might even have a hose in the garage. If not, we can pick one up on our way into town. Come on in and get some breakfast, and you can ride into town with us to pick up Greg while Meredith and Jennifer unpack. Your mom's busier than a stage director with hives this morning, but as soon as Greg gets here, all her chicks will be back in the nest and maybe she'll settle down."

Stephen winked at Mike and put an arm around his shoulders. He tried to put the other arm around Maggs, but she ducked away, laughing as she hugged Mike and kissed Jennifer and Meredith. Jennifer had a big mug of hot chocolate and Molly was pouring coffee for Meredith and Mike. In short order, Molly had food on their plates, Sassie and Leah had rushed in with hugs and kisses, and Jason and Melody waited impatiently for Jennifer to finish eating.

Maggs stood in the doorway and watched them, her heart full as she saw how happy they were. She was right—this was what was important. For now, it was all she needed.

After everyone had scattered in separate directions, Maggs inspected the table for tonight's buffet and took care of some last-minute arrangements. She was in high spirits, and the day flew by. Everything was ready for tonight. Everyone would be here. And everything would be fine.

When she heard the car pull up in front of the house, she came downstairs eagerly to meet Greg and his guest. He crossed the foyer swiftly, lifted her off the floor, and swung her around in a circle. "Greg, you're making me dizzy," she laughed. "Put me down so I can look at you."

He put her down, keeping an arm around her. She looked at him closely, taking in every detail of his appearance. Greg was the only one of her children who had her coloring. Taller even than his father, and more muscular, his blonde hair was short and his deeply tanned skin made his eyes look very blue. He looked happy and fit.

The striking young woman at his side watching the animated reunion was obviously pleased to be with him. Prominent cheekbones and dark eyes hinted of Indian blood in a not-too-distant heritage. Shiny thick hair curved around her shoulders in a dark cascade. She held her head proudly while her eyes smiled an invitation to be inspected and accepted by Greg's family. Maggs was struck by the quiet composure and the openness with which the young woman met their inquiring faces.

Greg said, "Mom, this is Raven Whitecloud. She's a first-year geologist on our project and one of the brightest we've got. She's a native of Oklahoma, and this is her first trip to the South. Mom, Dad, I've asked Raven to marry me, and she's accepted. We plan to be married next spring unless you all act so crazy while she's here that you scare her away."

Greg laughed as everyone crowded around to congratulate them and look at Raven's engagement ring. He hugged Maggs again. "It's so good to see you, Mom. I've missed you so much. I've missed everybody. As much as I love Oklahoma, it's not home. I've discovered that the South doesn't just get in your blood, it *is* your blood. Raven and I have both been offered a job working off the coast of Louisiana starting next spring, and we're considering it. It would be great for me, but it's a long way from home for Raven."

He lowered his voice. "I hope you'll like her, Mom. She's a very special person. And she's a lot of fun, once she gets to know you."

"If you love her, I know we will love her too, darling. I'm so happy you're both here. It's been so long since I've seen you. This is going to be the best Christmas we've ever had."

They stood with their arms around each other while his siblings vied for Raven's attention. When their excitement subsided, Maggs walked over and embraced her.

"Welcome to our family, Raven, and welcome to Myrtlewood. We're glad you're here. We're a big family, but there's always room for one more, and we're happy you've agreed to become part of it. Your engagement will make our Christmas even more special."

Raven seemed grateful for Maggs's acceptance. With Maggs's arm around her waist, she faced them and said, "I'm very glad to meet you all. Greg has told me so much about you, and I know how much he misses you. It seems he didn't exaggerate about his family. I'm happy to be sharing the holidays with you." Her voice was musical and very beautiful, and she spoke with dignity and confidence. She wouldn't be easily intimidated, Maggs thought.

Maggs squeezed her shoulder. "Well, you just make yourself comfortable, and let us take care of you. Ask for what you want, and do exactly as you please. We're having a big Christmas party tonight. It will be a wonderful opportunity to announce your engagement, if you and Greg would like to do that. After this party is out of the way, you'll find we're pretty informal. We generally come and go as we please during the day, and those of us who are here gather for dinner around eight."

"Sassie, would you show Raven to her room? I'm sure she'd like to rest before it's time to get dressed. Greg, do you want to rest a while too?"

"No, Mom, I'm too excited to finally be here. I'll be down after I get Raven settled." He lifted the bags and followed Sassie upstairs. When he came back downstairs, Stephen said, "Come with me, son. I've got just the job to settle you down." He took Greg by the arm, beckoned to Mike and Matt, and they went out to the garage.

"Stephen, please don't get so involved that you forget the time. It's not long before time to get ready. Are you listening?" she called after them in exasperation, knowing her words would have no effect.

Leah and Meredith took the children upstairs for a nap, and Sassie went to make a telephone call. Maggs looked in on Molly to see if she needed any help before the maids and the bartender arrived and found everything progressing smoothly.

Upstairs, she closed the bedroom door behind her, relishing the quiet. She loved having everyone together, but she had forgotten how noisy it could get. She imagined Raven was grateful for a respite too. Maggs took a long bath and did her hair and makeup so she could relax a few minutes before getting dressed.

Her beautiful dress hung on the closet door. Cream-colored satin with a heavily beaded bodice that flared into a very full skirt scattered with tiny, intricately patterned crystals. The form-fitting bodice accentuated her full bust and small waist, and the scalloped neckline was provocative but not immodest. The dress made her feel like a princess, but she had made three trips to the dress shop to try it on before deciding to buy it. She finally justified the cost because of the special occasion.

Beaded satin slippers complimented the dress, and the ruby and diamond necklace and earrings that Stephen had given her on their twenty-fifth wedding anniversary would add the perfect finishing touch.

She poured a glass of sherry and curled up in the chair in front of the fire Molly had somehow found time to build while Maggs was in the shower. She had forgotten to take the rubies out of the safe and went to her desk to get the combination. When she lifted the notebook where the combination was recorded, a photograph fell to the floor. It was a picture of her and Christopher made by the attendant at the marina the day they had sailed the Mon Coeur around the island. An unbearable pain twisted inside her. She stared at the picture while the wind growled outside her balcony doors.

She gazed at their smiling image, arms around each other, obviously in love. They had been so happy. She unwisely allowed herself to remember that day—and the other blissful summer days before reality confronted them with choices that couldn't be avoided. Those few shining days seemed years ago.

She remembered the expression on Christopher's face last night when he saw her. He had been as astonished as she was to find themselves face-to-face. But he had handled the unexpected encounter far better than she had. She closed her eyes and saw him standing in the foyer, elegant in his dinner jacket, the champagne glass held carelessly in his hand. His beautiful eyes, so blue and deep, were shadowed with a secret regret only she could read.

Tears filled her eyes. She bit her lip to keep them from overflowing. She slid the picture under some papers in the desk drawer and closed it firmly. She went to her vanity and dabbed gently at her eyes.

To the image that looked back at her, she said, "You don't have time for emotional indulgences. Tonight is too important. Snap out of it." She turned from the mirror, slipped out of her dressing gown, and removed her dress from the padded hanger. She stepped into the gown and zipped it up. She dabbed her favorite scent behind her ears and between her breasts, lifted her head, and went out into the hallway, turning off the light and closing the door behind her.

She looked in on Sassie and Leah, who were helping each other with makeup and hairdos, laughing and giggling as they used to when they were children. She stopped next at Raven's door, tapping lightly.

"Do you need any help, dear? Can I get you anything?"

Raven opened the door and smiled shyly at her. Maggs found herself almost speechless at the beauty of the girl before her. She was wearing a floor-length sheath of buttery-colored material that gave the appearance of very soft leather. But it wasn't leather, at least not any leather Maggs had ever seen. It skimmed Raven's figure lightly, revealing the perfection of her body and accenting her unusual coloring. But Raven's bearing was more impressive than her dress.

Her only jewelry was a necklace and earrings of small turquoises separated by tiny silver beads. A silver clasp held her hair at the crown of her head before it fell in soft ringlets down her back. Maggs understood clearly why Greg was drawn to her quiet dignity.

"Do I look okay?" Raven asked with complete candor. "Greg didn't tell me I would need an evening gown, and this is all I brought with me. Will it be dressy enough?"

"Oh, my dear, you could have looked forever and not found anything more stunning. You will surely outshine us all tonight. I can't wait for everyone to see you."

Maggs kissed her on the cheek and said, "I'm going downstairs to check on a few last-minute details. You may join me if you wish. It's early yet, but our guys are probably having a drink in the library."

"I think I'll wait for Sassie and Leah and Meredith. They said they'd come get me when they started downstairs."

Maggs found Stephen and the boys in the library as she had expected. They gave admiring whistles when she entered, and she bowed her head to acknowledge their appreciation.

"Thank you for your compliments, but wait until you see the real star of the evening. She's going to knock your socks off." She laughed.

She went to the safe and removed the case that held the rubies. Stephen took them from her and fastened them around her neck. He kissed her shoulder and said, "You do them full justice, Maggs. I'm very pleased that you chose to wear them tonight. May I get you a martini?"

She squeezed his hand. "Yes, please. Let me check just once more to be sure Molly has everything under control, and I'll be right back. The girls should be down shortly."

Everything was in order in the dining room as well as the kitchen, where Molly was instructing the maids on their duties. She caught Maggs's eye and nodded her reassurance.

When Maggs returned to the library, the girls were surrounded by a circle of admiring males. Unaware of her presence, they reminded Maggs of jeweled Faberge eggs, each girl brilliant and perfect in her own right. Sassie had chosen a wine velvet gown with soft lines that didn't disguise her generous curves. Leah was lovely in midnight blue chiffon, and her eyes were brimming with happiness. Meredith wore an emerald green sequined sheath which emphasized her cool blonde beauty.

The children were beautiful too. Jennifer had on a floor-length green velvet dress with a hand-embroidered lace collar, and Jason and Melody wore matching outfits of red and green plaid. They brought tears of joy to Maggs's eyes.

"Come here, my darlings, and give me a big hug! You look fabulous! And I'm so happy you're here. You make me very proud." She knelt and gathered them to her, inhaling their wonderful fragrance, releasing them reluctantly when they began to wriggle in her embrace. As she stood up, she looked at her assembled family. "You all do," she said.

The doorbell rang, and the evening was under way. The entire county seemed to have turned out for her party. The house was filled with music and laughter and the clink of china and crystal. The air was full of the smell of delicious food and fresh evergreens and scented candles, stirred by an occasional gust of fresh air ushering someone in out of the cold night.

The children stayed downstairs until dinner was over, and then Molly took them to the nursery to get them ready for bed. Maggs went up later with Leah and Meredith to tuck them in and kiss them good night. They had added extra meaning to this special evening.

Stephen was an excellent host, ably assisted by Mike and Greg and Matt. The party flowed with the happy rhythm that occurs when good friends gather to celebrate. The food was wonderfully prepared and served, the music suited the occasion, and there seemed no room for improvement in any part of the evening.

In the cold starry hours of the early morning after everyone had gone home, Maggs stood with her family in the foyer. She was exhausted but exhilarated. She leaned over and removed her shoes and said, "I think Molly is brewing hot chocolate. Last one there has to lock up."

They raced toward the kitchen, laughing, stocking feet sliding. Molly was standing at the stove stirring the chocolate. The kitchen was already restored to order, and the extra help had gone home.

They sipped the hot chocolate and discussed the success of the evening. At last, weary and sleepy eyed, Maggs said, "I hate to be the wet blanket, but I'm running on what is just about my last drop of energy, and I'm going to have to call it a night, my dears. Thank you for making this such a wonderful evening. I'll see you all at breakfast. Don't stay up too much longer. Lots to do tomorrow to get ready for Santa."

"Wait, Maggs, I'll walk you upstairs," Stephen said. "I can't hold out any longer either. Good night, boys and girls. This old codger is hanging it up too."

He held Maggs's hand as they walked up the stairs together, opened her bedroom door, and kissed her softly. "Tonight was supremely well done, Maggs. I don't think I've ever admired your strength as much as I do right now. Now get some rest. See you tomorrow."

Maggs closed the bedroom door behind her and stepped out of the beautiful gown. She washed her face and put on her nightgown. Tired though she was, she sat down and brushed her hair. At last, it was over. The party had been weeks in the planning and preparation, but the hard work had paid off. She had established her undisputed position in this community, and she had done it admirably.

She crawled between the soft sheets of her bed, thankful that now she could relax and enjoy the rest of the holidays with her family.

Chapter 26

The rest of the holidays swept past in a blur of last-minute shopping and secrets and snips of wrapping paper and ribbon and making fudge with the children and roaring fires that burned brightly while the adults sat on the floor until way past midnight laughing and putting together toys that had uncountable pieces and parts and innumerable decals to be placed in just the right place and being so sleepy when the children clamored to go downstairs Christmas morning that it took great effort, not to mention the stimulus of many cups of coffee, just to get awake enough to pay attention.

And kisses and hugs and belly laughs and good food and long walks in the woods and fireworks New Year's Eve. And brothers and sisters reunited with enough love for each other, their parents, their partners, and their children. Especially their children.

And then a flurry of suitcases that needed more packed into them than they held when they arrived and cars packed to the brim and flight schedules, and promises to write and to call and to visit again soon. And more hugs, this time accompanied by tears.

Sassie and Stephen were the last to depart. Maggs and Stephen spent relaxing hours before the fire in the library and walking in the woods while Sassie was entertained by one local youth after another. Finally Stephen and Sassie were gone too.

Maggs's routine reverted to what it had been before the holidays: an early breakfast, a morning spent writing, lunch and a brief rest, dinner at home, or occasionally as someone's guest. If she didn't write after dinner, she usually retired early. She slept better than she had in years.

After the holidays, Maggs thought a lot about the encounter with Christopher, intending to call him as soon as things were back to normal. But an unexplained reluctance to actually pick up the phone had overtaken her, and she postponed making the call time after time. Eventually it was something she was no longer comfortable about doing at all. She didn't know why. Molly seemed to sense her reluctance but kept her own counsel.

Maggs was busy, her days were full and satisfying, and she finally came to the conclusion that perhaps that was enough. If she dreamed more frequently than she admitted about Christopher's strong arms and the sweet pressure of his mouth on hers, she told herself it signified nothing. She wasn't responsible for her subconscious, thank God.

As spring approached, Stephen called to tell her that he and Angeline Montgomery planned to marry in October. Maggs was genuinely happy for Stephen. She told herself that emphatically. And she really was. It was just that his impending marriage left her feeling a little bereft, a little disconnected somehow. Stephen had become such a good friend since they had resolved their differences.

Sassie called frequently. She was doing well in school and had her job lined up for the coming summer. Peace evidently ruled in Leah's home; Matt and the children were well and content. Mike was enthusiastic about finishing his first year of law school. The relationship between him and his father was developing slowly into what it should always have been, and he and Stephen had even made plans for a deep-sea fishing trip when school was out for the summer.

Greg wrote that he and Raven had accepted the job in Louisiana. They would be married in Oklahoma first and would send details as soon as they had set a date for the wedding.

The days grew a little longer and a little warmer, and nature's annual renewal was slowly but surely unfolding. The squirrels and rabbits and raccoons were nesting, and the birds were once again competing for territory with fierce and raucous screeching as they proclaimed and defended their chosen sites in rituals that had taken place since time began.

When the days warmed enough to permit it, Maggs and Molly set about spring cleaning, and Maggs threw open windows and doors to the fresh spring breezes for as long each day as the warmth prevailed. Maggs began to write in the gazebo or sit on the bench under the willow tree when the days were too perfect to spend indoors. As the Carolina spring unfolded, Maggs's spirit was exalted by the rebirth of all that surrounded her. On one such glorious morning, Maggs decided it was time to return to her sandbar. She stuffed her writing materials into her knapsack and went to the kitchen to make a lunch while Molly was out of sight. To no avail, because just as she was stuffing her sandwich into the knapsack, Molly came into the kitchen and realized what Maggs's preparations were for.

"Where are you going, might I ask?" was Molly's predictable response.

"I'm going to work at the sandbar today. And before you even get started objecting, I'll take a sweater, I'll watch for snakes, and I'll be careful. So don't get in a snit, Molly, please. I just can't bear to be inside when the weather is this perfect."

"All right, but if you come back with the sniffles, don't say I didn't warn you. It's not as mild out as you might be thinking. And you'll need more for lunch than just a sandwich. Let me fix you a proper lunch while you're getting ready to go."

"Molly, you're a saint, but you worry way too much. I have all I need. I'll change and be down in a few minutes."

Maggs dressed warmly and came downstairs with a spring in her step. She picked up her knapsack and the blanket she would sit on. Determined to have the last word, Molly called out as Maggs went down the back steps, "Now don't be staying out there until the afternoon chill sets in. You hear? And where's your hat?"

Maggs ignored the questions, striding rapidly to the path that led into the woods. The sun was shining, and though the breeze was brisk, the sun felt balmy on her face. She removed her sweater and tied it around her waist long before she reached the clearing.

The tall hardwood trees were putting on leaves, and the wild dogwoods were flowering. Sunlight dappled the clearing in a way that would not happen once the canopy overhead thickened. The first bees of the season buzzed around the wild berry vines while the tight buds of wild hydrangeas and honeysuckle vines were just making promises.

Everything smelled so good—fresh and earthy and new. Spring was unquestionably a reward for enduring the long winter months. She closed her eyes to better absorb the sounds and smells that filled the air. She spread her blanket and went to gather firewood. In no time, she had a respectable fire burning and a small supply of wood to keep it going. She got out her paper and pencils and sat down on the blanket.

The lush promise of a new season seemed to encourage an abundance of ideas as though part of the same cycle, and when she paused to look at her watch, it was past noon. She ate her sandwich while she continued to write. When she had finished eating and poured herself a second cup of coffee from the thermos, she scouted the edges of the clearing to replenish her stack of firewood. That done, she lay back on the blanket offering her face for the dappled kisses of the sun.

She dozed without meaning to, and almost immediately, she was dreaming of Christopher. He was standing over her, calling her. She wanted to go to him, but she was too drowsy. She smiled at him instead, and he called her more urgently. She had to make an effort to respond. She wanted to talk to him.

Struggling to break free of the lethargy that consumed her in the dream, she awoke with a start. As her eyes opened, she saw a tall form looming over her. There was no definition to it; it was just a very large, threatening shape between her and the sun. She was desperately frightened. The thought flashed through her mind that she should have listened to Molly. Anyone on the river could come ashore at this sandbar. She was alone and had nothing to protect herself with.

Fear paralyzed her. She couldn't utter a sound. She instinctively began to push herself backward, pulling with her hands and pushing with her legs. The towering form reached out for her. As she opened her mouth to scream, she recognized a voice. A voice she knew well, one which never failed to stir her heart.

"Maggs, it's me—Christopher," the voice said.

"Christopher!" she screamed in relief. "You frightened the daylights out of me. I've never been so terrified in my life!"

She was half-laughing and half-crying and reaching for him all at the same time. In an instant he knelt beside her, his arms gathering her close. She felt his heart beating steady and strong as he crushed her against him. It had all taken place in the matter of a few seconds, but it had seemed to happen in slow motion.

"Oh, my darling. I'm so sorry. God knows, I didn't mean to frighten you. I saw the smoke from the river and stopped to investigate. I couldn't believe it when it turned out to be you. Again. Asleep in this very spot where I found you that other time. I tried to call your name quietly so I wouldn't startle you, but I guess it didn't help. I'm so sorry," he repeated.

He was rocking her gently back and forth, holding her tightly. Maggs couldn't stop shaking. She was stunned at his unexpected appearance but so happy to have his arms around her. She felt as if nothing could ever threaten her again. She remained silent, and her heartbeat gradually slowed and the shaking subsided.

Christopher moved her gently away from him so that he could see her face. "I seem to be making a habit of discovering you when I least expect you to be around. What are you doing here? Where is Stephen?"

"Christopher," she said slowly, grasping for words, "have you not seen Uncle George?"

He looked at her in puzzlement. "No, he's away visiting an old friend. He didn't know I was coming. I didn't actually know it myself. I needed a breather and decided impulsively to get away for a while. This winter in Maine has been a terror."

He paused, still looking at her with a question in his eyes. "Why? Is anything wrong with him?"

"No, no, don't be alarmed. He's perfectly fine. I just didn't know he was away. I thought he would have told you by now. Obviously you still don't know."

"Don't know what?"

She took a deep breath and looked down at her hands while searching for the right words.

"Christopher, Stephen and I are divorced. We have been divorced for almost a year. I came back here to live.

"We tried hard to work things out, but it just wasn't possible. Too many things had happened that changed us both. I wasn't willing to live a life I wasn't content with any longer, and Stephen didn't want anything less than a total commitment, which I could no longer give him. There were some angry confrontations at first, but I think he was actually as relieved as I was when we both admitted it just wasn't going to work. In the end, it was settled without getting ugly."

Once she had begun it was as if a dam had burst, and the words came out in a breathless rush. Christopher made no comment. He watched her intently, sitting very still.

"The children were my main concern. Of course you knew that. But they've been wonderful. Leah had more of a problem than the others, but that was to be expected. Even she has finally agreed that we're both happier now.

"Stephen has accepted what happened, and I believe he's happy now. He's planning to be married soon, in fact. We've come out of this ordeal very close. I don't think many divorced couples are that lucky. But we have children who are important to us, and we have a long history. Neither of us wanted a situation where one couldn't be a part of something if the other was, just because we decided to separate our lives. I guess I should say because I did.

"That's why he was here at Christmas. It was the first Christmas we faced apart, and the children were kind of torn about whom to spend the holidays with. Rather than having them run back and forth in an attempt to spend a little time with each of us, it seemed the only rational solution was to invite them all here, Stephen included. He was glad to be here, and I was glad he came. It was a wonderful time. It gave us a chance to heal as we started a new year. Stephen and I are friends, and we can be comfortable around each other when our family is together.

"I wanted to tell you all this at Christmas. I called the morning after Uncle George's party, but you had left town as if your coattails were on fire. I understood your need to put distance between us, but I was upset that you didn't give me a chance at least to talk to you. I intended to call you after everyone went home, but I put it off—at first—because I was hurt and a little angry. After a while, I didn't know what to say that wouldn't sound like a plea for you to come back. And I didn't know if you still wanted me. So I just didn't do anything."

She had watched his eyes as she talked. His expression changed from surprise to regret, then to hope, and finally to something she couldn't read. She looked out toward the river and saw his canoe where he had pulled it up on the sandbar. There was a name painted in small red letters across the bow where none had been previously. *Pocahontas*, it read.

He followed her glance, and when she looked at him with surprise, there was a smile in his eyes. He said, with a touch of embarrassment, "I didn't think I'd run into you again on this river, so I had it put on after you left last summer. Kind of silly, I guess, but it comforted me at the time."

He reached over to add wood to the fire, which had turned into smoldering embers while she talked. When it was blazing again, he faced her. He reached for her hand, checked himself, and dropped his own.

"I don't know what to say, Maggs. I had no idea you and Stephen had divorced. Uncle George hasn't mentioned it when I've called. So when I met Stephen at Uncle George's party, I just assumed the two of you were still married. And I liked him very much, though I didn't want to.

"I could barely look at you that night without wanting to pick you up and carry you away. By force, if necessary. But if you were happy and things had worked out with Stephen, I couldn't let you know how I felt. You were so beautiful that night that I had trouble focusing on anything else. My heart was so heavy I had to force myself to stay until the party was over.

"I had come on an impulse, much as I did this time, so I made up some mumbo jumbo about having to be back for a meeting right after Christmas and left on the first available flight. It was months before I conquered my desire to call you just to be sure you really were happy. But Stephen was so solicitous of you that night, and you seemed so frozen when you were in my arms that I concluded it was just wishful thinking that you might still care.

"I had an awful time after you went back to Mobile, and frankly I didn't want to put myself in the position of having to overcome all that pain again, so I didn't call. I wasn't sure I could come back here at all, and when I did, I certainly didn't expect to find you in my uncle's home. And now, here . . ."

He paused. "Isn't it strange, Maggs, how some things get so far out of kilter without anyone realizing what's happening?" He gazed unseeingly toward the river. He seemed as empty of words as Maggs was.

She waited and then said softly, "How long will you be here?"

"I had planned to stay two or three weeks, depending on how I felt after I got here. My time is my own for a while, so I took the opportunity to get away and relax. What are your plans for the summer?"

"I'm waiting for my novel to be published. I submitted it to the publishing house you recommended, and they liked it very much. I'm working on another one. It's going well, Christopher, and I owe it all to you. I don't believe I would have continued writing, much less been brave enough to submit the manuscript to a publisher without your encouragement. I know that's what made it happen. It meant so much to me that you believed in my talent.

"Stephen never did, and that was part of our problem. He never could see me as 'Maggs, the person' rather than 'Maggs, his wife.' And I just couldn't do that any longer. I'm at least as responsible for that as he was, of course. I lent myself so willingly to being an extension of him and the children that I can't really fault him for doing the same thing. It was only later that I discovered what a mistake that had been, and by then, it was too late to reclaim the separateness I had given up so readily and suddenly needed so desperately."

She paused. "I made the right decision this time. It was just too late for us. But I don't regret that I gave it one last chance. My questions are answered, and I'm happy with my choice."

Christopher remained silent. It wasn't a stony silence—more a reflective one. She forced herself to remain silent too. He would need time to decide how he felt about what she had told him.

Finally he said, "Maggs, do you still have feelings for me? Do you still think we have a chance? Because, to be honest, I've forced myself to accept that it was hopeless. I let go of the dreams I had for us. And I can't easily undo that. I don't think I can do it at all unless there's good reason.

"I want you to be very sure before you answer. You need to think about it. In fact, I think we both should take some time to think about this."

He stood up and extended his hand to help her up. Her feet got tangled in her knapsack, and she stumbled. He caught her arm to prevent her from falling. He looked annoyed with her then suddenly pulled her hard against him, and his arms tightened around her. Her arms found their way around his neck, and she lifted her face.

She thought she had remembered how good it felt to be in his arms, to have his mouth on hers, insistent, searching, but somehow reverent. But she hadn't allowed herself to remember everything. She hadn't remembered her immediate response to his touch. She hadn't remembered the dizziness or the weakness in her knees or how she lost track of everything but the hope that he wouldn't let her go.

But at length he did let her go. He held her at arm's length, his hands firm on her shoulders. He was shaking with emotion, just as she was.

"This isn't exactly giving ourselves time to think. Come on, I'll row you home."

He kicked sand on the fire, which had almost burned out by now, and walked toward the canoe without offering to help her pick up her belongings. Wordlessly, she gathered them and followed him to the canoe. He helped her in and then rowed in silence until they reached the pier at Myrtlewood. He tied the canoe to the piling and helped her out.

"Would you like to come up for a cup of coffee? Molly would be overjoyed to see you. I'm sure she's watching from the back porch, so she knows you're here."

"No, Maggs. Not now. I'm not in the mood for chitchat, even with Molly. Say hello for me, and tell her I'll see her later. You too."

With that impersonal comment, he abruptly turned his back to her, untied the canoe from the pier, and paddled off in the direction of Riverside while she stood and watched him out of sight. Thoughtfully she walked up to the back porch where Molly was standing with a mouth full of questions.

"I'll tell you later, Molly. Not right now," she said as she went through the back door which Molly held open, put the knapsack, and hamper on the table and said, "I'll have dinner in my room tonight, please, dear. I've some serious thinking to do. Don't go to any trouble, anything will do. Oh, if anyone calls, please say I can't come to the telephone."

After a hot shower, she put on a dressing gown of apricot satin, slipped her feet into matching slippers, sprayed herself with her favorite scent, and went out onto the balcony. She sat in the swing, one foot tucked under her, and pushed herself slowly back and forth with the other while she brushed her hair.

Molly brought her dinner and built up the fire while Maggs ate. "I'll be back for the tray in a bit. Will you be wanting coffee, darlin'?"

"Yes, and bring the brandy when you come back, please."

When Molly returned, Maggs poured a generous portion of brandy into her coffee while Molly cleared away the dinner tray.

When Maggs volunteered no information, Molly was forced to ask, frustration evident in her voice, "Well, are you going' to tell me what's going on or aren't you? He finally comes back and instead of a smile from ear to ear, I see only doom and gloom? Whatever's the matter, Ms. Maggs?"

"I'm not sure anything is, Molly. There's really not much to tell. Christopher came in unexpectedly yesterday. While he was canoeing, he saw the smoke from my fire and stopped to investigate. He was pretty shaken when he found out Stephen and I are divorced. He thought he had closed the chapter on us, and he needs time to decide how he feels about me now. At least, that's what I gather from what little I got out of him. That's all there is to tell.

"He said he wants me to think about how I feel too. As if I haven't thought about it almost every night since I've been back. I know he was terribly hurt when I went back to Stephen, and I guess he's afraid to believe that I won't hurt him again. I guess I deserve his reservations. Besides hurting him, I injured his pride."

She refilled her cup and added more brandy.

"I have to give him time to figure this out his way, Molly. I can't tell him how I feel until he's worked his own feelings out. I have to sit here and wait regardless of how terrible it's going to be or how long it takes. I have a feeling this is going to be a long sleepless night, maybe one of many. Would you bring me another pot of coffee? Then go to bed, Molly, and get some rest. No need for both of us to go without sleep."

"Very well, dear, but you know where I am if you need someone to talk to. I probably won't sleep much myself. I'll be back in a bit with more coffee." She left the room, clucking to herself.

Maggs took her coffee and went back to the swing. Night was closing in rapidly, the way it does only in early spring, as if twilight had been declared by nature to be unnecessary. The air was cooling rapidly, and she pulled her robe more snugly around her and tightened the belt. She would keep the fire going in her room; it would likely be very welcome before this night was over.

Molly came back with the coffee and stirred up the fire. "You should go to bed, Ms. Maggs. Nothing will be gained by waiting for the sun to come up. It might be days before Mr. Chris lets you know what he's decided. Things will either work out, or they won't. I'm betting my money they will. In the meantime, the clock'll not be ticking any faster for you staring at it the blessed night long." She turned down the bed and fluffed up the pillows. "Take my advice and get some sleep. Good night, darlin'."

"Good night, Molly."

When the door closed behind her, Maggs blew out the flame in the hurricane lamp and lay back on the chaise lounge. It was cool against her back, and she pulled the afghan up around her. She stared at the river for what seemed like hours, but no clue enlightened her frazzled mind and nothing reassured her aching heart.

She understood the conflict Christopher must be feeling, but if he loved her as much as she had thought he did, as much as she loved him, surely they would be together now that there were no more obstacles to their love. It seemed to her that the very fact of its possibility should take priority over everything else.

The hands on the clock moved slowly around its face. The more Maggs thought about the outcome, the more concerned she became. Uncertainty was her demon, torturing her through the long hours. What if he didn't care anymore? How could that be? She didn't believe it. Or did she?

When she was too cold to stay on the balcony any longer, she rose to go inside. The river had no answers. Molly was right as she had so often been when it had come to Christopher. As Maggs went through the balcony door, she heard a faint scraping sound. She turned and thought she saw a shadowy form at the pier. She tiptoed to the rail to see better. As she peered into the mist that hung above the river, the form stood upright, and her heart started beating wildly.

Someone had been bent over tying a boat to the pier, and that someone had stood up and was now coming silently and swiftly across the lawn to the back of the house. She knew with certainty it was Christopher, and joy flooded her heart. Then she thought, with a thud of her heart, *maybe he's come to tell me he no longer wants me. Oh, dear god, please don't let that be why he's coming! I don't think I can bear it.*

She put her hand to her mouth to keep from crying out, and he was alerted by the movement in the dark. He was close to the house now, and when he looked up, he saw her standing at the railing. He was headed for the steps leading up to the back porch but swiftly changed direction and went to the lattice that supported the roses at the end of the porch.

He climbed agilely and quickly while she stood silent and still, too frightened at the thought of what he might say to make a sound. He swung one leg over the rail, and then the other, and stood facing her in the utter blackness of the starless night. For what seemed eons, he glared at her with an intensity that gave no clue about his intentions.

At last he took her roughly by the shoulders and said, angrily,

"Now, goddammit, Maggs, you've got to promise me you won't go away again. I didn't mean to love you, but I did. And I loved you with everything I had in me. And when you left, I had to learn to live with ice in my heart again. I can't do that anymore. No, I *won't* do that, ever again! Do you hear me?"

He was shaking her, but she knew he didn't realize it. He was also about to cry, and she knew he didn't realize that either. She put her hands firmly on his face and held them there until he was still.

"I'm not going anywhere, my dearest. Ever again. Except wherever you take me. And that will be anywhere you want to go."

She was laughing and crying at the same time when he pulled her to him and covered her face with kisses. When he finally released her, she took his hand and led him inside to the fireplace. She added wood until the flames filled the room with a kaleidoscopic glow and then she stood before him in front of the fire and undressed him.

He remained completely still until she was finished, and he stood strong and powerful before her. He seemed oversized in her very feminine bedroom. He reached for her and removed her robe. He lowered the straps of her gown, and it puddled on the floor at her feet. She shivered as he lifted her in his arms and carried her to the softness of the huge bed, but she didn't think it was from the cold.

As he covered her face with kisses and her body with his own, she laughed in his ear and said, "What do you think Molly is going to say when she comes upstairs in the morning and finds you in my bed? How will I explain this to her?"

"Well, first of all, you aren't going to be able to explain anything to anyone. And secondly, unless she picks the lock, she isn't going to find us together, so whatever she thinks is going on in here, she can't prove. Now do be quiet. I have to show you something."

Hours later, snuggled deep under the covers, Maggs's head on his shoulder, they watched through the open balcony doors as the sun lightened the sky and spread the countryside with a pale rosy light. Neither wanted to leave the warm bed to go and close the doors.

"This is the most perfect sunrise I've ever witnessed," Maggs murmured. "And I do believe I can sleep now."

She snuggled deeper under the covers and closer into the curve of his body and closed her eyes.

"Well, maybe you can, but I, for one, have got to get out of here before Molly makes her morning rounds and finds me totally compromised."

"I thought you didn't care what Molly said." She laughed as he got up, shivering, and tiptoed over to close the doors. He found his clothes and dressed quickly while she watched him, unabashedly enjoying the movement of his body, a satisfied smile on her face. "Come back to bed."

"You, madam, are shameless. You should be helping me get away from here before we're discovered instead of tempting me back to bed."

"I'm not shameless at all," she protested. "I'm in love. Totally and completely and undeniably in love, and I don't care who knows it. And if you weren't so intent on playing the naughty schoolboy, you'd come back over here where you should be and forget about what anybody else thinks."

"Well, I'm not going to. You may not be afraid of Molly's tongue, but I've been on the wrong end of it before, and I guarantee you, I don't have the strength to defend myself against her righteous indignation this morning."

He put his shoes on, came over to the bedside, and bent down to kiss her. "Good morning, my love. I'll call you later. Right now I've got to get out of here."

He removed her arms from his neck and kissed her exposed shoulder. He replaced the covers around her and went out to the balcony and quickly down the trellis.

Maggs lay in bed laughing softly, knowing that whether he thought so or not, Molly had probably known exactly when he arrived last night and would know exactly when he left this morning. And although he might think otherwise, she knew that Molly wouldn't pass judgment on them.

She thought about their future, too excited to sleep, impatient for the hours to pass until she would be in his arms again. How unpredictable life was. After their last encounter, she thought she had lost him forever.

She threw back the covers and hurried into the bathroom. As she stepped under the hot water, she realized Molly had been right once again. Their last dance at Riverside's Christmas party hadn't been the end of anything. Here, in what she had begun to think of as the Indian summer of her life, she was claiming a future that held infinite and delicious possibilities; and she would spend the coming years with someone who would bring all the seasons alive.

She couldn't wait to tell Molly!

The End

Begun May 1994
First Draft completed Aug. 22, 1995
Second Draft completed Jan. 8, 1996
Third Draft completed Feb. 27, 1996
Fourth Draft completed July 8, 1997
Fifth Draft completed February 28, 2001